THE
DEUCE

THE DEUCE

A NOVEL

MIDTOWN  BLUE
SERIES

F. P. LIONE

Revell
Grand Rapids, Michigan

Published by Fleming H. Revell
a division of Baker Publishing Group
P.O. Box 6287, Grand Rapids, MI 49516-6287

Printed in the United States of America

Library of Congress Cataloging-in-Publication Data
Lione, F. P., 1962–
  The deuce : a novel / F. P. Lione.
      p.   cm. —(Midtown blue series)
  ISBN 0-8007-5960-5 (pbk.)
  1. Police—New York (State)—New York—Fiction. 2. New York (N.Y.)—
Fiction. 3. Conduct of life—Fiction. I. Title. II. Series.
PS3612.I58D48 2005
813'.6—dc22

2004021709

This book is dedicated to Jesus, the author and finisher of our faith, who loved us and washed us from our sins in his own blood and has made us kings and priests unto his God and Father.

And to Georgie, champion, overcomer, mighty man of valor. You have always been such a wonderful son.

*T*imes Square, where Broadway crosses 7th Avenue, is known as the crossroads of the world. Millions of people from all walks of life come to New York every day, and the Port Authority, Penn Station, and Grand Central Station deposit them into the melting pot of midtown Manhattan. When I came here as a rookie cop, I didn't realize that in crossing the Narrows from my little world in Staten Island I would leave behind my innocence, my optimism, and my faith. I must have had some faith. The years I spent getting slapped around the halls of St. Michael's by Sister Bernadette gave me an awareness of God, and definitely a fear of him. But after a couple of years on the job I wasn't sure he existed. If he did exist, how could he sit up in the heavens indifferent to the evil going on below? Once, induced by alcohol and depression, I asked him, "Where are you, God?" At the time I didn't think he'd answer me, but he did.

I was hungover the day my life was about to change. It was nighttime, actually, and I had just started my last midnight tour of the week. It was late June and New York was in the grip of a heat wave. We had a week of over ninety-degree temperatures that were supposed to climb to one hundred as the Fourth of July approached. The humidity was oppressive, and my vest was already sticky, pushing the heat up the front of it to my chin.

I was in my tenth year as a New York City cop, and I was trying not to dwell on the fact that I had just marked my thirty-second birthday, my girlfriend had run off with her boss, and my partner had blown out his knee. He'd tripped on the curb the night before while chasing a perp. He brought the perp down but tore a ligament in his knee and was probably going to need surgery. It didn't look like he'd be back anytime soon, and I found myself anxious at the thought of working without him. Funny that it was more traumatic to lose my partner than my girlfriend.

I was standing at roll call trying to convince myself that the sweat dripping down my face and back was from the ninety-degree Midtown temperatures and not from sweating out all the booze I drank after ending my tour that morning. I had stayed in the bar on 9th Avenue until about noon, not wanting to go home to an empty house. I had gone out with five other guys from the midnights, with every intention of being home by 11:00. I got into a deep conversation with Mike Rooney about the job and the fact that the perps in Central Booking had air-conditioning and we don't. We actually have to open the windows in the cells because they're so cold. I was pretty lit by noon, so I took it easy driving home.

I got only four hours sleep. Since I had promised my brother I'd work on the deck we were building on our house, I stayed up and worked on it until about 4:00, drinking cold ones to keep me going in the midday heat. I slept until 8:00 p.m., showered, and ordered out some pizza. I called my partner, John Conte, to see how he was doing.

As I stood in the muster room that night, the glare of the overhead lights made me squint. The glare was new—the panels that cover the lights are usually so dirty that they give the room a yellow cast. When Hector, our maintenance worker, cleaned the lights the inspector had seen how filthy the room was, and now they're painting the cinder block an ugly two-tone blue. It's funny; a couple of years ago the department did a survey on what color car had the least amount of accidents. They found out that it was white. We now have a new fleet of white Chevy Impalas with NYPD emblazoned in blue on the front doors. The back doors have CPR imprinted on them: Courtesy, Professionalism, and Respect. We still have some of the blue ones, but eventually they'll all be white. You would think they'd take their cue from that and paint the walls white, but I think they try to depress us on purpose.

The muster room is where roll call is held; it is one large room, about thirty feet long by thirty feet wide with a wall of gated windows on one side. There is a podium that the sarge speaks from when he addresses us. An old metal desk sits behind it. The walls were decorated with biographies of wanted perps and missing persons with sketches or pictures to go with them. There are vending machines for soda and candy, and scarred wooden benches anchored to the floor running along the walls. Above the benches are crime statistics, quality of life problems, all garbage to appease the public and the brass, to make it look like we're keeping up on what was going on.

So there I was, my head pounding and stomach burning, with Sergeant Hanrahan's voice droning in my ears as he gave out the sectors.

"O'Brien."

"Here."

"McGovern."

"Sarge."

"Charlie Frank, 4:00 meal," the sarge directed them. "Fiore," he continued.

9

"Here, Sarge."

"Cavalucci."

"Here," I answered.

"David George. Five o'clock meal."

Fiore and Cavalucci? I thought. *What's that about?*

O'Brien and McGovern started snickering and making the sound of a bomb dropping, a long whistle followed by an explosion. Apparently they found the boss putting me with Joe Fiore funny. I didn't. The boss even smirked.

I waited until the boss finished roll call with, "It's hot out there, a lot of tempers flaring, just be careful," before I grabbed him.

"Boss, can I talk to you?" I asked quietly, not wanting to draw attention to the conversation.

Sergeants are addressed as either Boss or Sarge; both are interchangeable and show respect. I liked Pete Hanrahan. He was somewhere in his mid-thirties with salt-and-pepper hair that didn't age him. He was tall, at least six feet, with deep blue eyes enhanced by his recent tan.

He put his head down, shuffling through his papers, waiting for the rest of the platoon to file out. "What's on your mind, Tony?" he asked.

"Who am I working with tonight?" I asked, acting confused.

"Were you asleep during roll call or is David George your sector?"

"It's my sector, but what's the deal putting me with Fiore?" I said, my voice rising.

"Well, since your partner's gonna be out for a while, and Mazella went to Harbor, you and Fiore are the only ones in the squad not partnered." He leaned on the podium, put his hands out, and raised his eyebrows. "Is there anything else?" he asked. As he leaned down to say something he got close enough to smell the alcohol on me. Realization seeped into his face, and he straightened back up. Disappointment and concern showed at the same time. He picked up his papers and started walking away.

He was a good boss, knew the job, always backed his guys, and went by seniority. He had seven years on patrol before he made sergeant, and for seven of my ten years in this command he was my boss. I never had a problem with him, until now.

"Boss, why can't you put me with Romano?" I asked, annoyed.

"Romano's a rookie, and he's babysitting an EDP down at Bellevue who thought he was Superman and flew through a plate glass window on the four-to-twelve. You're working with Fiore. Fiore's a good guy." He turned away again.

"Boss, I'm not saying Fiore's not a good guy."

"Then we don't have a problem, do we? Besides, you could learn a lot from Fiore."

Just then the lieutenant called him to the desk to give the rundown on the sectors to Central by phone. Central stands for Central Communications, the faceless voices that transmit our jobs from the 911 operators. Each operator works one division made up of three commands. When 911 gets a call from the public, they relay it to Central, who in turn transmits to us.

Like I said, Fiore wasn't a bad guy. But I didn't think there was anything I was gonna learn from him. He came to Midtown from Queens a couple of years ago and worked day tours. Our paths rarely crossed until last year when he went to midnights. He had some time on, he was active, and he made good collars. Not as good as mine, but still one of the leaders in the precinct in arrests. He was a nice enough guy, always said hello, always showed up to jobs for backup. I was just tired and sick and didn't want to deal with a new partner who had more time on than I did. I was five and a half hours away from my meal and all I wanted to do was sleep.

11

I pulled a pack of Marlboros from inside my shirt and lit a cigarette to calm down. I stood next to the interim order posted that said No Smoking, trying to figure out how to get out of working with Fiore.

I finished my cigarette, crushing it in the ashtray next to the No Smoking sign, and headed over to the radio room to pick up my radio and shoot the breeze with Vince Puletti, the old-timer who runs the radio room. He was sitting at the desk, mopping his forehead, when I came in. A little three-blade fan was perched on a shelf above his head, blowing shafts of hot air my way every time it rotated. He's got about thirty years on the job and wouldn't talk to anyone who has less than five. The first year he spoke to me, I finally felt like a real cop. If a rookie tries to talk to him he just grunts, not acknowledging that he even sees them. He sits all night playing with his deferred compensation investments, waiting out his time. At this point he was probably losing money, but I don't think he has a life outside the job. He's a short, beefy man in his late fifties. He has no hair on top of his head, almost like a horseshoe that goes around the back of his head connecting his ears. His fingers are like sausages and he's big in the gut, the buttons of his shirt straining against his stomach. His voice is gruff from forty years of smoking, and I always wondered if he'll have a coronary before collecting his pension. I think he'll die if he retired anyway; what would he do with himself? He stood as I came in.

"Rough night, Tony?" he asked, hooking his fingers in his belt loops and hoisting up his pants.

"Ah, ya know," I said, shaking my head.

"Heard you're working with Fiore," he said as I signed for my radio.

"Yeah, John's gonna be out a while with his knee."

"I heard he's having surgery. Is he coming back?"

Vince hears everything.

"He said he'll be back but not for a while. After the surgery, he'll need a few months of physical therapy, then maybe he'll be back limited."

He looked up at me. "It's good you're working with Fiore, he's a good guy," he said, nodding seriously.

"That's what I keep hearing."

He laughed. "Take care, Tony."

"You too, Vince."

I headed back to get the keys to my RMP (Radio Motor Patrol), only to find out that Fiore had already gotten the keys from Rice and Beans (Alvarez and Rivera). I lit another cigarette on my way out and tried to figure out how to handle who was gonna drive. This may sound trivial, but believe me, it's important. With John I always drove, for several reasons. First of all, I had more time on than he did. Second, he couldn't stay awake all night and had a tendency to fall asleep at red lights as the night wore on. Of course, Fiore had more time than I did, so technically he would be the one to drive, but this was my sector. I felt it was my responsibility to cover my own sector. If it was Fiore's sector, he would be the one to drive.

Midtown is made up of several sectors. These include Port Authority, Penn Station, Grand Central Station, Times Square, the Empire State Building, Madison Square Garden, the Garment District, 34th Street, and 42nd Street between 7th and 8th Avenue, which all the old-timers call the Deuce. There are a lot of things to consider with handling each sector. Time of day, time of year, politics, and public opinion all play a part. A heat wave would bring people out, like a blizzard would keep people in. A police corruption scandal would lower public opinion of cops, resulting in more open disrespect and hostility. In a heat wave like we'd been having, if you add drugs or alcohol to the equation it always means trouble. Bar fights, domestic disputes, and summer tourists all point to a busy night. If this had been a weekend it would have been worse.

Fiore was waiting out front listening to his radio when I came out. He tossed me the keys.

"Wanna drive?" he asked as we approached the car.

"Sure, no problem," I said, relieved.

"We got an alarm on 39th Street between 7th and 8th. Let's answer that first and then we'll stop and get coffee at my place."

"Sounds good," I said.

Cops all have their favorite places to go to. Some for coffee, some for good bagels in the morning.

As we got in the car, Fiore checked the backseat and the trunk. He cleaned out the cups and wrappers from the four-to-twelve guys but left the newspaper. I wondered if he heard about my tendency to throw any garbage out onto the street if someone left my car dirty.

I got in the car and jammed my nightstick between the seat and the console. I slid my cuffs, mag light, and mace forward, otherwise they would dig into my back as I drove. Fiore put his radio in the notch of the door's elbow rest. This way he could answer it easily and wouldn't forget it when leaving the RMP. I put mine in the driver's side door. We tossed our memo books on the dashboard and our hats on the backseat. I set the car radio to the classic rock station and turned up the AC as we drove off.

"Classic rock okay?" I asked.

"Anything but Howard Stern."

"I think he's on in the morning," I said with a chuckle.

The first thing I noticed about Fiore was that he smelled good. Clean, like he'd just showered. I figured I must stink, I was sweating so much. I'd showered almost two hours ago, but my clothes were soaked. Fiore was fresh and unwrinkled; I felt like a slob.

I studied him out of the corner of my eye as I drove down 9th Avenue. There were similarities in our looks. We were both Italian and looked it. But he was a couple of inches taller than I was, probably about six feet. His hair was dark, almost black like mine, but wavy. I had a long nose; his was a little wider. He was built, but you could tell he didn't power lift like I did. We were both clean shaven. His eyes were darker than mine—my eyes are light brown, almost hazel. I couldn't gauge his age but knew he was older than me. He wore a wedding ring and an expensive-looking watch. I tried to remember what I knew about him, but there wasn't much.

I made a left onto 34th Street, passing the Manhattan Civic Center just before 8th Avenue. The overhead was lit up, but the center was empty this time of night on a Thursday. I made a left onto 8th Avenue, past the New Yorker Hotel, where a doorman was coming out to meet a cab. I took 7th Avenue to 39th Street.

Midtown traffic is a nightmare during the day, all one-way streets, no turn signals and thousands of pedestrians. If it had been something serious and not an alarm I would have shot up 39th Street from 8th Avenue the wrong way.

"So how's your partner doing?" Fiore asked.

"He's hurting, blew out his knee."

He nodded. "You still playing softball with the commissioner's league?" he tried again.

"Yeah, we made the playoffs."

"What do you play?"

"Third base."

We went into it about the league and how the championship game was always played at Yankee Stadium. A couple of years ago a cop sued the Yankee organization because he got hurt while playing there. That was the last time the championship game was at Yankee Stadium.

15

"Cops always ruin it for themselves," Fiore said, shaking his head.

I had to agree.

Fiore gave me the particulars about the alarm, 257 West 39th Street, Galaxy Fabrics. It was a first-floor showroom with the iron gates pulled down for the night. It appeared secure, gates locked and in place with no sign of entry. We couldn't get access through the back so Fiore radioed back 90 Nora 3, which meant "unfounded, alarm secure."

While Fiore filled out the unnecessary alarm form, we got a radio run for a 31 on West 38th Street, right around the block from where we were. A 31 is a burglary in progress, so I hurried to get there. Central said there were two male Hispanics breaking in and that the super would be waiting outside for us. I went the wrong way down 8th Avenue using turret lights. I made a right onto 38th Street, shutting them as I parked. The super was outside when we pulled up.

Fiore radioed back Central, notifying them of our arrival at the scene. He requested backup to wait outside the freight entrance while we did a search of the building.

The building was fourteen stories and covered with scaffolding with a walkway underneath for pedestrians. The super said he was there on overtime because a new tenant had moved in. He saw two Hispanic men, one dressed in black pants and black shirt, the other in black shorts and white shirt. They went into the freight elevator about ten minutes earlier. The super said he tried to chase them, and they called him some colorful names, but "old man" seemed to irritate him most. He went to grab a pipe so he could teach them some manners. He called 911 and came back to find them gone. He saw the lock on the stairwell door jimmied and waited outside for us.

The guy was about sixty, short and grubby. He had arms like Popeye and a tattoo of a topless mermaid on his right forearm. He still carried the pipe, which Fiore politely asked him to get rid of.

He rode us up to the fourteenth floor, and we checked the roof and found it secure. We started the long walk down the stairwells to check each floor to see if any stairwell doors had been tampered with. The building was hot, and I felt like I was suffocating. The odor of urine, stale cigarettes, and who knew what else hit us the whole way down. I was feeling nauseous to begin with, and the stench was making it worse.

Fiore, on the other hand, was lively as ever, asking me questions that I had to suck in air to answer. My back was drenched with sweat, and perspiration from my forehead was starting to drip into my eyes. I turned the questions on him and quietly asked him some so I wouldn't have to talk.

The stairwells in most buildings of that type are used for fire escapes, with access allowed every fifth or sixth floor. In this building there was no reentry to the stairwell until the tenth floor. I motioned Fiore for quiet, and we walked onto the tenth floor to see if it was secure. Our footsteps echoed in the empty building, and we kept our voices low so they wouldn't carry in the empty corridors.

Between the tenth and fifth floors I found out that Fiore had twelve years on the job, two more than I did. He was thirty-six years old and lived in Holbrook, Long Island. He grew up in Bay Ridge, Brooklyn. He worked in Queens for most of his career but got tired of driving. He now took the Long Island railroad for free into Penn Station and could read and sleep on the train instead of driving. I also found out that he loved to fish and was a diehard Yankee fan. Last year he'd caught the World Series detail at Yankee Stadium, which he calls the highlight of his career. He also added that his father was a Met fan and loved the Brooklyn Dodgers.

"Don't you mean the Los Angeles Dodgers?" I asked. "The Dodgers left Brooklyn back in the fifties."

"He's one of those people who could never accept the 'Brooklyn Bums' moving to California." He chuckled. "He knows more about baseball than anyone I know, and he never lets me forget that the Brooklyn Dodgers beat the New York Yankees in the 1955 World Series. It doesn't matter to him that the Yankees have won more championships than any other team in baseball; in his mind the Dodgers were the best. He grew up in Brooklyn and used to watch them play at Ebbets Field. Once they moved to California, he had no use for them."

I'd met some old-timers like that. I'm a Yankee fan myself.

We reached the fifth floor reentry and found the floor undisturbed. There was no sign of break-in on any floor. The men must have left the building when the super went to get his pipe.

My head was really starting to pound after walking down all those stairs, but Fiore was throwing the bull with the super like we had all night. Two more alarms came over the radio while we stood there, and I was getting aggravated. I wanted some aspirin and a cold soda and it didn't look like Fiore was going to shut up anytime soon.

"Joe, we're getting more jobs, and I want to get something to drink," I said impatiently. I looked at my watch for effect, and Fiore finally said good night to Al, the super. He tried to get away, but Al kept talking. There were two more handshakes and some more talk about Al's friends who worked days at our precinct. Al swears he gives us information on truck burglaries and that once he'd chased down three guys who robbed an old man. He'd then flagged down an RMP to take away the offenders. I rolled my eyes until Fiore finally wrapped it up and suggested we head to a deli on 43rd Street.

"Are you gonna do that at every alarm?" I asked as Fiore finished writing up his unnecessary alarm form.

"Yeah," he said, still writing.

18

"So if we have twenty alarms, you're gonna do all twenty?"

"Yeah, why?" He looked over at me.

"Cause you're better off not filling them out."

"Why?"

Now at this point I decided to let Fiore know I'm as stupid as I liked people to think. In fact, I had a college degree. An associate's degree, but a degree all the same. I didn't go to John Jay and study criminal justice; I went to the College of Staten Island and studied biology for two years. I left school when my parents started having problems, and worked as a carpenter until I went into the police academy. With my credits from the academy I'm only about thirty credits shy of my bachelor's. I keep saying I'll go back and finish. I just never seem to get around to it.

I lit a cigarette as I explained it to him.

Fiore cracked his window.

"The unnecessary alarms won't matter to the nickel-and-dime burglars who hit delis for cigarettes and cash out of the registers. It won't even matter for the more ambitious one that does the offices for computers. But for the serious guys who are purposely tripping the alarms three times so they can hit for a hundred grand in garments or a million in diamonds, then we got a problem. They know that once three of those forms are filled out within a month, Central is notified not to give that alarm out anymore." I flicked an ash out the window, took a drag off my cigarette, and paused to look at him. "Sooo, when they hit, we won't respond until the security company lets us know that there's a confirmed burglary at that location." I finished the last drag of my cigarette, tossed it out the window, and blew out hard for effect.

"I get it," Fiore said, nodding. "So which ones should I fill out?"

"None of them," I said with a smile.

Fiore digested this and then continued to write. "Tell you what," he said. "I'll fill out one for every job. At the end of the night you pick out the ones that I can give in, I'll save the others and hand them in at the end of the month. That okay with you?"

I shrugged. "As long as you're the one filling them out."

By this time it was 12:30, and we still hadn't stopped for coffee. We drove to a deli Fiore wanted to stop at on 43rd and 8th. I didn't understand why he would go there, maybe the coffee was good. He got a cup of joe for himself and a package of Tylenol and a Coke for me. I popped the Tylenol and guzzled the Coke, hoping to sit down and read the *Daily News* Rice and Beans had left from the four-to-twelve.

I didn't have time to let the aspirin take effect before the radio got busy and the night got chaotic. We had a family dispute on 9th Avenue, and then we answered a job on Broadway where the address was no good. Heading back from that, we answered a bank alarm out of our sector. We had a robbery at 34th and 8th and canvassed the area with the two complainants. We came up negative and filled out a complaint report. We had a robbery in progress on 39th and 7th, and on the way to the robbery we had an 85 (officer needs assistance) so we went there first. A foot post cop in Times Square had an arrest, so we were going to take the complainant back to the precinct while McGovern and O'Brien took the foot post and the perp.

While we were in Times Square with the foot post, a leggy blond who was centerfold material tried to get Fiore's attention. She looked like a model or some big shot's girlfriend. McGovern and O'Brien were tripping over themselves to get her attention. Even in my declining physical state I had to wipe the saliva from the side of my mouth. She was beautiful, tall, and wearing a short black skirt and a black halter top. She had on high-heeled sandals, not the thick ugly kind but the kind that made her legs look a mile long. Her blond hair went down to her waist, and she had big blue eyes, slightly slanted at the corners.

She didn't notice us—it was Fiore she was after. In a purring voice she said, "Officer, can you help me get to Penn Station?"

O'Brien offered to carry her there, but she said, "I'm asking him," and pointed at Fiore.

Fiore looked up at her, then looked back down at what he was writing and answered, "Walk straight down 7th Avenue to 32nd Street."

I started to wonder if he was human.

By this time it was 2:00, and because we responded first to the officer needing assistance, we had to go back to the robbery in progress on 39th and 7th.

The robbery in progress complainant turned out to be what we call a walking 61. A complaint report waiting to happen. We found him sitting on the corner of 39th and 7th with his head in his hands. He started yelling at us the minute we pulled up.

"Where were you guys? I'm bleeding, they took all my money, look!" he said, showing us his shorts.

When he stood up I almost laughed out loud. Both sides of his shorts had been cut with a razor. It looked like he was wearing a loincloth with black and red bikini underwear showing underneath. I thought about what my mother always said about underwear and accidents.

The liquor on his breath was obvious. He was about fifty years old, with a slight build. He had a European accent I couldn't place, but I guessed Scandinavian. He wore a button-down white shirt over dark green cotton shorts that were slit up the sides, and brown leather sandals. I summed him up as wimpy. He should have just put a sign around his neck that said: Drunk Tourist, Rob Me. His left leg was bleeding, but it didn't look serious. I could see where his tan line ended and his underwear started. He looked ridiculous.

"Come on, get in the car, and we'll look around," I said and drove down 39th Street toward 8th Avenue.

Fiore started getting a description of the two perps. According to the wimp, two males in their teens slit one side of his pants. When he realized what was going on, one of the kids punched him in the face. They then slit the other leg and took his wallet, which had 530 dollars in fifty-dollar denominations and two traveler's checks worth a thousand dollars each in it. The guys then ran up 7th Avenue. One kid was wearing black shorts and a big red T-shirt. The other wore black shorts, a tight, shiny silver shirt, and a red hat. The complainant told us he'd put his wallet and money in his front pockets because his tour book told him about the pickpockets that frequent midtown Manhattan.

"Well, buddy, I guess they were on to you," I said dryly.

"Were the colors they were wearing significant?" he asked. It sounded like "seeknificant."

"Why, those colors didn't look good on them?" I asked.

"No, were they gang colors?" He managed to say all this with his lips blown up like an inflated tire tube.

I assured him it wasn't gang related.

Fiore put this over the radio as I drove toward Port Authority. It was about forty-five minutes after the robbery, and the perps were probably long gone. I figured they'd already run to the subway station at 40th and 8th, making this canvass useless.

Port Authority was still somewhat busy despite the late hour. A group of five teenagers was standing in a circle talking, and there were people coming in and out of the building with a scattered few taking refuge from the heat. Every time the automatic doors opened a blast of cold air would rush out from inside.

"Take a look over there," Fiore told the complainant we now knew as Carl Hansen. "There's a guy in that group with a silver shirt minus the red hat."

I slowed almost to a halt so he could get a better look. Hansen rolled the window down and squinted at the group, who paid no attention to us.

"That's him! That's him! That's the guy right there, he cut me!" Hansen screamed out the window.

I shook my head at his stupidity. Fiore got out of the car, walking quickly toward the front of Port Authority. I shut the car off, grabbed the keys and my nightstick, and followed Fiore. Before I could stop him, Hansen jumped out of the car after us and started yelling and pointing, "That's him, silver shirt, silver shirt!"

I sighed audibly. I wasn't in the mood for this.

The kid saw us coming and tried to act nonchalant; his friends looked confused. Hansen was acting like the kid coming back to the school yard with his big brother after the bully had slapped him stupid. Fiore had the radio in his left hand and his right hand on his gun.

The kid's eyes widened when he saw Hansen coming up with Fiore, and then he bolted. He ran down to 41st Street, heading west toward 9th Avenue. Fiore was about half a block ahead of me. I groaned and took off after them, passing Hansen, who was running after Fiore and looking like a stripper with a breakaway skirt. The material was flapping up, and his bikini underwear showed off his backside.

The whole time the kid yelled, "I didn't do nothing, I didn't do nothing!" while Hansen yelled, "That's the guy! Get him!"

I could hear our footsteps echoing under the overhead walkway connecting the Port Authority buildings, my handcuffs jiggling as I ran. Forty-first Street was deserted except for a few postal trucks parked for the night in back of the post office. Garbage bags lined the streets, waiting for the private sanitation pickup. I caught whiffs of the trash as I ran past. I thought the kid would continue to run westbound, but instead he cut through the bus ramp that would bring him over to 40th Street. I saw Fiore was keeping up with him and turned right on 40th Street. We passed two Port Authority cops who joined in after me when they realized we were chasing a perp.

From there the kid ran diagonally toward 9th Avenue. As he approached West 39th Street, he saw a sector car going the wrong way north on 9th Avenue. Fiore must have put it over the radio as I heard another car coming south on 9th Avenue. When the kid realized he had nowhere to go, he slowed down near the corner.

As I approached, Fiore grabbed the kid from behind and put him up against a private sanitation truck parked on the corner. By this time I was sucking wind. I heard myself gasping for breath, and I listened to my heartbeat slamming rapidly in my ears. I was sweating profusely and slowed myself down to a walk, taking in big gulps of air.

Fiore held the kid against the truck as he put his cuffs on him. He took the kid's right wrist and put it behind his back. The Port Authority cops caught up with us as I held the kid's left arm and shoulder against the truck.

The smell of the truck hit me so hard I stepped back. My mouth watered, and I felt bile rise in my throat. I came back up and tightened my grip on the kid. I was able to turn my head a little to the left before my stomach heaved. My last thought was that there had to be rotting fish in that truck.

2

Since I had vomited on the perp he automatically became my collar.

Mike Rooney started making gagging sounds as soon as he was on the scene. He was thrilled, because he still hadn't lived down the time he lost a prisoner. Last year he left a female prisoner handcuffed to a bench inside the precinct while he went for a sandwich. She was double-jointed and got out of her cuffs, walking out unnoticed. I could understand how it happened; the station house is always crowded by the time the day tour starts. You don't know who's who around there unless they're in uniform. Rooney walked for thirty days and lost a week's vacation, but the guys won't let him forget it, especially me.

Emptying my stomach on my prisoner took Rooney out of the limelight. And he took the lead in playing up my embarrassment, holding his side and laughing it up. Guys howled until tears rolled down their faces.

Fiore was the only one who didn't think it was funny, and he got control of the situation in spite of the meatballs. He cuffed the perp and called Central, telling them to slow it down, we had the guy in custody. He asked me if I was okay. I nodded, breathing in deep breaths as the complainant caught up with us. He was gasping for breath and his sandals were making a scraping sound on the pavement.

"That's him! You got him!" he yelled, still pointing, holding his chest.

The perp yelled to Hansen, "Yo, dude! I helped you!" He bent at the waist to accommodate his hands handcuffed behind him. "Tell them, that guy dissed you, man, punched you in your face and took your money. Remember I chased him? He dogged you, punched you in the face, look at your lip, man! I helped you, tell them!"

I should add here the reason Fiore didn't tell him to shut up. At this point anything the perp says is considered a spontaneous utterance. Since he wasn't questioned on it and blurted it out we can use it in court. What he was saying placed him at the scene with the other offender.

"Well, who cut my pants?" Hansen lifted his pants to assault us again with the sight of his bikinis. "Who did this?" he yelled. "You did! I saw you. I'm bleeding!"

Everyone started laughing again, agitating the handcuffed kid, who thought they were laughing at him.

"I didn't do anything. I try to help someone, and this guy—" he looked at me, "pukes all over me."

Fiore leaned over and spoke quietly to the kid. "Buddy, what's your name?" he asked.

The kid put his head to the side as if to control his anger. "Darrell," he spat.

"Okay, Darrell, he didn't puke all over you, he got a little on your shirt. And if you hadn't made him chase you, he wouldn't have gotten sick. I'll tell you what, let's go back to the precinct, I'll get you another shirt, and we'll straighten this whole thing out. Let me search you, and we'll head back," Fiore finished calmly.

He asked Darrell if he had anything sharp on him, and Darrell said he might have something sharp in his right back pocket. Fiore found six crisp fifty-dollar bills in his front left pocket, a crumpled five and two singles in his right front pocket, and a box cutter in his right back pocket. He patted him down to check for other weapons, finding none.

While Fiore took the perp back to the precinct, I walked back to 8th Avenue, spitting and swallowing to get the taste of vomit out of my throat. I picked up the car and drove it back to find Sergeant Hanrahan at the scene. He told us good job on the collar and asked if I was okay.

"I'm fine, just a little out of shape," I lied.

By the time I got back to the precinct everyone had heard about it. They cheered when I walked in—this would go down in history. I thought about banging out sick for the next month, and I was already dreading roll call on Sunday. Cops are ruthless, me included. I've taunted every cop who ever did a stupid thing, so I was in for it.

I went to wash up, and Fiore had Darrell put in the holding pen. Fiore ran his name and found out that our Good Samaritan was working up a pretty good resume. He was convicted of petit and grand larceny in '96, graduated to robbery in '97, and did six months for robbery in '98. This latest charge would introduce him to hard time.

Since I was taking the collar, I was buzzed in to the arrest processing area. I went straight through to the holding pen area so I could watch Darrell while I did my paperwork. I sat at the table to the left of the pen. The holding pen was a big black cage, about twelve feet long by about six feet wide with a bench inside running the length of the cage.

I noticed the perp was wearing a blue Nike T-shirt. Fiore must have given it to him.

"Your partner's all right, man," Darrell called from the cell.

I ignored him.

"Yo, you didn't have to puke on me, I was just trying to help the guy."

I won't repeat what I said to him. Needless to say he was nothing but respectful after that. He dropped the small talk and asked for a soda and candy bar, which I got for him. He was asleep as soon as he finished eating.

The rest of the night went without incident. I stayed in the precinct, got a bacon, egg, and cheese on a roll from the deli at the corner, and slept for an hour. I felt a little better and left at 10:00.

I was going to head straight home, but instead I went over to the bar on 9th Avenue to face the guys. I had changed into shorts, sneakers, and an oversized T-shirt to hide my gun. I drove my Pathfinder, putting my NYPD parking plaque in the windshield. The sky was cloudless, the sun hot, with temperatures already in the mid-eighties.

The bar is out of the confines of my command, so technically I wouldn't get in trouble for drinking there. It's a small neighborhood bar that used to be a real dive. In the spring they had put red brick on the front with green shutters and brass lights; now it's just a dive on the inside.

The interior was dark until my eyes adjusted. The bar is a narrow *L* shape, running along the left side with stools all through. There is a shuffleboard table in the back with a joker poker and a pinball machine.

Rooney, Garcia, and Connelly were the only ones left when I walked in. They repeated their laughs, gestures, and other nonsense for a full ten minutes. If all this were happening to someone else I would have laughed right along with them. The truth is I was humiliated. Rooney started calling me Ralph. Actually it came out Rrraaaalph, like vomit. Funny guy. I wondered what other names they'd come up with by Sunday. Since I'm usually the "name man" I doubted they could come up with anything as creative as I could have. I'm famous for making up names. I named Alvarez and Rivera "Rice and Beans" for their partiality to Spanish food, Frankie Mazza and Billy Chin "Cheech and Chong" (Italians call anyone named Frank "Cheech"), and two female partners in our squad "Cagney and Lacey." All the names stuck. In the back of my mind I was making up names I hoped no one would call me.

I had two beers and tried to talk to Rooney about Fiore. *Tried* is the key word—Rooney had been drinking for two hours and was feeling good. He was a big Irishman, wavy light brown hair, blue eyes, and a deep hearty laugh. Built like a linebacker. Nice guy too, I liked him. He'd been friendly with Fiore's old partner, Mazella.

"Mike, what do you know about Joe Fiore?" I asked.

"Great guy, real super," he said.

"What's so great about him?"

Mike seemed to think about this, scrunching up his face in concentration before he answered. "He's a real gentleman. Nicest guy you're ever gonna meet. He worked with Mazella since he came to the South. Nothing ever bothers him, he's easy to work with. He won't bother you about the God stuff unless you ask him."

I groaned. "Not one of those." If Fiore was a Jesus freak, he was gonna have a field day with me. I drank, I smoked, and I slept around. You name it, I did it. I wondered what he thought of me already.

"What kind of God stuff?" I asked. "Are we talking snakes and poison, or just pious self-righteous stuff?"

He laughed. "I don't know, good guy stuff. Always helping out, letting you know he's praying for you, crap like that. He won't bother you, Tony, he's probably praying for you right now." He waited a beat and added, "Praying you're not gonna be his partner anymore!" With that he cracked up laughing again, ending his laugh with dramatic gagging and retching sounds.

I rolled my eyes.

I left not long after that, walking out into the morning heat, squinting at the sun. At that time of day most traffic was inbound to the city. I took the West Side Highway downtown, passing the meat-packing district and the Chelsea piers and seeing the World Trade Center buildings in the distance. I took the Brooklyn Battery Tunnel since the Brooklyn Bridge is always backed up. I caught some construction but still reached the Verrazano Bridge in record time, twenty-four minutes. I took the lower level of the bridge and sat in traffic for an extra five minutes, then drove one minute home from the bridge. An even thirty minutes. I time myself every day; I don't know why, just a quirk that I have.

I live in an old section of Staten Island called Shore Acres, nestled between Fort Wadsworth and Rosebank on the East Shore. The strait of water that runs along the side of my house was called the Narrows. It ran under the Verrazano Narrows Bridge, connecting upper and lower New York Bay. My parents were native Islanders; my grandparents moved here from the Lower East Side in 1940. Before the bridge was opened in 1965 the Island was pretty rural. My grandfather had the house built when my grandmother was pregnant with my mother. The house sits at the end of the block, right next to the water. My grandfather worked on the docks and the boats all of his life, and he loved the sea. I'm a lot like him. I love the water. I grew up running along the waters of the Narrows, sneaking into Fort Wadsworth, playing in the underground passages, fishing under the bridge.

Fort Wadsworth is one of the oldest military bases in the country, named after a Civil War general. Along with Fort Hamilton on the Brooklyn side, it has guarded the entrance to the Narrows for centuries. It goes back to the Revolutionary War. It's a Coast Guard base, but it's open to the public. It has the most awesome view of the bridge. You can walk up on the bluff and see the whole harbor—it looks like a postcard. They have a section where you can see the stages of the bridge being built. I don't remember a time when the bridge wasn't here, but most people were sorry to see it go up.

My house is an old colonial at the end of Harbor Road. Most of the houses are older, built on oversized lots that sell for a fortune now. Giant old oak trees grow along the street, buckling the sidewalks, but the trees taper off as you get near the beach. I live in the last house on the block and have access to the beach. My house faces the Verrazano, but the other houses across the street keep us from getting a clear view. We have a bay window in the front of the house and a set of French doors leading out the side to a deck we were building. The kitchen has a big window in the back, giving us a view of the water on three sides.

By the time my parents got divorced, the house had become run down. I guess they were both so miserable that the house wasn't a priority anymore. After they both moved out, my brother and I renovated the house; the last thing we did was add the deck and new French doors. The flooring was almost done, and we just had to add the railing. We wanted to finish it for our Fourth of July party the following week, and it looked like we'd make it. My brother, Vinny, invited our dysfunctional family for a barbecue, along with our closest family friends. Since the divorce, we haven't had a family gathering that didn't end in fights, drunken dramatics, and other domestic incidents.

Vinny has never grasped the idea of inviting our parents over separately. He likes to think of us as one big happy family. That was never gonna happen. When I was a kid I thought I had the perfect family. Then my father announced one night over dinner that he and my mom were getting divorced. He hadn't bothered to tell my mother; I guess he just wanted to say it once and get it over with. I never knew they were un-happy—they never said anything about it. I was in college then, partying with my friends and seldom home. My father had made detective in the fifth precinct and had an affair with Marie, who was a PAA in his command. PAA stands for Police Administrative Aide, civilians who do clerical work for the department. She was twenty-two years old at the time and married to an ironworker. Her husband was smarter than she thought; he had her followed by a private investigator and called my mother with the goods about the affair.

My mother didn't take it well. She had spent all her married years taking care of her family. She had never worked before and had no job skills, just a high school diploma and a lot of domestic experience.

I think my father came around a lot at the beginning to lessen his guilt. My sister Denise was sixteen and Vinny was fourteen, and they took it hard, but I was almost twenty so it didn't affect me the same way. Then my mother stopped him from calling the house, and if she found out we saw him she would cry and carry on that we didn't love her. I don't know what she expected us to do.

My father moved back and forth a couple of times when Mom tried to kill herself. She didn't try too hard—she'd swallow a couple of pills and pretend to faint, or cut her wrist enough to draw blood but not enough to need stitches. Just enough to get attention. My father would be full of guilt and come home for a while. He finally moved out for good and supported her for a few years until Marie cut it off. That's when my mother took up drinking. She had always been a social drinker, but after my dad cut her off she got serious. When Vinny was twenty-one she went to live with Aunt Patty in Pennsylvania, in the Pocono Mountains. She got a job in the cafeteria of an elementary school, which gives her benefits and a pension. My mother is very bitter and makes it hard for anyone to be around her for any length of time.

My father has changed just as much. I can't believe he's the same caring father I had as a kid. He had been a family man. Church on Sundays, company for dinner, fishing, camping, baseball, he was always home with his family. Now you can barely get him to commit to dinner for birthdays or holidays. He sees my grandmother, but I rarely see him.

I heard the phone as I unlocked the front door. I dropped my gym bag and keys and crossed to the kitchen to pick up the cordless. The house was hot and stuffy, so I opened the side doors and stepped out onto the deck to say hello.

"Tony, is that you?"

I smiled. "Yeah, it's me, Grandma."

"Are you coming for dinner tonight? I made fish." On Fridays she always made fish.

"I'll be there, Grandma."

"Good, and don't forget to tell Vinny to bring the bread." Vinny's girlfriend's family owned a bakery.

"I'll tell him, Grandma," I said.

"Come at 6:00, and I love you very much and I'll see you tonight."

"I'll be there, and I love you too," I said and hung up.

My grandmother is my favorite person in the world—eighty

years old with a sharp mind and a constant smile. She still works as a sales "girl" in a religious store, taking two buses a day to get into Brooklyn. She sells statues, crucifixes, and other religious objects. When I became a cop she gave me a St. Michael medallion to wear with a prayer card to stick on the inside of my hat. She always gives me angel pins to wear on my uniform and pictures of dead saints to put inside my undershirts. I never wear them but don't have the heart to tell her. She is also the best cook I know, and I eat at her house at least once a week. She lives in a rent-controlled apartment in Clove Lakes. She's smart, tough, and spunky. I wish I could meet someone just like her, only younger.

I felt better after talking to her and went inside to the fridge. I grabbed a slice of cold pizza and went back out to the deck to watch the water traffic. The bright sun was dancing off the reflection of the slow-moving current. Some of the ships were already coming into the harbor for the celebration on the Fourth. I lay down on a lounge chair on the finished part of the deck. I closed my eyes, listening to the screech of the gulls. In the distance I could hear the beep-beep of a truck backing up. I must have dozed off. I woke up sweating with my exposed skin burning from the sun. I downed two glasses of water and went up to bed.

I slept until about 5:00, putting the air conditioner on full blast. I've never understood why we do that—make our house sixty degrees in the summer and eighty degrees in the winter. I showered and changed, finding myself alone in the house again. My note for Vinny to bring bread was still on the kitchen table, and it didn't look like he had been there. He's not home much; his girlfriend lives in New Dorp and he's always there.

I drove to my grandma's apartment building, parking in the spot reserved for 4A. That may sound rude, but I know for a fact that 4A doesn't have a car. I park in his spot every time I'm here. I saw Vinny's Jeep parked in 2C and hoped he remembered the bread.

My grandmother lives on the ground floor of a red-brick six-story apartment building full of mostly senior citizens. My grandparents moved here five years ago when my grandfather had a stroke. He died last year.

I stood in the front vestibule and rang 1C. Grandma buzzed me in to the lobby, and I could already smell the food, a hint of garlic and tomatoes. Vinny and his girlfriend, Christie, were already there eating antipasto when I came in. They remembered the bread, Italian with seeds and plain semolina.

My grandmother gave me a kiss and a bear hug, ushering me to the table. She must've gotten her hair done that day. Every week she has it teased, curled, and sprayed until it looks like a dish of rotini on top of her head. She had it tinted a peach color and accented the look with gold balls hanging from her ears. She wore red shorts, a white blouse, and gold slip-on shoes. She smelled the way she always does, a combination of garlic and hairspray.

I took a dish and was piling mushrooms, peppers, and olives on it when the door buzzed.

"That's your father," Grandma announced and buzzed him in.

I wondered how she knew it was him until I saw she had her TV tuned to the "lobby" station. If you were bored enough you could spend your evenings monitoring the activity in the front of the building.

A minute later Marie and my father came in bearing pastry and giving cheek kisses all around. My father hugged both Vinny and me and kissed Christie on the cheek. Marie looked about twelve, wearing a pink sleeveless shirt and white shorts, with her dark hair pulled back in a ponytail. My father wore a tight black T-shirt, faded jeans, and work boots. He's a good-looking guy for his age. His hair is combed back with some kind of grease that hides the gray, and he has piercing blue eyes that everyone but me seems to have inherited. At fifty-two he's still built, thinner than I am but with well-defined arms and a flat stomach. Tonight he looked uncomfortable, not meeting anyone's eyes as we sat down. Since we hardly ever see him, I wondered why he was here.

My grandmother had made clams, mussels, and shrimp in a red gravy with linguine. There was also broccoli rabe with garlic and oil and a green salad. We were interrupted again when the buzzer rang; we all turned to see my sister, Denise, standing in the front vestibule crossing her eyes and sticking out her tongue at the camera.

It's funny that no matter how old you get, when you're with family you automatically revert back to your childhood routine. I was the hothead, Denise the screw-up, and Vinny the baby. Denise and I are more alike, in the sense that we're tough and aloof. Vinny is innocent. His eyes are the same as Dad's and Denise's but rounder with a perpetual surprised look to them. He's about five-nine, with a small build. He has the same dark, almost black hair that we have. He doesn't work out with weights, but he runs three and a half miles a day on the South Beach boardwalk.

My sister, Denise, has always been different. Not really a screw-up, just kind of aimless. She's never held a job for long, and loses interest easily. She signs up and drops out of college or trade school at least once a year. So far she's been to secretarial school, bartending school, beauty school, and dog grooming school, never having graduated from any of them. She gets a job, gets an apartment, loses the job, and moves back in with Vinny and me. She's never gone out with any guy who wasn't a meatball, and I've even had to tune up one or two that dared to slap her around. She's four years younger than me, never married, and in our very Italian family is considered an old maid. She swears she'll never get married and ruin her life for a man like my mother did. She resents our father, yet he is the first one she runs to when she's in trouble. He, in turn, sends her over to me. She hates Marie passionately and doesn't bother to hide it.

Denise came in wearing denim shorts that were tiny enough to offend and a tight white tank top. Her long, dark hair hung straight past her shoulders with a zigzag part in the middle, and her blue eyes were heavy on the liner. She is tall with long legs and a Victoria's Secret model's build. She is usually pretty conservative when it comes to clothes, but when she knows she's going to see my father, she'll wear something to get a reaction out of him. When she's dressing the way she was now, a fight is pretty much on the menu. I reached for the wine. This was gonna be a long dinner.

We barely started the meal when Marie informed us that they had been in court that day. I could feel acid building in my stomach over this particular topic.

"Where's Mom?" I sighed.

"She went home with Aunt Patty," my father said. "She's not too happy."

"Oh yeah?" I asked tiredly. "And why is that, Dad?"

My parents have been involved in a lawsuit for the past two years. When they got divorced they used my father's lawyer, a friend of his who got out of the department on three-quarters and went to law school. He never put the issue of the sale of the house in the divorce decree. My grandfather, my mother's father, had sold my parents the house for ten thousand dollars when they got married. My mother felt the house was rightfully hers, regardless of the fact that she no longer lived there. My father's beef was that he supported her and paid the bills on the house for so many years. Quoting Marie, he said, "It was part of the marital assets." Marie wanted the house sold and the money split. My mother wouldn't sell, and the issue finally wound up in front of a judge.

I tried not to think about having to leave my home. I've never lived anywhere else, never wanted to.

"The judge ruled in our favor," Marie said smugly. "Your mother's gotta sell the house."

"Is that keeping you up nights, Dad?" Denise asked. "Ripping off Mom's childhood home must be breaking your heart. I wonder what you and Marie will think of next. Maybe you should just—"

"This is none of your business, Denise," Marie said.

"Come on, guys, it's their house," Vinny pleaded to Denise and me. "It really isn't our business."

"Not our business?" I said. When my family fights they are very explosive, me included. "Not our business?" I said again, in case he didn't hear me the first time. "The house we live in? The house we pay the bills for? Are we talking about the same house? The one I broke my back fixing all these years? It's my business, Vin, and yours too." I was seething. I turned to Marie. "I bet you wish my mother lived there so you could have the judge put her out on the street."

"Yeah," Denise said. "But Marie would have waited until it was winter to put her out."

Denise and I went back and forth, adding wheelchair and deathbed scenarios until Marie stood up.

"Shut up, Denise," she yelled.

"Tony—" my father started.

"Don't *Tony* me, that wasn't your house. Grandpa sold it to you and Mom cheap because you were married. He'd be turning over in his grave if he knew what you are doing." I turned to Marie. "You really get off on this, don't you?"

"It's half your father's house," she yelled. "Your mother—"

"Don't you talk about my mother!" Denise shouted.

"Don't tell me what to do!" Marie yelled back.

Denise stood up, and so did Marie. I stood up and got in front of Denise, blocking her way.

I won't go into detail about the rest of the fight. To recap, Denise and I screamed at my father and Marie. They screamed back. Marie is from Brooklyn, making her heavy on the accent with a tendency toward finger-pointing. She got in Denise's face, her index finger going a mile a minute to make her point. I was holding Denise back while she yelled at Marie. Grandma started crying, Vinny tried to calm everyone down. Denise and I both got mad at him, and I told him to stand up for something for once in his life. I felt bad afterward. He was just trying to keep the peace. Marie and my father stormed out, and Vinny and Christie left shortly after.

Denise and I sat with my grandmother for a couple of hours. She understood how we felt about my father and Marie. She blamed Marie for the whole mess—my father had been blindly seduced, just being a man. Of course, it takes two to tango, but Italian mothers never grasp that. You'd think that after all these years, time would heal the wounds in my family. If anything, it's gotten worse.

We ate as much as we could; Grandma had cooked for a crowd. She put some leftovers in Tupperware and wrapped up some bread to go with it.

I told Denise I was going up to Dave's Tavern, our neighborhood bar.

"I'll come," she said, getting her pocketbook.

"No way, Denise. If you want to dress like that, go out with your friends. I'm not up to a brawl tonight."

She pulled a folded button-down white shirt out of her pocketbook and unrolled her shorts.

"You took that off before you came in? Why do you do stuff like that?" I asked, shaking my head.

"Because it aggravates Marie," she giggled.

"And Dad," I added.

"All the better." She went into the bathroom to change. She came out with her hair pulled back into a ponytail at the base of her neck, the zigzag part gone, her shorts long and her shirt tucked in. All class. People have told us all our lives what a good-looking family we were. That's Denise and me, good looking with an attitude to cover up our insecurities.

We got to Dave's about 10:30. The bar was empty for a Friday night. Most Staten Islanders spent their summer weekends down on the Jersey shore. Dave was bartending, and two or three locals sat at the bar. Dave's bar has been in the neighborhood for over thirty years. His father, also Dave, ran it until a couple of years ago when he started having heart trouble. The bar was pretty big, with a regulation-size pool table and a bowling machine. A decent-sized kitchen in the back served club sandwiches, pan pizza, buffalo wings, and hot sandwiches until 2:00 a.m.

Dave's face lit up when Denise walked in; he was madly in love with her. She stopped to say hello to a few of the neighborhood guys playing pool, and I went over to the bar to see Dave.

Dave is in his early thirties, never married, and looks like a biker. He wore a black T-shirt with a Harley Davidson emblem, a black leather vest, and faded torn jeans. He has friendly green eyes, and a harmless nature. He has the kind of facial hair never quite filled in. If I don't shave every day, I look like a desperado.

Denise came over, and Dave served us our drinks. I was drinking beer, alternating with vodka on the rocks. Denise was drinking Sea Breezes. We asked about Dave's father, who recently had heart surgery. When Dave got busier, Denise wanted to talk about our mother.

"I can't believe she didn't bother to call us. She's never here, and she comes all the way in from the Poconos and not even a call. The last time we saw her was in March for Vinny's birthday," she said.

I peeled the label off my bottle. "Why do you let her bother you?"

"Because she let Dad ruin her life. She stopped living when he left. If it were me I'd never let him know he hurt me. I'd be out having the time of my life, whether I felt like it or not. Not her. She gave up everything—her home, her kids. How do you walk away from your kids? Who is she to make us choose between them? Not that either one of them cares about us."

"Yeah, they both stopped caring about us a long time ago. They were too busy getting off their next shot to see who they were hurting."

"Why don't they hurt Vinny?"

I shrugged. "Because Vinny's Vinny. He's the baby, the glue trying to hold it all together. No one wants to hurt him."

"They're selling our house," she said sadly. "Vinny doesn't care. He wants to marry Christie some day and move to Jersey. None of them care that it's our home. Where will I go when I want to come back? Where will you go?"

"I don't know. But we're too old to still be together anyway," I said.

"Yeah, and too screwed up for relationships."

"That too."

We depressed ourselves with family talk until 2:00 and drove back to the house. Denise decided to stay over. She said she wanted to sleep in her old room. We never changed it—she moved back and forth often enough.

We were pleasantly numb from the drinks and sat on the deck watching the boats and the bridge. It was actually chilly there, a cool breeze blowing in from the water.

"Tony, do we drink too much?" Denise asked in a sleepy voice.

"No, we drink socially," I murmured. The lights from the bridge made it hard to see any stars. The moon over Brooklyn was shrouded in a haze.

"Do you drink alone?" she asked.

"I'm usually in the bar," I said with a laugh. "Why?"

"Every day?"

I thought about that. "Do you?" I asked.

"Just the weekends," she said. "Well, Wednesday nights at the bowling alley."

"I didn't know you bowled."

"I don't. It's ladies night, half-price drinks."

I mulled this over. I went to the bar on the mornings I didn't collar. I used to take a collar to get a day off from drinking, but not in a while. Every day I find a way not to go home to my empty house—the house I'd have to leave soon. If I didn't go to the bar, I'd come home sober. Then I'd have to look at how empty my life was. At least in the bar I wasn't alone.

I woke up Saturday morning uncertain of the time—I sleep odd hours and tend to get disoriented. It was freezing in my room, so I got up to shut off the air conditioner and jumped back under my blanket. I hadn't heard the rain; the hum of the air-conditioning had blocked it out. I lay in bed listening to the sound. I could hear a foghorn. On days like this the fog would get so dense on the bridge that they had to close the upper level. I heard the soft ping of a buoy and another foghorn close by, probably a ship right offshore. I couldn't remember what the weather forecast was. Maybe it would rain all day.

The clock showed it was 10:15. A dark and overcast sky lured me back to sleep. The phone rang twice then stopped. I forgot Denise was there until I heard her yell. I figured it was Marie, throwing her next grenade. I sighed. I wished Denise would get married. Then I wouldn't have to worry about her anymore. I pulled a pair of sweats out of my drawer; I was still freezing. I went downstairs to see what was up.

Denise was wearing red plaid boxer shorts with a black top while doing the Cavalucci temper proud. She tossed out threats of bodily harm and property damage so unique that even I was impressed. This went on for a couple of minutes until she slammed down the phone. Since the phone is cordless and you have to press the "talk" button to shut it off, I could still hear Marie screaming.

"Marie said to be home by 9:00 Monday morning because she's sending an appraiser over," Denise said. She shook her head. "I hate her."

"Me too," I said. I really did hate Marie. I blamed her for everything that was wrong with my family. The way I feel is that if you break up a family, the least you could do is be nice about it. She enjoyed what she did to us. I knew my father was as much to blame. He was just stupid, but Marie was mean. Anger burned inside me. This woman was an outsider yet she affected our lives more than our parents did.

"I hope I can make it home by 9:00," I said innocently. "All kinds of things come up at work. I never know what time I'll get home."

"Marie said if you're not home by 9:00 she'll make Dad throw you out of here." She raised her eyebrows. "You're not going to put up with that, are you, Tony?"

"He's already throwing me out of here," I said. Who was Marie kidding? My father couldn't throw me out. Now just out of spite I wouldn't be home on Monday.

We kids spent the rest of the weekend together. For once, Vinny stayed home without Christie. The rain changed our plans to work on the deck so we spent the afternoon lounging on the couch watching movies. The three of us rode over to Blockbuster and rented some family favorites on Saturday night. *Return of the Jedi* for me, *The Good, the Bad, and the Ugly* for Vinny, and *Fatal Attraction* for Denise. Denise was in the mood to see it—she calls Marie a "bunny boiler," kind of a pet name for her.

We ordered Chinese food—chicken and broccoli, steamed dumplings, house lo mein, and sesame chicken—watched our movies until dinner, and played cards while drinking three bottles of merlot. I think all three of us knew we wouldn't be together like this much longer and wanted to enjoy the time we had. We were all kind of sad about saying good-bye to a part of our lives we would never get back. We talked about when we were little—our home, baseball, St. Michael's, and even Sister Bernadette (we all hated her). By the time the conversation swung around to the present, we were feeling no pain, laughing about all the sick things my parents and Marie have done to each other. It wasn't funny, but we laughed all the same.

Sunday morning dawned clear and bright, cooler than the past week and without the humidity. I showered and went downstairs to the kitchen, following the smell of the coffee. I poured a cup from the pot on the counter and stood by the screen door looking onto the deck. Vinny and Denise were both gone. I didn't see a note and figured they hadn't gone far. We always leave each other notes—"I stopped by" or "Pick up bread," stuff like that.

I went out to the deck with my coffee, breathing in the cool scent of the ocean. The sun was bright, dancing on the water. A Japanese ship was cruising through the Narrows toward the harbor. People were out along the beach waving as it went by. I looked to my left and saw the Staten Island Ferry making one if its daily treks to the city. I went back inside when I heard a car pull up and then Denise and Vinny laughing. They had gone to Montey's deli for potato, egg, and peppers on rolls. Montey made the best around, and I ate two of them.

Vinny had cleared the day with Christie so we could finish the deck. But I didn't want to finish it now. All I was doing was raising the property value for Marie and my parents. Vinny hemmed and hawed until he talked me into it. "We have to finish what we started," and "We were doing this for ourselves," blah blah blah. I don't know who he gets it from. Denise and I would have ripped the whole deck out just to spite Dad and Marie. But I love Vinny and I admit I'll do anything for him, plus I was sorry I made him upset at Grandma's. He didn't feel the same way Denise and I did; he was moving on. He was looking ahead to a future with someone he loved, he had a good job, and things were happening for him.

I was happy for him but sad for me. I would miss him. I loved it here, and I didn't want to leave. I had hoped to be married now, raising my kids in my childhood home. I looked out at the view, trying to memorize it. Depression threatened at the edges of my mind, and I had to fight to shake it. I snatched up my tool belt and headed outside.

My mother used to love gardening, and there were still signs of it in the yard. Every year roses, lilac, and my mother's wisteria tree bloom along with a strawberry patch and an apple tree. They probably needed to be pruned. I never touched them yet they came back year after year. Denise makes apple pies in the fall, and we eat the strawberries; other than that, the garden's on its own. There were roses in bloom now and other varieties of flowers I couldn't name. Denise worked around the yard, pulling up weeds in the still-damp ground. She'll never admit it, but there were some things she inherited from my mother.

"Hey, Tony, who's coming on the Fourth?" she called from the rosebushes.

"Ask Vinny," I called back. "He's the party planner."

"Mom, Aunt Patty, Dad and Marie, Grandma, Mike and his girlfriend, Frank Bruno, and Sal Valente," Vinny said. "You guys invite anyone?"

"Not on your life," Denise answered.

Denise and I made it a practice not to bring anyone to family parties. Mike was Vinny's best friend. Frank Bruno had been my father's partner on the force. His wife was Caroline, and they have a daughter Nicole who they bring to every family gathering in the hopes that she and I would hook up. But Nicole is a spoiled daddy's girl, and I stay far away.

Sal Valente was a few years older than I was. His parents live across the street half the year, when they're not in Florida. Sal had moved in their house a few years back when he divorced his lunatic ex-wife. At the moment he's estranged from his children and devastated because of it. He was a good guy, very gullible, which was probably why he'd married that man-eater in the first place. Vinny brought us up to date on Sal's situation while we worked. Sal was a fireman in Brooklyn. He loves to cook and garden, and he restores antique furniture on the side. I think he has a crush on Denise, but it's hard to tell since he's that nice to everyone. Denise helped him plant vegetables in the spring, and they were constantly talking about the progress of their garden. I'll just be happy to have beefsteak tomatoes in August.

We put the rest of the floor down on the deck. The navy warships had started to arrive for the Fourth of July celebration in the harbor. We all stopped to stare as the USS *John F. Kennedy* aircraft carrier passed under the Verrazano Bridge. It was a powerful, imposing ship. The USS *Nassau* and the USS *Mount Whitney* came through later on, along with some of the tall ships that were here for the festivities.

At 3:00 we grilled steaks and burgers and boiled water for corn on the cob. We had potato and macaroni salad from Montey's, and we ate on the deck admiring our work. We drank very little, a couple of beers, and I took a nap from 6:00 to 9:30.

When I woke up it was dark and everyone was gone. The house was warm because we'd been outside all day and never turned on the AC. Denise left a note saying she had gone back to her apartment and Vinny had gone to Christie's. I threw a leftover cheeseburger in the microwave and ate it with some of the potato salad. I hurried through my shower and shave, knowing there might be traffic on the bridge from everyone coming back from the Jersey Shore.

I left for work by 10:30. It took me forty-one minutes to get there, leaving me four minutes to change into my uniform. I barely made it to the muster room for roll call by 11:15. I heard Sergeant Hanrahan's "Fall in!" as I entered.

He got behind his podium. "Attention to the roll call. The color of the day is green." The color of the day let us know a plainclothes cop from street crime, anticrime, or narcotics, who all work out of uniform. We often identify them by asking, "What's the color of the day?"

He gave out the sectors.

"Rooney."

"Here."

"Garcia."

"Sarge."

Sergeant Hanrahan went on without any indication he was about to humiliate me in front of the ranks.

"I have been informed by the CO that our command has not been answering back 84 to Central," Sergeant Hanrahan said. When we arrive at a job we're supposed to radio back to Central "I'm 84" or "I'm on the scene."

"In fact," he continued, "the CO states that we are number one in the city for not answering 84." He looked around to see if we were digesting this.

Mike Rooney started clapping. "Yeah! We're number one!" Yells, claps, and high fives echoed around the room until Hanrahan smirked. "The Borough wants to monitor the radio and see if we're putting over 84. I know you're at the job, but Central can't put it in the computer until you say it. The CO is making this a priority.

"The inspector has also advised me that a duty captain found a couple of foot posts and a sector car socializing in the sub station in Times Square Thursday night. Needless to say he was not happy. I understand you have to use the bathroom, but do me a favor and go somewhere else until this blows over."

He wrapped it up with, "Good job, Fiore and Cavalucci, on the robbery collar, and before I forget, we've been given a new piece of equipment to add to your vehicle. These are to be stored in the storage pocket of the driver's side doors of the RMP."

He held up a barf bag, the kind they give out on airplanes. "We can thank Tony." He smirked. "Don't forget to pick one up on your way out."

The ranks roared with laughter. Garcia held one up painted with red lips and long black eyelashes. He sang in a girly voice, "Poppy, my tummy hurts!" I shook my head and walked away. Everyone used the bags as puppets, making gagging and vomiting sounds. Mike Rooney's wife is a stewardess, so I didn't have to figure out where those came from. The platoon filed out, laughing and joking, ready for the night.

Fiore got the keys from Rice and Beans, and I went to pick up my radio. On the way to the sector car, Fiore tossed me the keys again. He cleaned out the garbage from the four-to-twelve guys, saving the *Daily News* again.

Fiore was wearing that same cologne, his clean scent clashing with my Paul Sebastian. I purposely put on cologne to make up for my polluted smell the other night. Fiore sneezed twice and opened the window. I adjusted my belt and turned on the radio. We tossed our hats in the back, books on the dashboard, and we were on our way.

"South David," Central came over the radio.

"South David," Fiore answered.

"There's a 53 at West 36 and 7th, no injuries."

"Ten-four," Fiore responded.

We headed to the car accident. I ignored the urge to stop for coffee. Fiore had gotten me a coffee, but it was cold by the time I got to it. When we arrived, Fiore the Boy Scout radioed back an 84.

A couple in their fifties driving a Jeep Cherokee with Jersey plates was hit by a cabby cutting across 7th Avenue to pick up a fare. The fare had gotten into another cab, leaving the cabbie without a witness.

The cars were still in accident position, the cab angled toward the curb and still attached to the front driver's side of the Jeep. There was damage to the driver's side of the Jeep and the back passenger side of the cab. The cab driver was irate, yelling at the couple, pointing to the damage on his cab. The couple from New Jersey looked unharmed but shaken. I told the cabbie to back up his car and park, and I told the Jeep to pull his up. The metal made a sickening screech as the cars moved. Traffic was starting to slow down due to all the rubbernecking onlookers.

I took the information while Fiore did the report. I questioned each party, and Fiore wrote their statements down verbatim. He then drew a diagram of the vehicles and made a determination of who was at fault. He decided that the cabbie was responsible for the accident.

We were driving toward 35th Street to stop for coffee when a 10–11 came over. A safe alarm had gone off on the south side of 38th Street between 5th and 6th Avenue at a place called Seville Jewelers. We were to meet Holmes Security outside.

Fiore radioed back 84 when we arrived. The Holmes security guard was waiting in front of the building when we pulled up. He was in uniform. The guy was at least sixty years old, out of shape with a pasty complexion and a protruding belly. He had a shock of white hair and wore thick-rimmed glasses. He carried a Smith and Wesson 38 service revolver.

The old guy seemed relieved to see us and said that he had gone up to the twelfth floor and found the door to the premises intact. He was smart enough not to try to enter the premises on his own. Considering his physical shape and the peashooter he was carrying, he probably couldn't do much anyway.

The old twelve-story building had Seville Jewelers on the top floor. The guard had keys and let us in the front entrance. The foyer and elevator lights were on, but most of the building was dark. The old-timer keyed the elevator and rode us up to the twelfth floor.

We stepped off the elevator, and I crossed to the stairwell. I quietly opened the door, listening for footsteps either up to the roof or down. The building made plenty of nighttime noises, pipes creaking, vents going on and off, and I heard a phone ringing somewhere. We crossed to Seville Jewelers to enter the office.

The door is what's called a mantrap door. It opens into a small foyer with another door inside that gave actual access to the office. Both doors could not be opened at the same time. There was a receptionist window similar to what tellers have in a bank—bulletproof glass with a small opening at the bottom to put paper through. This kind of setup would save the company on insurance. If a perp tried to hold up the place from outside the cashier's window, she could lock him in there while waiting for the police.

The guard, Fiore, and I squashed into the vestibule to close the door behind us so we could open the inside door. The guard opened the door and shut the alarm, punching in the code key. We asked where the safe was, and he said it was in the back.

We walked past a reception desk with two partitioned work areas beyond it on each side of the room. A hallway led to four other rooms, which we checked. Across the hall was a large room with eight ancient jeweler workbenches in natural wood. There were four on one side, four on the other, facing each other. Four of the desks had lips carved upward, I guessed to keep the jewelry from falling off. I noticed tweezers, picks, and magnifying glasses.

The other tables must have been for different types of jewelry. They each had three types of small drills shaped like cigars hanging from a partition in front of them and small jars, different sizes, that held liquids. A small, green, free-standing combination safe was off to the side. Each of the rooms had cameras and sensor alarms.

Another office had to be for the boss. It had a massive mahogany desk with a matching wall unit. The shelves were full of awards and pictures, including a caricature of a man leaning on a golf club wearing a truckload of gold jewelry. In the center of the wall unit was a picture of a rabbi who looked vaguely familiar. He must have been a big shot rabbi; I'd seen him before.

In the back I saw a walk-in gray steel safe about nine feet high built into the wall. A metal protrusion covered the hinges and looked to be three or four inches thick. The safe had two keypads and no handle on the door, but a wheel projected out. Everything appeared to be in order. The guard punched in four numbers on one of the keypads and reset the alarm.

Down on the eleventh floor we checked the office below Seville Jewelers. This office had recently been vacated, and the security guard didn't know if it had been rented again yet. I put my ear to the door and listened for sounds from inside. I made a mental note of the recent change of business. A good burglar would rent the floor above or beneath a company and break in to the safe from the floor or the ceiling.

In the hallway we checked windows. An alley ran behind the building and cut into the back of a parking lot. Someone could cut through and escape easily.

We gave the job back to Central premises secure. We wouldn't put in the unnecessary alarm form, just in case something was cooking. We said good night to the guard and headed out for some coffee.

I drove over to 35th and 9th to the all-night deli on the corner. Since this was my place, I got us some coffee and muffins. They baked their own stuff, and by the time we got in, the muffins are the only thing edible. I normally would have gotten bagels, but at 1:00 in the morning they're all stale. I got a cup of regular joe and a blueberry muffin. Fiore wanted light, no sugar, and anything but bran. I got him a banana nut. He tried to give me money as I got out of the car, and I looked at him like he'd lost his mind.

We sat in the car. I read the *Daily News* while I ate. Cops read mostly the *Daily News* and the *New York Post*. It takes three days to read one issue of the *New York Times*, so most guys don't read it. Plus it's the kind of paper that you have to unfold; it's long and doesn't fit in your lap. Personally, my favorite is the *Post*. Their political cartoons get to the heart of what the everyday Joe is thinking, and they have the guts to draw what everyone is thinking but is too afraid to say. The cartoons are hysterical, and a lot of them make for locker room decorating among the cops. On any given day you can find a copy of the *Daily News* or the *Post* in the lounge, the RMPs, anywhere throughout the precinct.

"How was your weekend?" Fiore asked.

"Good," I said with a nod.

"Do anything special?"

"Nope."

"Are you ever gonna answer with more than one syllable?" he asked seriously.

I smiled and thought for a minute. "I went to my grandmother's for dinner on Friday and hung out with my brother and sister for the rest of the weekend. We finished building a deck on my house."

"You do carpentry?" he asked.

"Yeah, I used to be in the union until I came on the job."

"What kind of carpentry?"

"I built free-standing partitions in office buildings."

"So how'd you learn to build decks?"

"I used to work with my father; when he retired from the department he did some general contracting. Restorations, stuff like that."

"Why'd you come here?"

I looked over at him. He seemed interested, and who knows, maybe he just wanted to bond. I humored him.

"I couldn't see myself building offices until I was sixty-two. Here I'll be out in twenty. I'll be forty-two years old. If I want to stay longer I can, but I have the option to retire at twenty years."

He nodded. "Are you married?"

"No, I just broke up with my girlfriend."

"What happened?"

I shrugged. "I guess her boss was more interesting than I was. He definitely had more money."

"If that's the case it's better you found out now."

"I guess. What about you? Are you married?" I knew he was married, he wore a ring.

"Yup. I've been married for ten years." He sounded proud of it.

"Any kids?"

"Just had my third. A girl, she's two months old, and I have two boys. Look." He pulled a picture out of his wallet. I studied the wallet-size family portrait. His wife sat holding a pink bundle while the two boys sat on either side of her. Fiore stood behind her with his hands on her shoulders. The kids were cute, dark like Fiore with big smiles. His wife was kind of plain, not what I expected. She had dark brown hair and dark brown eyes, and she looked a little chubby. Maybe it was from the baby. Joe pointed them out, giving their names. "There's Joey and Joshua." He showed each of the boys. "The baby is Grace, and this is my wife, Donna."

"Nice kids. Cute," I said for lack of anything better to say.

"My family is a real blessing to me," he said, still looking at the picture.

I didn't know how to respond to that. Most guys complain about their wives, saying they went to work so they didn't have to stay home with them.

Central interrupted my thoughts. "South David."

"South David," Fiore spoke into the radio.

"We have a male drunk, walking in traffic, possible EDP on West 40 and 8."

"Ten-four."

I parked near the corner of West 40th Street, and we got out of the car to walk to the intersection. Fiore radioed back 84 as we approached.

A white male of indeterminate age lay sprawled out on his back in the intersection, partially in the crosswalk. He had greasy, matted, shoulder-length hair, and his beard was long and grisly. He wore a shirt that probably had been white once with buttons missing and sweat stains in the armpits. His dirty underwear showed from his ripped and cutoff shorts, and emitted an offensive, rancid odor.

"Buddy, what are you doing?" I asked as I bent down to talk to him. "Get out of the street."

"I want an ambulance," he slurred.

I looked down 8th Avenue. The lights were red down to 34th Street. If I'd had the time I would have pulled the car into the intersection and put the lights on, grabbing a pair of gloves while I was at it.

"Get out of the street," I repeated.

"I want an ambulance," he slurred louder.

I saw the light turn green at 34th Street and a sea of head-lights move forward.

"Get out of the street!" I yelled, my voice getting frantic.

The green lights were turning in succession, 35th Street, 36th Street.

"I want an ambulance!" he screamed.

Fiore radioed for an ambulance as the army of yellow cabs approached, speeding up to catch as many green lights as they could. Thirty-seventh Street, 38th. I don't know why I looked back to the sector car; it was still too late to move it. My tunnel vision didn't include Fiore as the cars approached 39th Street. I grabbed the guy's boots and pulled him toward the corner of 40th Street, thinking that in about ten seconds he wouldn't need an ambulance, he'd need a medical examiner.

I heard Fiore's "Hey!" He tried to grab the man's arms as I dragged. Fiore got one arm and picked it up so we were dragging only one of his shoulders along the pavement. We got the guy to the corner and dropped him next to his pushcart crammed with shoes, blankets, pieces of pipe, bottles, and other miscel-laneous items of garbage.

As soon as we dropped him on the sidewalk I felt the *swoosh* of the cars zooming by and throwing up waves of hot air and exhaust into our faces.

"What are you doing?" Fiore yelled.

I looked up at him. "What?" I asked, confused. "What's wrong?"

"What's wrong? You didn't have to do that!" he yelled, his face contorted in anger.

"Did you want me to stand there and dodge cars, hoping nobody ran this guy over?" I yelled back.

"All you had to do," he said quieter, through clenched teeth, "was ask me to grab his arms, and we could have carried him."

Meanwhile the guy on the sidewalk lay arching his back, moaning and bleeding which in my opinion was better than smashed up and dead.

"Hey!" I pointed at the guy on the sidewalk. "He's wasted, he's filthy, and he smells like a sewer. I didn't want to touch him, all right?"

"I know you didn't want to touch him, but you grabbed him anyway, didn't you? All you had to do was ask me to help you. He's a human being. How—"

"Oh, cut the liberal crap, he's a skell," I shot back.

Skell is our name for any kind of street scum. Crackheads, homeless, junkies, drunks, anything that has been reduced to the bowels of humanity we call a skell.

"And if he died here," I continued, "no one would have cared."

"God would have cared," Fiore spat.

"If God cared, this bum wouldn't be lying in the middle of 8th Avenue waiting for a cab to hit him."

Fiore looked at me funny. "Who told you that?" he asked.

I didn't get to answer him because EMS pulled up. We gave them the particulars. Technically the guy wasn't an emotionally disturbed person because he was rational enough to ask for an ambulance. Besides, he was intox. Aside from the fact that he was lying in the middle of 8th Avenue, he didn't seem to be trying to harm himself.

EMS was ticked off; they hated picking up smelly drunks. They calmed down some when I explained that we had to drag him off 8th Avenue to keep him from getting hit by a scud missile. We called cabs *scud missiles* because some drivers use them as assault weapons on unsuspecting New Yorkers. The EMS guys took him as an intox-aided case so I didn't have to ride with them.

There was an odd silence between Fiore and me once EMS drove away. We hadn't spoken directly to each other since they pulled up, both of us directing the conversation to the EMS workers. I thought about the way I handled the guy and didn't think Fiore had anything to yell about. I mean, I got the guy out of the street.

I was batting a thousand with this Fiore. Everyone who knew him said what a great guy he was, that nothing ever bothered him. Two days with me, and he was about to rupture a neck vein.

"Listen, Joe," I began, "I wasn't trying to hurt the guy, there wasn't much time—"

"Tony, I'm sorry I yelled at you, and I understand why you did it. But you didn't have to drag him that way. That's not the way I operate, and it's not the way God wants me to operate."

"Oh, come on." I ran my hands through my hair, then looked at them wondering if I should have washed them first. "It wasn't a conscious decision to hurt the guy, it just happened. I'm not gonna worry about what's politically correct for every skell I come across."

"It's got nothing to do with being politically correct. It has to do with how I feel about God and how I behave. My behavior has to line up with the Word of God and my commitment to my faith."

I looked at him like he'd lost his mind. What was he talking about? I shook my head and walked back over to the sector car, slamming the door as I got in. I lit a cigarette, taking a deep drag. Fiore stood there a minute and walked to the car and got in.

"Tony, you said before that if God cared about that guy he wouldn't be lying in the middle of 8th Avenue," he started.

"Yeah, so?" I wondered where this was going.

"Do you think God had any part in that man's life?"

I shrugged. "I doubt it."

"So why is God responsible for his misfortune? You and I both know that guy drank or drugged himself into the gutter on his own."

"God helps them who help themselves, right?" I quoted Sister Bernadette.

"What does that mean?" Fiore asked.

"It means God couldn't give a crap either way," I said. (Actually, I didn't say *crap*, but at the time my vocabulary was different.)

Fiore put his head down. I thought he was done talking, but he surprised me by saying, "I'll never understand why people would rather believe that God is cruel. They live their lives without him, patting themselves on the back when they succeed at something, yet blame him when they fail. Every tragedy is called an act of God. The problem is most people don't make an effort to know God, to have a relationship with him."

"How can you have a relationship with someone you can't see? Someone you don't even know exists?" I couldn't believe I was having this conversation.

"If you ask him, he'll make it real to you," Fiore said.

"Who will make what real to who? What are you talking about?" I didn't get any of this.

"If you ask Jesus into your heart and into your life, he'll give you everything that matters."

I was quiet for a minute, actually thinking about what he said.

"Well, what about the ones that can't ask him?" I challenged.

"That's where his grace and mercy come in. Take the guy tonight. He was put in front of me, and I prayed for him. I prayed that he would come to know God, to believe that Jesus died for him, and to give his life to him."

"You pray for everyone you come across?" This surprised me. We meet so many people, he'd be praying all night.

"Just about. When I answer a job I pray for the people involved."

"What about that blonde the other night?" I smirked.

"What blonde?" He seemed clueless.

"The one in Times Square who asked you for directions." Personally, I'd never forget her.

"In fact, I did pray for her," he said seriously.

"I prayed for her too," I said with a smile. "But she didn't come home with me like I wanted."

He shook his head. "Tony, that blonde is the last thing you need right now."

"How do you know what I need?" I could feel myself getting angry.

"Because it's the same thing everyone needs, a relationship with Jesus."

"Do you really believe all that stuff in the Bible?" I asked.

"What stuff?"

"All those stories about Jesus. Don't you think they stretched them? I mean, who's gonna know? It happened a couple of thousand years ago. By the time it got to us, don't you think the story changed?"

He closed his eyes and composed himself. "Tony, the stories in the Bible are true. No one stretched them, they wrote them down exactly as they happened." He sounded like he was talking to an idiot.

"So you expect me to believe that Jesus took a couple of loaves of bread and a couple of fish and fed five thousand people?" That one always bugged me.

Fiore shrugged. "I support a wife and three kids on our salary."

I guess he had a point.

We parked on 39th Street, eating sandwiches in the car. I had a roast beef and Muenster with mustard and tomato. Fiore had turkey, lettuce, tomato, and mayo. We talked about everything but God.

Before my partner got hurt we had been trying to figure out the MO on some burglars called the Harper brothers. They were hitting garment and jewelry manufacturers. All of the hits were on 39th Street between 7th and 9th Avenues. We knew their name was Harper because a cop on the four-to-twelve working South David grabbed one walking on 39th Street. He had a big army backpack with a thick rope hanging out of it. The cop stopped him, looked in the bag, and found a grapnel hook attached to the rope. The guy was taken back to the station house and questioned. His backpack also held gloves, a flashlight, a crowbar, and a handheld hatchet with a hammerhead tip. Unless he was going rock climbing in midtown Manhattan, he was up to something.

His name was Terence Harper, brother to William, Daniel, and Robert Harper. All locked up twice for the same burglaries—garments. Two other guys were caught with them and suspected to be working with them. They were all from Hell's Kitchen, which is in the north precinct.

Over the past couple of months six big garment companies were hit for a hundred grand in garments each. Every time, the thieves hit on a midnight that I was working. That was when I stopped handing in my unnecessary alarm forms. The alarms had been tripped three times, and Central wasn't putting them over anymore. Technically it wasn't my fault, but it was my sector all the same.

Now Fiore and I were on surveillance, watching in particular three addresses. Fiore asked for details, so I explained this to him that these three buildings were connected by roofs and had been hit twice already. The way I figured, the thieves were entering the building in the late afternoon, early evening. The garment workers exited the building between 6:00 and 7:00 p.m. Most of the workers don't speak much English so no one would question anybody. All the perps would have to do was wait in the lobby and grab the stairway door as workers came out. Then the perps could go up to the roof and wait it out. The roof doors open from the inside, and there are ledges in the back of the building every two or three stories. This would be where the grapnel hooks came in handy. Since the three buildings were connected, the perps could jump onto another building, exiting from that one. Every building in Midtown has an alley behind it.

The super at one address said he saw one of the Harper brothers talking to the workers unloading trucks. The guy was probably trying to find out what was going on in the area or who was finishing up on large shipments of garments. The super also said he found ropes and a crowbar on the roof. These were taken into evidence at the last burglary since the super said they weren't his and didn't belong there. Unless the CO made it a priority and put some plainclothes on it, catching the Harper brothers would be difficult, relying on the alarms. If we stayed in the area we might get lucky and catch them going in or out of a building.

Like I said, we talked about a lot of things on this watch. Fiore asked me what Times Square was like when I came on the job. Having come over from Queens two years ago, he missed seeing it before the Disney invasion, back when Midtown was a war zone.

When I started here twelve years ago I walked a foot post up on the Deuce. These days people came to Times Square to see *The Lion King* or *Beauty and the Beast*, *Good Morning America*'s studios, and other tourist attractions. Back in the late eighties and early nineties when I came on, Midtown was full of welfare hotels. Places like the Strand Hotel, the Meridian, the Elk, and the Holland were some of the worst. Some are closed now, but in their heyday, something was going on every night of the week.

It was then I learned what the department was really about. The NYPD was all about numbers. Fudging the numbers to make it look like they were keeping crime down when all they were doing was banging down the charges. Robberies got banged down to grand larceny, grand larceny to petit larceny, or if the person didn't see who took his property, it became lost property. The bottom line is how many collars you get, how many tags you write, and whether they were parking or moving violations. The NYPD keeps numbers on everything, like a business. They rate each precinct in the city for stats on how long it takes for each job to get answered. If more than three jobs weren't given to patrol in a certain amount of time, we fall into what's called backlogged. COs will do anything not to be one of the top five commands for being backlogged or not answering 84 on the scene.

Back when I first started I thought I could change things,

make a difference somehow. It didn't take long to realize that not only did the public hate us but also that the brass was willing to feed us to the wolves if it served their purpose. The old-timers who were about to retire used to say they felt sorry for us. I figured they were just old and nostalgic about the way things were when they came on. Nothing could have prepared me for the things I would see.

I've worked the midnight tour my whole career. I was thrust onto a foot post in the middle of Times Square where my academy training was basically useless. The sector cars would come on backlogged forty or fifty jobs from the four-to-twelve with more jobs coming in. The foot posts like me would have to go off post within a block to answer jobs for them. The Police Department does not want backlog, so we would have to have everything answered by the time the day tour started. Meals weren't taken until 5:00 or 6:00 a.m. after the bars closed and things quieted down. We used to close off 42nd Street between 7th and 8th Avenue because of the volume of people walking around. Back then if you had a collar, you processed the arrest yourself. Drugs were rampant, and shootings, robberies, and domestic disputes happened every night of the week. Crack was the up-and-coming drug, and prostitution was the way to get it. I saw starved, filthy street whores who would do anything for a vial of crack.

I remember trying to cuff a guy who had smashed in the face of an elderly man coming from the theater with his wife. The perp had hit the man with a pipe as he walked past, grabbed his wallet, and left him bleeding on the sidewalk. I saw him do it from across 7th Avenue and caught up with him half a block down. As I was trying to cuff him one liberal woman stood there and asked in her cultured Upper East Side voice if it was really necessary to throw him on the ground that way. I showed her the elderly man, whose face was now unrecognizable with all the blood and exposed tissue. I told her to go ask him if I was using unnecessary force. She had the nerve to curse at me.

We pulled so many weapons off the street we didn't have time to voucher them all. A gun collar I always vouchered, but knives, box cutters, and razors I collected in a box in my locker and disposed of regularly.

After my third year I had more knowledge than cops with ten years in quieter precincts. I would psyche myself up with the other guys in the locker room by playing Guns and Roses' "Welcome to the Jungle" before going out. As we pumped up to the music we would turn our hats backward and slap our nightsticks into our hands while we made our way out.

The Deuce was the busiest street in the city. There were more jobs handled there than in any other block. Plenty of 85s with officers needing assistance for arrests and 13s where cops were involved in shootings every night of the week. Probably more robberies and commercial burglaries happened in midtown Manhattan than in anyplace else in the city.

Specialized foot posts were assigned to 42nd through 45th streets between Broadway and 7th because the employees coming in and out of the *New York Times* were being robbed almost daily by perps using guns and knives.

Then the police commissioner came up with "Operation Take Back." This ingenious action was geared to "take back the streets" in the precincts where crime was rampant. Along with Times Square, the 75 precinct in East New York, the 34 precinct in Washington Heights, and any other busy precinct would have cops from all over the city volunteer or be forced to work overtime. Everyone thought they would be getting the overtime until the lieutenant came around and gave out minor violations and took the overtime away. Out of twenty cops who came, at least sixteen would get minor violations.

The lieutenant would say your hair was too long, your shoes weren't shiny enough, you forgot your watch, or you had two sets of cuffs on your belt, and then hit you with a violation. That violation would take back your overtime. Imagine that—cops volunteering to work overtime in the busiest precincts in the city and the NYPD brass hammering them over the head with minor violations to swindle them out of the overtime pay.

I worked three years on a foot post and three years in a sector car in Times Square. Now crime is different in Times Square. With the tourists came the scammers and the pickpockets. Drugs are still a problem but on a smaller scale. The statistics say crime is down, but that depends on how you look at it. Violent crime is down, but the other stuff is still there. The prostitutes are still there, and so are all the triple-X places—they just don't advertise in the tour books. The city had been trying to move those places out of Midtown since Disney came along.

Fiore and I talked about the old Times Square until we went back to the precinct for our meal. We had eaten in the car, so I slept through my hour meal. The rest of the tour was uneventful.

Afterward I changed into beige Dockers shorts and a dark blue golf shirt and drove over to 9th Avenue to meet Mike Rooney in the bar. The morning was overcast and humid, one of those respiratory alert days. Mike was at the bar but didn't stay long as his stewardess wife had flown in the night before and wanted him home. He had a couple of beers with me and left by 9:15.

I stretched out my stay until 10:30, taking my time so that the appraiser would be gone by the time I got home. If Marie warned the appraiser to wait for me, he would have waited for up to two hours. She'd probably hear about it.

After Mike left I watched one of the talk shows on the TV

over the bar. An overweight sixteen-year-old with bleached-blonde hair was confessing that she was sleeping with her sister's husband while babysitting their three kids. The sister was off in a back room, oblivious to the drama being played out for the audience. When she came onstage, she hugged her sister and said that they were as close as sisters could be. Then the overblown little sister slams her with the fact that she's been sleeping with her husband, and baboom. It all breaks loose. The sisters started duking it out, and security guards pulled them apart while the girls yelled, "Bleep bleep, you bleeping bleep." I can read lips. They ended it with the husband coming on the stage and leaving with the little sister while the wife collapsed in sobs. What a world.

I left at 10:30. A closed lane on the Verrazano cost me three minutes, plus a ten-minute stop at Montey's deli for bread and cold cuts, and that put me at my door at 11:13. A red Honda Accord was parked in front of the house. When I got out of my truck, the guy who I guessed was the appraiser got out of the Accord. It was hot and sticky by now, but this guy was dressed in brown dress slacks with a light brown blazer. We shook hands, and he introduced himself as John Randazzo from East Shore Appraisals.

He was really a nice guy, so I felt a little guilty for making him wait. He didn't ask what took so long, just waved away my apology for being late. As we walked up to the house Denise pulled up, her sporty white Celica chirping to a halt at the curb. She went around to the back and pulled a box out of the hatchback. She obviously wasn't on her lunch hour since she was dressed in denim shorts, a peach tank top, and no shoes.

"What's this?" I asked, nodding toward the box.

"I thought I'd come and stay until the house is sold. It's the last time I'll be moving back and forth. Figured I'd spend my last summer next to the water," she said with a sad smile.

"Putting your furniture in the basement again?" I sighed. She nodded.

"No work today?"

"Called in sick. Can I use your truck later to pick up some of my stuff?"

"Sure. If you want I'll give you a hand later, okay?"

Denise turned to Randazzo. "So, what's it worth?"

He seemed taken aback, then shrugged. "A lot. The property alone is worth a quarter of a million. The size of the house and the fact that it's by the water will bring it over four hundred thousand. I've taken pictures of the outside and did some preliminary comparisons to other homes in the area, and it's impressive. Why are you selling, if you don't mind my asking? I mean, people don't sell much in here."

"My parents are divorced, and the house is being divvied up between them," I said.

Randazzo nodded. "The builders love it here," he said. "They tear down these older homes, leave up a wall or two to save on filing fees. Then they build something they can sell for a million or more."

I noticed he talked with his hands. I do too, being Italian. But not like this. His hands flew in every direction as he talked, his pen waving back and forth like a weapon. On closer inspection I noticed that Randazzo had an artificial tan from a tanning salon. My old girlfriend used to go tanning, so I can tell the difference. He also had a clear nail polish manicure and very white teeth. He seemed harmless, just a little vain.

The area we live in grew to be exclusive over the past decade or so when they started building co-ops with waterfront views. The properties here are bigger than other areas of the Island, and the views of Manhattan, Brooklyn, and the Verrazano Bridge skyrocket the prices. Most of the people who lived here were working class people. Many of them sold out to builders, so now doctors, lawyers, and judges are moving in.

"How long do you think it will take to sell?" I asked.

"Honestly? About a week."

"How long after that would we have to move?"

He shrugged. "It takes a couple of months to close, maybe by September."

We went into the house so he could finish taking pictures and measuring the place. I put my food on the table and grabbed my baseball bag out of the front closet. I went up to my room and got my baseball uniform and socks. This year's uniforms were black shirts with red letters and the Commissioner's league symbol in white. I had a doubleheader tomorrow morning after work and put my gear by the front door so I wouldn't forget it.

I saw Denise walk Randazzo out to his car, stopping to talk by the curb. I cut a whole loaf of Italian bread and put slices of mozzarella cheese along it. I layered Genoa salami and hot cherry peppers then drizzled some olive oil and a splash of vinegar on top. I grabbed two cans of Coke, glasses, and ice and put half the sandwich on a plate for Denise. I used the wax paper from the salami as a plate and was chomping away when she came back in.

"I tried to get Randazzo to sabotage the appraisal, but he said he could get fired," she said.

I smiled. It wasn't beneath my sister to use her looks to get what she wanted, and usually it worked. We sat at the kitchen table and ate our lunch, leaving the doors to the deck open. The sandwich was delicious—the mozzarella was so fresh it was still warm, and the saltiness of the cheese complemented the bite of the hot peppers and the paper-thin salami. As we ate, I filled her in on Fiore and some of the stuff that had been going on at work.

"Why didn't you tell me your partner got hurt?" she asked between bites. She waved her hand in front of her mouth to show how hot the peppers were.

"I forgot. I went in hungover the next day and got sick on a prisoner—"

"Sick as in vomited?" She scrunched up her face.

"Yeah." I smirked.

"And you went back the next day? I would have quit."

I almost said that was her answer to everything, but I held my tongue.

"At least now everyone will forget about Mike Rooney losing the prisoner," I said.

"I would think so. Did they think up a new name for you yet, or do they expect you to do that?" she asked. She knew about my reputation for making up names.

"Not yet," I said. "But barf bags were handed out at roll call, a new addition to our gear."

She laughed hard enough to make me smile. Then she asked how I liked Fiore. I told her about the guy I dragged off the street and how mad he got about it. Then I told her about the God stuff.

"He sounds like Nancy," she said.

"Nancy who?"

"Remember that lady, Nancy, who worked with me at Macy's? The one I used to call 'Church Lady'?"

"The one who sat with you at the wake when Grandpa died?"

Wakes are very important in an Italian family. Besides the grieving spouse or child repeatedly throwing themselves on the ninety-year-old body of the deceased, screaming, "Why, God, why?" there is a certain conduct that must be observed. Flowers must be sent. And if a family member does not attend the wake, there is at least a twenty-year waiting period until the mourners will speak to you again. Friends who come more than one day to the wake elevate their status in friendship—they become like family. Sending food to the family in the days that follow is also a plus.

I remembered a nice older woman sitting next to Denise at the funeral home and being in St. Michael's for the funeral mass. The day after the funeral she sent an expensive fruit platter from a very good Korean market to my grandmother's apartment. The family was impressed.

"She's been like a second mother to me," Denise said. "I love her. She's one of those born-again Christians. She always prays for me, teaches me verses and stuff. I went to church with her a few times, remember?"

"Not really. I remember her, but not you going to church with her. What church?"

"Abundant Life Christian Center on Richmond Avenue."

"The big brick one?"

She nodded. "That's the one."

"What's it like?"

"It's nice. The music is different and the way they pray is different. But it's so peaceful. I still go once in a while." She paused. "Why? Do you want to go?"

"Why would I want to go?" I asked, surprised.

"It would give you something to talk about with your new partner."

"I'm sure we can find other things to talk about," I said dryly.

She shrugged. "If he's anything like Nancy, he's okay."

"He's okay," I said. "I just hope he's not shaky."

"Meaning?"

"I don't know. I guess someone so bent on always doing the right thing that he'd rat to the bosses about some petty thing he should be keeping his mouth shut about."

"Like what?"

I shrugged. "Like some guy at a deli not charging you for your food. So you throw a couple of bucks down on the counter to cover it because he won't ring you up." Some guys don't throw money down, but I do—probably not what it would cost me, but I won't take the food for free.

"Nancy wouldn't rat on me," Denise said. "She would talk to me, try and show me how to do the right thing. She'd never hurt me."

Actually, I'd never heard that Fiore had screwed anyone over. And I'd found him pretty interesting in the couple of days I'd worked with him. He was smart and funny in a G-rated kind of way. And I found out he did a lot of fishing off Long Island and goes out for shark and tuna every year out of Montauk Point. He said he was going fishing at the end of August and asked if I wanted a spot on the boat. I guess fishing was one thing we had in common. My best friend, Mike Ellis, had a house down the Jersey shore this summer, and I was going there next weekend. We did a lot of fishing and waterskiing or tubing with his boat. We'd charter a boat and go out to fish for shark and tuna or whatever else was running. There's nothing like it.

Denise and I spent the next hour or so going over the food for our party. Denise said she would shop because I wouldn't have the time. I had to work that night and had a doubleheader in the morning. Then I had grand jury on Wednesday for the robbery from the other night. I had taken Thursday off for the Fourth of July, and I was going down the Jersey shore for my weekend off.

Denise said she would be going back and forth to her apartment with my truck for the rest of the day to move her stuff. I put my air conditioner on high so I wouldn't hear her moving around as she unpacked. It was now 1:00, and I set my alarm clock for 8:00 p.m.

I got up at 8:27, having hit the snooze button three times. I showered and shaved and put on old faded jeans and a black T-shirt. I kept my gun in my workbag since I wouldn't be wearing it at my game tomorrow and would have to keep it somewhere.

I could smell the food from upstairs, so Denise must have cooked. I looked in her room. Boxes were strewn everywhere, and there was a new bedcover on her bed and new curtains. I could hear her talking to someone as I came down the stairs.

She turned to me as she hung up the phone. "Dad said they listed the house with a real estate agency. Mom was supposed to have done it already and the judge got mad and listed it himself."

"That was Dad on the phone?" I asked.

"Yeah, he said they would be here on Friday to put up a sign and asked us not to take it down."

"I won't take it down."

"I will." She giggled.

"Denise, we're too old to play the 'Let's make everyone think the house is haunted so they won't buy it' game. They're gonna sell the house."

Denise changed the subject. "You hungry?"

I nodded. "What smells so good?"

"Sal sent over dinner, and it's incredible. Salmon with tomato and artichoke hearts over bowtie pasta in a cream sauce."

My mouth started to water. I should've been a fireman like Sal—great food, great hours, and no guns.

I left at 10:15 and got to work early. It was still hot enough to use the air conditioner in the car. The roads were clear through to midtown. I changed, got a cup of coffee, and sat in the muster room listening to the bantering before roll call. It was too early in the season for anyone but the diehards to be interested in baseball; if the Mets and Yankees were still doing good in September, the room would be buzzing about that. There was talk about our playoff game tomorrow against the four-six precinct and a shooting on 8th Avenue during the four-to-twelve.

A rookie with less than six months on the job had shot himself in the leg trying to get his gun out, thus ruining his chances of ever having a career in police work. He'd chased a guy who stole fruit from an outdoor stand down into the subway. He said the gun went off as he pulled it from his holster. Trust me, he was running down the stairs with his gun out and his finger on the trigger when it went off. It's over, kid, go home and be an accountant, because you'll never live this down. At least the guys weren't talking about me puking on a perp.

Everyone filed in as Sergeant Hanrahan called attention to the roll call. "There is a thirteen-year-old black male reported missing from the 114th precinct. He was last seen outside Madison Square Garden wearing white high-tops, a yellow FUBU shirt, white shorts, and a black-and-yellow do-rag tied around his head."

"How do you spell do-rag?" Mike Rooney yelled out. Laughter echoed throughout the room, and the jokes continued as we filed out of the room.

Fiore got the keys from Rice and Beans while I went for my radio. When I got to the radio room, I threw the bull with Vince Puletti about the rookie shooting himself and met Fiore outside a few minutes later. He had cleaned out the car, saving the newspaper. We threw our hats in the back, books on the dash, and we were off. I found a barf bag stuffed into the side of the console and threw it out the window as I drove.

We stopped first at 35th and 9th where Fiore went into a deli.

I wanted a bagel, but since they were stale I got a soda instead. Fiore got himself coffee and a muffin. It was 11:30 and we had no jobs yet, so we drove over to the parking lot on 37th Street to eat. We heard Central put a job over for South Adam.

"You have a 54, possible EDP suicide at 79 East 32nd Street, apartment 4 George."

I pictured a possible domestic incident where an EDP threatens to kill himself and his family. I heard the other sectors respond, then Fiore.

We arrived around the same time as three other sectors. Out of the corner of my eye I saw Fiore put his head down before we got out of the car.

"Hey, Guts and Glory!" McGovern and O'Brien called out as we walked up.

"Shut up, O'Brien," I called back.

He laughed and asked how my tummy felt.

The building was old but well kept. The white cement face was accented with black window boxes that held flowers and vines on the first floor. Big containers in the front courtyard bloomed with flowers. When we entered the front lobby door of the building, the sergeant was coming off the elevator with the complainant. She looked like a bohemian, mid-thirties with curly brown hair. Her face was free of makeup, and freckles stood out on her face and arms. Her clog shoes made a clopping noise as she walked.

She said that her boyfriend had been depressed lately about the way his art career was going. He'd gone down to the laundry room to do wash about two hours earlier and hadn't come back. She was afraid to check on him because he had been talking about killing himself.

She showed us the door to the stairwell that led to the laundry room. The only light came from an alcove at the bottom of the stairs, making the stairwell dim and shadowy. The bottom of the stairs had an open doorway leading into the laundry room. The bright lights from the laundry room threw some light to the stairs. We walked down in single file, cuffs jingling and gun belts squeaking. My heart started to hammer as I approached the bottom of the stairs, and I could feel sweat trickle down my back.

We saw him as soon as we walked in the doorway of the laundry room. The sergeant, Fiore, and I walked inside while the rest stayed back near the entrance. The room had ten-foot ceilings with pipes running along the length of the room. He was hanging from the ceiling, a metal square-backed chair overturned beneath him. He had used several bungee cords and tied them together. I could see the tightened knots joining cords of different sizes and colors. The room was strangely quiet; there was no noise from the machines as he hung there.

His face was swollen and distorted, his dark eyes open and vacant as a doll's. His feet were swollen, his body limp. His body slowly swayed and made a rhythmic creak as the cord strained against the pipe. I swore the body was moving down closer to the floor. We stood transfixed watching him sway back and forth.

"I guess he didn't have enough change for the machine," Mike Rooney barked out.

Everyone laughed nervously. Leave it to Rooney to snap us out of it. Fiore walked over and grabbed the guy's arm to stop him from swaying. I was glad he did; it was bothering me. The heat must have been getting to Fiore. I noticed even he had started to get damp. We all got quiet again and watched the now-still corpse.

Most cops never get used to seeing things like this. They don't teach you how to deal with it in school or the academy. The stuff nobody wants to talk about. This guy we would think about long after we left here. The emptiness we didn't want to feel.

There was a letter, along with a pair of flip-flops, by the second washing machine. The laundry he would never do was in a basket on top of the machine. It was addressed to Devon, who I guessed was the girlfriend. The note said he was sorry he was such a failure. He didn't want her to blame herself, but he was tired of feeling this way. My hands started to shake, so I put the letter down. In an abstract kind of way I wondered what it was that threw him over the edge and made everything so meaningless. He obviously had some money, his girlfriend was pretty—what was the deal? What was so bad in his life that he didn't want to fight for it? What made him hang himself in the basement for me to find him?

We didn't hear the girlfriend come down the stairs; she just appeared in the doorway. She covered her face with her hands and sobbed, "No, no!" The sergeant put his hands on her shoulders and moved her out of the room, back up the stairs. He turned to us before he went up. "South Adam will handle this with us. You guys go back to patrol."

We went back upstairs where a small crowd had gathered in the lobby to see what was happening. We walked through them and outside to our car.

I lit a cigarette as soon as I hit the street, my hands shaking as I struck the match. Fiore put over to Central that we were 98, driving off back to our sector.

Mondays are usually quiet, so I had too much time to think about the guy hanging in the basement. It was still pretty early, almost 1:00, too early for me to go to the bar and drink until he disappeared from my mind. I couldn't have a drink until the morning, after my ball game. I never gave much credit to the Alcoholics Anonymous people, but even I knew that wanting a drink in stressful situations is a sign of trouble.

I threw my cigarette out the window and headed west. Fiore was quiet, his head down. I guessed he was praying; normally I would have thought up some wisecrack, but this time I wanted to let him pray.

"That was pretty sad," I said a couple of minutes later. He nodded.

We were quiet again.

"I bet his friggin' art is worth something now," I finally said. "It's always worth more after you're dead."

"I doubt his girlfriend sees it that way."

"Yeah, she was pretty torn up."

I parked on 37th Street in an empty parking lot by some office buildings. The street held mostly office buildings ranging from about twelve to twenty-eight stories. Most of the ground-floor gates were locked down for the night. We watched the rats, continuing the conversation.

"Did you know that next to eating your gun, hanging is the next favorite form of suicide among cops?" I asked Fiore.

"Really?" He looked surprised.

"Yup. I mean, cops eat their guns like ninety percent of the time, but the rest is mostly hanging. After hanging, it's jumping off bridges or buildings, I'm not sure which, the city has so many of both."

Fiore stared at me with a funny look on his face. "How do you know all this?" he asked.

"Remember when Tommy Moffit ate his gun last year?"

He nodded.

"Well, they sent some people to the precinct after that. They were talking about suicide among cops. They gave us the phone number for the confidential help line. They were talking about stress on the job, crap like that. It just stuck with me, you know? I mean, if you have a gun, why would you hang yourself?"

I didn't like the way he was looking at me, so I turned my attention back to the rats. I lit a cigarette and cracked my window. The garbage from the offices sat by the curb, waiting for the private sanitation truck to pick it up. The rats ran back and forth in a straight line, three or four at a time, to the garbage and back to whatever hole they'd crawled out of. I could hear the bags rustle as they scavenged through them and feasted. These were healthy rats, the size of small cats. During the next half hour or so, I watched twenty to thirty rats go back and forth to the bags.

The sanitation truck finally made it to the block. I could hear the brakes squeak from three blocks away and wondered why all garbage trucks squeak like that. As it got closer I could hear the clamor of the compressor on the truck. It stopped a couple of feet past each building as it made its way down the block. The driver passed us, and I could see his partner standing on the back of the truck, holding the handle and jumping off before the truck stopped. I was curious to see what would happen when he hit the rats, but apparently he'd done this before. He kicked the bags, and the rats ran as he flipped the bags at lightning speed into the back of the truck.

Watching the truck distracted me from thinking about Tommy Moffit and the day he died. We had worked together the night before. My partner John was off, and the boss put me with Tommy. He was a nice guy from Long Island, with a couple more years on the job. He was in a different squad than me so he had to be back the following night. We had a good night at work. We went out for drinks the next morning and got pretty lit. Something hilarious had happened the night before that I can't remember now, but I do remember both of us laughing about it at the bar. We laughed so hard that tears ran down our faces and our sides hurt.

Like I said, we had a good night and plenty of laughs the next morning. I never knew anything was wrong. He went home, had a fight with his wife, locked himself in his bedroom, and ate his gun. There was a rumor going around that his wife shot him and tried to make it look like a suicide. I never believed it. I don't know why, but I knew she didn't do it.

Statistically more cops die committing suicide than are killed in the line of duty. Significantly more. Most of them are white males, patrol cops, not sergeants, detectives, or lieutenants. And most are in their thirties, and alcohol and relationships play a part. The suicides seem to happen in waves. If a lot of cops are killed in the line of duty that year, there is less suicide. If a police corruption scandal comes down, there is more suicide. Less crime, more suicide; more crime, less suicide. Go figure.

It didn't escape my notice that I fit into the category most at risk for suicide. I drank too much, slept too much, and spent most of my waking hours without sunlight. Lately I had no interest in women, which was a bad sign. I guess when I packed up my old girlfriend Kim's stuff it opened my eyes to the shallow relationship we had. After two years all that she'd left behind fit into a shoe box. A tube of crazy glue for those acrylic nails she was so obsessed with, two CDs of Mariah Carey, a pair of drawstring pajama pants, and a bottle of Midol. No love notes, no tears, nothing. The saddest part was I didn't even miss her.

"Joe, do you go to hell if you kill yourself?" I asked.

He thought a minute before he spoke. "I don't know. I know that God is merciful and that he loves us. He wants us to go to heaven." He paused. "You never know what a person does in the last moments of his life. Only God can judge, and like I said, he does it with mercy. Why?"

I shrugged. "I think God is far away."

"I don't think it's God that's far from us. It's more that we're far from him. He's always there waiting. We're the ones who walk away."

"Are you Catholic?" I asked.

"No."

"What are you?" I asked like he was some unknown species.

"I'm a Christian."

"Aren't Catholics Christian?"

"Sure."

I changed directions. "Do you believe in those TV preachers who are always asking for money and going to jail for it?"

"I believe in Jesus, not any man. If those people ripped anyone off, they deserve to go to jail. But God forgives them just like you and me." He paused. "Tony, do you remember your confirmation prayer?"

I made a face. "No, I was in the sixth grade when I made confirmation."

"Well, your confirmation prayer is the prayer of salvation. The problem is it usually dies there. Salvation is about a relationship with Jesus."

"You said that last night. How do you have a relationship with someone you can't see or talk to?" This baffled me.

"You can talk to him, pray, read his Word. That's how you get to know him."

"I don't know, Joe, this is confusing. Those people always seem fake to me, like they're scamming to make money."

"Talk to me, Tony," Fiore said sincerely. "Ask me anything you want about God, and I'll try to answer it for you. If I don't have an answer, I'll find someone who does."

"Okay. Why is there so much wrong in the world?"

"Oh, I can answer that," he said with relief. He started to talk and I cut him off.

"Forget it, I don't want to know."

"Tony—"

"Not tonight, okay?"

He paused, then nodded. "Sure, no problem."

I lit a cigarette and drove the car over to the deli at 35th and 9th. I went inside, got coffee, and picked up a stale buttered roll for each of us. I drove back to 37th Street. The block was quiet, and in the distance I could hear an occasional horn or siren and the squeak of a truck brake. We sat in silence drinking our coffee and eating our rolls. I was glad Fiore didn't try to continue the conversation, and I realized what Mike Rooney had said was true. Fiore didn't push it. When I asked about God, he answered, and when I told him to back off, he did. I could tell he wanted to talk more but held his tongue.

About 3:30 a.m. we spotted a white male, about eighteen years old, exiting a building a couple doors up, which made no sense since the building was dark. He was carrying an overstuffed cardboard box. He came out the door, saw us, and turned to go back into the building just as the door slammed shut. He turned back around and toward us. Fiore and I gave each other a look and watched him as he came toward us. The driver's side of the car was on the left side of the street so he had to pass me as he walked by. I rolled down my window the rest of the way.

"Hey, buddy. Anything good to sell?" I asked as he approached the car.

"No, nothing good here," he said and tried to keep walking.

I opened the door and stepped out, leaving Fiore in the car. I was in front of the kid so he couldn't walk past me, and the box was kind of bulky so he'd have to drop it first if he decided to run.

"Hey, let me take a look," Fiore said as he leaned over toward the driver's side of the car.

"No, it's nothing good," the kid said.

Now he was in front of me, so I got a better look at him. He wore ripped jeans and a faded T-shirt, and his sneakers were old and filthy. He was too skinny to have been eating properly, and he had a nervous air about him. He was short with a scar by his left eye. He looked young and old at the same time, and something about him gave me the impression he was homeless.

The kid had no choice but to lean in and show Fiore the box, thus trapping himself between the car and me. In the box was a small fax machine, a phone, a radio, some cassette tapes, Post-it paper, and other assorted office supplies. As he leaned in he saw Fiore's hand on his gun, and I went for my cuffs as I put one hand on his back.

"Put your right hand behind your back," I said.

He did and I cuffed his right hand. Fiore got out of the car, and we cuffed his left hand too. We called Dogman, the K-9 cop from our command, to come to the scene. K-9 is called whenever there's a possibility of a burglar in the building. Then we tossed the kid and found out he had no weapons, no ID, nothing on his person. We sat him in the backseat until K-9 got there. He told us he worked in the building and gets out late, but he couldn't even give me the name of the company he supposedly worked for.

Dogman arrived with Shane, his German shepherd, and the two of them watched the kid, who was looked nervously at the dog. Shane barked up a storm, thinking he'd get a steak later if he got a collar.

The door to the building had a magnetic lock on it. Fiore and I wrestled with it for a few minutes and finally pulled it open. The building had six floors, with the elevator in the immediate lobby. The elevator door was open but the panel was unscrewed and hanging by a wire. I wasn't sure if we should take it but figured we could radio back if we got stuck. I would have taken the stairs but the stairwell door was locked. We pressed two on the hanging panel and the elevator closed, humming as it ascended to the next floor. The second floor was dark when we stepped off and found the door across the hall open.

We turned on the lights, revealing a small office. We took about twenty minutes in the office and called the sergeant to the scene. We would have searched the other floors, but their lights wouldn't come on in the elevator. We pressed the button for the lobby and went back down.

The boss was there when we came back out, and we showed him the office goods and told him about the break-in. We thanked Dogman and patted Shane good night. Everyone left, and we went to take the kid back to the precinct when he asked if we could stop and get his stuff. He said it was on 8th Avenue in a studio where bands go to jam. He was pleading, saying it was all he had in the world and if he left it there he would lose it.

"No problem, buddy, we'll stop," Fiore said. "Where is it?"

"Right where those guys are on the sixth floor, as soon as you walk off the elevators, first door on the right. Tell Daz to give you Albert's stuff."

To tell the truth, I was feeling sorry for the kid. He wasn't a bad kid. He had a sad, resigned look in his eyes. Having everything he owned fit into a couple of bags wasn't new to him.

I pulled up to a rundown apartment building. A few freaky-looking guys and girls were hanging out in front. They looked nervous when we stopped and I got out of the car. I got the kid's stuff from Daz, a wicked-looking guy with tattoos from his shoulders to his wrist and a nose ring with a chain connected to his ear. I came out to find Fiore in deep conversation with the kid.

"Look at this, Tony," he said as I got in the car. He held up a cuff key.

"Where'd you get that?" I asked.

"Our buddy Albert," he said with a nod toward the back. "He had the key in his mouth and was gonna run off. Because we were good guys and let him get his stuff, he decided to tell me."

If we had lost Albert, we would have walked a foot post for thirty days and lost a week's vacation. This made me feel worse for the kid. When we got back to the house to process him we found out he had a record. He did time for burglary and got out four months ago. You could tell this life was all he'd known, all he'd ever know.

"You looking tonight?" Fiore asked, to see if I wanted the arrest.

I said no. I had a ball game at 9:00, a doubleheader. We'd already had to forfeit twice because of guys not showing up.

We stayed inside the rest of the night, processing the arrest. I got in an hour's sleep between 5:00 and 6:00, hoping it would give me some energy for the game.

I changed into my softball uniform at 7:30, leaving my sneakers on until I got to the field. We were playing the four-six precinct from the Bronx. The sun was already hot, with the humidity climbing. I parked my truck on the sidewalk and put my parking plaque in the window to avoid a ticket. The DOT loves to ticket us, but there wasn't much they could do with twenty cars parked with police plaques in the windshields.

Rooney, Garcia, and Rice and Beans were already at the field tossing a ball around when I got there. I saw Dennis Fitzpatrick, our pitcher, pull up, and Connelly got out of the car with him. Seven guys this early was a good sign—if O'Brien and McGovern showed up we'd be set. Paddy Mullen came in; it was his RDO (regular day off) so he brought his little girl, since his wife was working.

The park takes up the whole block. There was a playground on one side with swings and a sprinkler and the ballpark on the other side. It's a regulation softball field on grass, not concrete. The dirt has a reddish tint to it and stains my socks and pants so bad it never comes out. I put bleach to get some of it out but it doesn't help. Mike Rooney says he never washes his, just throws them out at the end of the season.

The team from the Bronx was good. We split the games, winning the first one 7–4, and losing the second 5–2. I batted three for four in the first game, with two doubles, scoring twice. Mike Rooney racked in a home run in the first inning, starting us off. Garcia had popped out, O'Brien had a single, I got on second, pushing him to third, and Connelly brought us home. The Bronx scored two in the second inning and two in the fourth. At the top of the fifth, bases were loaded and Mike Rooney hit a grand slam, cementing the win.

By the second game we were pretty tired. Everyone except Paddy Mullen and Rice and Beans had worked a midnight and showed signs of fatigue. Fitzpatrick's arm was hurting, and Paddy cut up his leg sliding into home after I hit a pop-up out to right field in the first game. The guys took turns watching Paddy's daughter, a three-year-old blonde demon who kicked everyone who came near her in the dugout. We had eleven guys, ten playing the field, so one of us had to stay with her when the other team was up. I never had to watch her, since I played the whole time both games.

In the second game they got two runs in the first inning and one in the second. By the fourth inning the score was five-zip. I hit a single, followed by a double by Rooney, and we both scored when O'Brien hit deep into right field. We ran out of gas by then but were able to keep Bronx from scoring anymore. Since we won one and lost one, it was pretty much a wash, and we'd have to play them again.

I stayed at the field with Mike Rooney, Garcia, and Connelly drinking a six-pack. Rooney's wife was working so he planned on drinking for a while. He would then get something to eat and sleep at the precinct until our tour that night. I was off because Fiore and I had court in the morning. I tried to get the ADA to wait until Friday so I could pull a tour of overtime on my day off, but she wanted to get it done before the holiday. I would work a day tour tomorrow at court, stay at the precinct for the four-to-twelve, and then work the midnight. I would get home on Thursday morning and hopefully get a couple of hours' sleep before the dysfunctional family picnic. I had three days off this weekend and wouldn't have to be back to work until Monday night.

Garcia and Connelly left at 1:00, and Rooney and I went to the bar. Rooney was feeling no pain by then, joking about the rookie who shot himself the night before. I wasn't finding anything funny. I kept thinking about the guy who hung himself last night and my last conversation with Tommy Moffit in this very bar the day he killed himself. I alternated beer with vodka on the rocks, hoping it would improve my mood. Rooney started to slur at around 2:00, and I drove him back to the precinct.

I headed home, aware of the fact that I'd drunk too much

to be driving. I swerved once, cutting off a cab. That sobered me a little, and I lit a cigarette and blasted my air-conditioning to stay awake. I cut over to the West Side Highway, driving in bumper-to-bumper traffic all the way downtown. It took me an hour to get home. I pulled in front of my house at 3:05 to find a Century 21 For Sale sign hammered into the ground next to the mailbox.

I let myself in, threw my bag on the floor, and checked the messages on the machine. Marie had called to tell me the realtor was showing the house at 7:00. The house was hot and quiet. I left a note on the table saying not to wake me up and went upstairs. I stripped off my uniform, red dirt sprinkling the floor as I peeled off my socks. I threw them in a pile in the corner of the room and turned on the air conditioner. I wanted something to eat but was too tired. I fell on the bed, asleep almost instantly.

Someone knocked on the door at 6:00. I knew it was 6:00 because I rolled over and looked at the clock, yelling at them to go away. I woke again at 8:30 with a headache and a mouth full of cotton. I jumped in the shower, letting the hot water pelt over my sore muscles. I assessed the damage—slide burn on my right calf, bruise on my upper left arm where a ball shot up at me—not too bad. I brushed my teeth but didn't shave, figuring I'd wait until morning. I picked up my dirty clothes and headed downstairs.

Denise was sitting on the couch polishing her toenails.

"Hey, feel like going up to Dave's?" she asked.

"Sure, I'll go, I just want to eat something first. Did you eat?"

"I stopped at Grandma's. She sent over a chicken cutlet sandwich for you."

"All right, I'll eat and then we'll go up. I can't stay too late. I'm working a day tour tomorrow."

"What for?"

"I have court for that robbery collar the other night," I answered.

"You washing clothes?" She nodded toward the pile I was holding. "I have some towels to throw in; we're running low." She went upstairs and came down a minute later with her arms full of towels, adding them to the clothes I was holding.

I went down to the basement, which was now empty except for the washer, dryer, and a freezer. We didn't use the freezer anymore. My parents used to stock up on food, but it had been empty for years. The basement is unfinished, but the cement floor and walls were painted with an oil-based gray that kept it looking neat.

The basement floor was cool against my bare feet. I put my baseball uniform in with the towels and set it on warm. I waited until the water started to agitate before I added the soap and threw in some softener. Vinny and I used to put the laundry in one big hamper, but he never understood the concept of separating whites and colors. I wound up with pink underwear and socks too many times to count. Now I do my own laundry, and Christie does his.

I went back to the kitchen. Denise had put my sandwich in the oven for me. It was breaded chicken cutlet with smoked ham and Swiss cheese on seeded Italian bread. I popped open a can of soda while waiting for the cheese to melt. I ate the sandwich alone in the kitchen while Denise went upstairs to change. I put on white shorts and a black T-shirt after my shower and went back upstairs to grab my sneakers.

Denise and I walked up the block to Bay Street, made a left, and walked another block to Dave's Tavern. The place was hopping for a Tuesday night. Mike Ellis, my best friend, was there with his girlfriend, Laura. The jukebox was blasting an Aerosmith song. The jukebox at Dave's was classic rock, no rap.

"Tony!" Mike yelled from the back of the bar as we walked in.

"Hi, Tony," Laura said as I approached them.

"Hey, Denise," Mike said in a taunting voice.

Denise rolled her eyes. She hated Mike. There was a time when she was madly in love with him, one of those crushes girls get on their older brother's best friend. They got together for a short time a few years ago. She never told me what happened, and I never asked her. I was mad at him for going out with my sister, and we took a couple of swings at each other over it. I know how he is with women and didn't want him near my sister. Denise hates him now and he does everything he can to get her to fight with him.

His girlfriend, Laura, was checking out Denise. My sister was dressed conservatively in a floral sleeveless dress and the ugliest shoes I have ever seen. They were black with a clunky platform and heel. All the women in Midtown wear them, so they must be in style.

Laura was pretty in a malnourished kind of way. She was tall with long brown hair highlighted in blonde. She wore a black workout outfit with white sneakers and still managed to look dressed up. She talked with her hands and had three-inch blue nails with American flags airbrushed on them.

Mike cheats on her every chance he gets. I doubt he told her he used to date Denise, but she seemed to sense that Denise was competition. Denise ignored Laura and stayed near the pool table, flirting with the guys, looking miserable.

Talking to Mike tonight was depressing me for reasons I couldn't fathom. Maybe it was him playing the devoted boyfriend when I knew that when we were away this weekend he'd be after everything with a pulse. I didn't talk with Mike and Laura for long. All that bogus lovey-dovey crap was making me nauseous. I played darts with a couple of the Bay Street guys, drinking beers and talking softball. Denise and I went home at 11:00.

I had slept until 8:30 so I wasn't tired. I watched *Friends* and *Seinfeld* reruns until midnight, then tried to sleep. I tossed and turned most of the night, finally falling into a deep sleep ten minutes before my alarm went off. I showered, shaved, and dressed by 6:15, and I was out to my car at 6:30.

It was a hazy, steamy day. It already felt like ninety degrees, and according to the weather forecast it would be. By tomorrow temperatures could hit a hundred degrees. Health officials were issuing warnings to stay out of the sun, drink lots of fluids, and wear loose, light clothes. I couldn't wait to put on my uniform, vest, gun belt, and boots.

The day tour was more crowded than the midnight, and parking was nil. Street Crime and the evidence collection teams now park at my command, making it almost impossible to find a spot. I finally angle parked on the sidewalk and threw my parking plaque in the windshield. I tossed two bucks to the skells hanging out there to watch my truck and got to the precinct by 7:15. Believe it or not, the skells really will watch your car if you ask. It gives them a place to hang out that doesn't interfere with us or with any pedestrian traffic. It also makes them feel like they're doing something important.

I told the desk officer I was there and signed the court sheet. I went downstairs to the locker room to change. The lockers had a lot of colorful pictures and stickers, but most of it was X-rated and pretty foul. I used to have two lockers but someone got wind of it and clipped one. Now I have stuff piled two feet high in my locker and nowhere to put it. A lot of people have two lockers. One for everyday stuff—toiletries, uniform, baton, gun belt, pants belt, and hat. The second locker is for your dress uniform, dress coat, winter coat, riot helmet, sleeping bag, and alarm clock. The sleeping bag and alarm clock are for when you work overtime and don't bother going home. We have a dorm on the third floor that sleeps about fifteen guys, but it's so disgusting I rarely slept there. If I do sleep there I zip myself in my sleeping bag and jump on the mattress without touching anything.

I changed into my uniform and went across the street for a cup of coffee. I grabbed a fresh bagel, still warm with butter. I met Fiore by the front door on my way back in. He was dressed in shorts and a short-sleeveed shirt and sweating from his walk from 35th Street. Despite the heat he was as bouncy as ever, giving me a big good morning. It was contagious—I smiled back.

Fiore signed in and let the boss know that we would both be heading down to court. I waited for him to change, teasing Clarice, our nicest PAA, about her new hairdo. Then we walked in the suffocative heat to catch the C train downtown. The train had emptied some at 34th Street but was still crowded with rush hour commuters. I leaned up against the door at the end of the car, bracing my foot against it while I held the pole next to the door. This gave me a view of what was going on in the train and kept me from bumping and swaying the entire time. Fiore stood across from me doing the same.

The train we were on had the new PBA posters taking up half the subway car. PBA stood for Patrolmen's Benevolent Association, our union. The new president had launched a campaign to get us higher salaries. Statistically we are one of the lowest paid police departments in the country, even with the legislation passed on the perb bill, a bill introduced into legislature to give the NYPD similar salaries to those of the surrounding police departments.

The posters were controversial because of their graphic content: an officer facedown next to his RMP with blood spilling from a gunshot wound. The flashing red lights on the car cast an eerie shadow over his face and upper body while the blood trickled down the sidewalk from a chest wound. The caption was about how most people wouldn't do this job for a million bucks, but we do it for a lot less. The poster bothered me; I guess that's what it was supposed to do. As I rode downtown I found myself stealing glances at the faceless dead cop, wondering what others thought when they saw the picture.

We got off at Canal Street and headed upstairs. We walked east toward Lafayette Street and passed a bar with a sixties theme. Peace signs and hippie collector's items decorated the restaurant, and on the front window was a painting of a flower child smoking a joint. Trucks were loading and unloading at this time of the morning, double-parked along the street. We passed a lumberyard, a shop selling ceramic dragons and other Asian images, and a store full of women's pocketbooks and accessories. Even at this hour of the morning the area looked dark and dingy.

As we approached Lafayette Street we could see that traffic was bumper-to-bumper on Canal Street, spilling over to Lafayette Street up to the courthouses. We walked two blocks south, cutting across the Civil Municipal Court building and Court Park, where sleeping skells were sprawled out on benches and in cardboard boxes.

We spotted the coffee vendor in front of the courthouse; the line was ten deep with suits and ties, so we waited for ten minutes and got coffee and bagels. The Asians were out, doing their Miyagi-style crane moves slowly as they faced the morning sun in Columbus Park. Some looked more than eighty years old and were there every time I came to court. We saw an early basketball game going on with a blasting of rap music from a boom box by the fence. We went down the ramp into 60 Centre Street to punch in with our ID cards and went across to the criminal court building and rode the elevator upstairs to the seventh floor to the assistant district attorney's office.

ADA Rachel Katz was handling the case. Both Fiore and I had worked with her before. She's in the special prosecutor's section dealing with felony arrests in burglary, robbery, gun possession, and assault one. We caught her as she was coming in, and she addressed both Fiore and me from memory.

"Good morning, Officer Cavalucci." Her face lit up when she saw Fiore. "Officer Fiore, it's good to see you again."

The ADA was heavyset, late thirties with frizzy brown hair, green eyes, and a big smile. She wore a maroon skirt with a white silk blouse. She hadn't changed into her work shoes and still wore socks and sneakers over her pantyhose. She was easy to work with, competent and pleasant. Whenever I'd dealt with her she tried to move the case along or at least let me know when we would be testifying so I could come back later in the day.

We sat down outside her office with our coffee and bagels. I had the *New York Post*, and Fiore had brought a book. The DA's office was chaotic, phones ringing, faxes beeping, people coming in and out from every direction. I tuned it out and opened my paper. There wasn't much going on in the city, just a lot of hype about the Fourth of July. The paper gave a schedule of activities around the city: the South Street Seaport had a free concert; the Intrepid Museum had exhibits and hands-on nautical crafts for children; the fireworks display in the harbor would start at 9:15 and continue until 10:00. I had a view of the harbor and I was sure my party would be in full swing by then.

I turned to the sports section. We had a good night in sports. The Mets beat the Braves 10–2. The Yankees beat the Orioles 9–8 with the Orioles giving up five walks and sixteen hits. Then I read the crime report. The city put out its crime report for the first half of the year, and apparently every crime but murder was down in the city. I would love to know who does those numbers and how much their nose grows each time they calculate the statistics.

Nick Caputo, who used to work with us, stopped to say hello to us outside the ADA's office. He was in a plainclothes unit now and was there on a gun collar, working with another ADA. After he left, Fiore and I went back to our reading until I got bored with the paper. I looked over to see what he was so interested in.

"Whatcha reading?" I asked.

He looked startled. "Oh, it's a daily devotional."

"What's that?"

"Every day it gives you a Scripture and then talks about that Scripture. Then at the end it gives you a Scripture reference. Today's is interesting," he said. "I think it's something you'd understand."

I took the bait. "So, what's it say for today?" I asked casually.

"You really want to know?" He looked skeptical.

I shrugged. "Sure, tell me what the word is for today."

"It's about protection."

I must have looked confused, because he chuckled. Actually, I almost asked him if he meant birth control.

"The verse is from Psalm 91, which is all about God's protection. It says in verse 11: 'For he shall give his angels charge over thee, to keep thee in all thy ways.' Do you understand what that means?"

"Like a guardian angel? My grandmother gave me a pin like that."

He thought for a second. "Kind of. You know how we're assigned to South David to protect it?"

I nodded.

"Well, the angel has an assignment to protect us."

"How do you know that?"

"I read it, just listen to what it says." He smiled.

He went on to tell me something about wings, feathers, arrows, and pestilence, along with other stuff I had no idea about. Then he came to the part about the reference verse. "Listen up, Tony, this is from Ephesians 6. I think you'll be able to relate to it. It's about protecting yourself."

I took his word for it, whatever it was he was talking about.

"Verse 13 tells us to put on the whole armor of God. Think about our uniform. 'Stand therefore, having your loins girt about with truth.'"

Loins?

"Which is like putting on my gun belt," Fiore continued, "except it's my integrity and faithfulness to Jesus. Then it says: 'And having on the breastplate of righteousness.'"

I could have guessed this one.

"Which is like our vests. Except that righteousness is what Jesus went to the cross for. He died to make us righteous with God even though we were sinners. The breastplate of righteousness protects our hearts from the enemy's attack, just like our bulletproof vest protects our vital organs from gunshot. You still with me?"

I nodded.

"'And your feet shod with the preparation of the gospel of peace.' This means that the strength I get from the gospel gives me peace so I can stand in battle. Just like the academy and intac training and all the other stuff we learn prepare us for when we're out there.

"This next part is good, 'Above all, taking the shield of faith, wherewith ye shall be able to quench all the fiery darts of the wicked.' The Roman soldiers used to have a shield made of wood, and it was covered with linen and leather to absorb fiery arrows. So what Paul was saying is that the shield actually consists of faith, and our faith in the Lord can stop all the flaming arrows that the evil one is throwing at us. Our shield is what stops the arrow. Our shield goes over our heart too; it may not give us power, but it gives us authority."

"How do you know Roman soldiers wore shields like that?" I asked, interested.

"I learned about it in church, but it's not anything you couldn't find in a history book." He checked again to see if I was following this. I guess I looked okay because he continued.

"'And take the helmet of salvation, and the sword of the Spirit, which is the word of God.' Think hats and bats—if we're in a riot situation, that helmet is hot and uncomfortable, but if someone tosses something off a building, our head is protected. At first salvation is uncomfortable. We're used to—"

"Joe?" I asked quietly.

"What?"

"Is this really what you do when you get dressed for work? Put on your gear and get ready to battle evil forces?" I could see a psych pension coming here.

"It's an analogy, Tony," he said patiently. "I'm giving you something to compare it to so you have a visual idea of what I'm talking about. Anyway, the sword is like our gun, used to combat the enemy's assault. The sword is the Word of God. This is the last part: 'Praying always with all prayer and supplication in the Spirit, and watching thereunto with all perseverance and supplication for all saints.' Prayer is communication. While we're out there, we have constant communication with Central with our radio, and prayer is our constant communication with God."

I just nodded.

He squinted at me. "Are you getting any of this?"

"Oh, I understand completely now," I said seriously. "Luke Skywalker and Darth Vader."

He smiled. "Sure, the force against the dark side."

"You're a meatball." I laughed. "Have you always been like this? With God, I mean."

He nodded. "I was raised going to my church. I gave my life to Christ when I was a little kid, never lived any other way."

Just then Carl Hansen, the complainant for our robbery collar, walked up. He was sober and dressed in a conservative suit. I had a hard time forgetting about his ripped shorts and underwear but managed to shake his hand without laughing. He told us he postponed his trip home two extra days so he could testify before the grand jury.

He was nervous and asked a lot of questions about testifying. We assured him not to worry, that the defendant and his attorney wouldn't be in the courtroom. Just ADA Katz asking him questions. He asked if we found the other perp who robbed him, and I told him no, but we were searching for him constantly.

ADA Katz came out of her office, and the three of us went in one at a time to talk about the case. Fortunately the case wasn't complicated, so the whole thing took only about a half hour. After that we took the elevator up to the grand jury room on the twelfth floor while Katz gave her paperwork to the court clerk. The clerk catalogued the order of cases to go before the grand jury, and because it was the day before the Fourth of July, the schedule was crowded. Katz told us we wouldn't go on until after lunch. The grand jury recessed from 12:00 to 1:00 so we wouldn't have to be back before 12:45. She was using only Fiore to testify since he was the one who handcuffed the perp and heard him place himself at the crime scene, and he was the one who recovered the money and knife.

We stayed in the courthouse until 11:30 then walked in

the heat up to Mulberry Street to get some lunch. There's an Italian deli called Luciano's where we eat whenever we're at court. It's pretty expensive, but the special of the day is usually reasonable. Today's special was turkey pastrami with smoked mozzarella and sun-dried tomatoes on a hero for six bucks. We waited in line for fifteen minutes, then took our sandwiches and ate in Columbus Park. The park was packed—even the midday heat couldn't keep everyone out of the sunshine. Music was blasting from a parked car with a guy and girl sunbathing on the hood. I envied their lack of clothes while I sweltered in my uniform.

The sandwich was incredible but salty. I drank a twenty-ounce Coke but was still thirsty. The conversation over lunch was mostly about fishing. Fiore was going out this weekend on his father's boat. I told him I was going down the shore and would probably do some fishing myself. The crabbing was good down there, but it was too early in the season for crabs. I didn't mention that I would be doing a lot of partying too. I didn't think he would lecture me, but I wasn't sure how much I wanted him to know about me.

We walked back to the courthouse at 12:40, and I spent five minutes trying to suck water from the water fountain. I hate the water fountain there; you never know what kind of germs were on it. If I wasn't so thirsty I wouldn't go near it. We waited until 1:15 for the grand jury to reconvene, and then our case went on. The complainant went in to testify first, and Fiore went in about 1:30. We waited for the count, and Katz let us know the perp was indicted. We said good-bye to Hansen and ADA Katz, went to punch out, and walked back toward Canal Street to catch the train uptown.

We passed Columbus Park again. Some guys were playing softball on the asphalt field, and we stopped to watch for a few minutes. There were still a lot of people around, dog walkers, roller skaters, but not any cops. A woman came up to ask us where the Department of Motor Vehicles was located, and we told her. Then a man asked us what would happen if he didn't show up for an arrest for urinating in public. Fiore told him that a judge would issue a warrant, which he wasn't too happy about but thanked us anyway as he walked away mumbling. We left after that. This wasn't our command, and we didn't know a lot about the area.

A hot dog vendor known to have clean hands replaced the morning coffee vendor outside the courthouse. Even though I wasn't hungry I couldn't pass up a dirty water dog. I ordered one with mustard and sauerkraut, paid a buck and a half for it, and ate it as we walked back to the train. You can't get hot dogs like that working midnight. It was delicious—soft roll, salty thin dog, with just the right bite from the mustard.

There are certain foods I will eat only in New York—hot dogs, pizza, and bagels. I traveled a lot when I was a carpenter, working jobs all over the country, and I've never found anyplace that comes close. You can get good Italian or even Chinese food in Chicago, L.A., or other big cities. But never bagels, pizza, or hot dogs. It's in the water; nothing tastes like New York tap.

The train ride back was less crowded than it had been in the morning. Rush hour wouldn't start until about 4:00. There were seats on the train, but we stood by the doors again at the end of the car. Without the crowds you could hear the conductor announcing the stops, and the screech of the train was more noticeable. A guy came through the doors from the car ahead of us, announcing that he was selling pencils. He was a skell but had cleaned himself up a little. He wore a short-sleeved white dress shirt and dark blue pants with sneakers. As he passed people he told them his sob story—he was out of work with children to support, down on his luck, blah blah blah. When someone gave him money he would loudly bless him or her while he walked almost drunkenly to the sway of the train.

I smirked when he saw us. He paused, and for a minute I thought he would run, but he went to walk past us so he could cut through the doors to the next car. Fiore threw him a buck. The skell looked as surprised as I was. I would never give a skell money. There were times when I wanted to, but if word got out that I was an easy target, skells would be lining up around the precinct for a handout.

"God bless you, Officer," he said.

"God bless you too, guy," Fiore answered.

6

*T*he subway was air-conditioned, but when we stepped out onto the platform at our stop, the air felt like a sauna. We walked up onto the street in sunshine so strong it made me squint. The smell of roasting peanuts and pretzels drifted over from the vendors' carts on the corner. We crossed the street and went into Starbucks where Fiore bought us each an iced cappuccino. We drank them as we walked back to the precinct.

We went inside to notify the desk sergeant that we were back from court. I didn't have paperwork to do, so I went downstairs to the lounge.

The lounge is in the basement, a twelve-by-twenty-foot room that holds four tables for eating. A foul-smelling refrigerator mottled with mold sits with a microwave on top of it. There are no windows, just panels of fluorescent lights that cast a dismal shadow on the already gloomy room. Black cushioned benches line three of the walls where most people sleep. Someone's old couch sits in front of the television. Four day-tour guys were watching reruns of *Law and Order*, so Fiore and I sat down at the table to watch with them. Fiore went up at 4:30 to sign out. I signed out for 4:30 but didn't do it until 5:00.

I changed into blue cotton shorts and a white shirt and went over to the bar on 9th Avenue with Frankie Amendola from the bike squad. Frankie played first base with us last year but hurt his arm wrestling with a pickpocket up on 34th Street. He was bummed out about missing the playoffs but would be back to play next year. Willie the bartender was engrossed in a heated argument with one of the day-tour guys, about his bar tab. He calmed down when he saw us all looking at him. I doubted he wanted to lose business over a bar tab.

I drank beers with Amendola until about 6:00, then walked over to my favorite Chinese food dump. I picked up an order of house lo mein and some chicken and broccoli. I walked back to the station house and ate my food in the lounge while watching the *Fresh Prince of Bel-Air*. Fiore was asleep on one of the benches in the back, the lights off on that end of the room. I finished my dinner, then napped until about 10:45 to sleep off the beer.

I washed and changed and went back to the muster room for roll call. Sergeant Hanrahan was out, and his replacement was Jimmy Yu, a new sergeant.

I met up with Fiore by our vehicle. He cleaned out the car again, saving the *Post* for me. We stopped for coffee on the corner of 35th and 9th. A red Ford Taurus was blocking the left lane, bringing traffic down to three lanes. The left front tire was up on the divider and the driver's door was open.

"What is this moron doing?" I said as I pulled up behind the car and gave the guy a whoop with my siren. I saw no reaction or movement inside the car. I whooped him again and turned on my turret lights as an old-time security guard in front of the post office on 32nd and 9th yelled over, "I think he's drunk."

Now I was mad—this guy was gonna get someone killed because he was drunk in the middle of traffic. We both got out of the car, Fiore more carefully because he was on the traffic side. Cars were slowing down to see what was going on. I stomped over, angry that I had to deal with this. The security guard called over again, "I called it in." Of course he called it in, to come and get me to clean up the garbage. I pulled the door open more and leaned down into the car.

"Buddy, what's the problem?" I got no response. His face was toward the passenger side so I added a little louder, "Have you been drinking?" I leaned in and saw him close his eyes. He was an older black man, about sixty years old and dressed in blue work pants and shirt. I didn't smell booze, but the car smelled faintly of urine. I tried to pull him out of the car, but his body was stiff. Fiore was looking in the passenger side window and must have seen the drool on the side of the guy's mouth because he motioned me with a wave. "Tony, I don't think he's drunk, but he might have had a stroke or something—he's trying to respond but he can't."

I leaned over him. "Buddy, are you having a heart attack or something?" His arms started to flutter but that was the extent of it. Fiore was already on the radio calling for a bus (ambulance), telling them we had a possible stroke victim and giving our location.

"Easy, buddy," I said as I patted his shoulder. "The ambulance is on the way."

He tried to nod.

"I'm gonna get your wallet," I said as I checked his back pants pocket on the left side. There was no wallet on that side, so Fiore leaned in from the passenger side and retrieved it from his right back pocket.

I stepped back outside to direct the traffic as Fiore came over to the driver's side and spoke to him in a soothing voice.

Now I felt terrible, because I realized the poor guy had tried to move his car out of traffic when he realized he was having a stroke. If the security guard had bothered to see what was going on, the ambulance could have been here sooner.

"So was he wasted?" the guard called from his booth, almost giddy.

"No, he had a stroke," I snapped. His face fell.

The ambulance arrived, parking in front of the man's car, and angled up on the divider so they weren't out in traffic.

"Do you need a hand?" the guard called again, now acting concerned.

"No thanks, pal, you've done enough," I called back.

Fiore took the information off the guy's license, and we waited until they got him into the ambulance. Fiore drove the man's car back to the precinct, and as I walked back over to my sector car the security guard yelled out, "I'm not allowed to leave the booth." I ignored him and drove away.

Once I got back to the precinct I dialed information and got the man's home phone number. A fragile voice answered and confirmed that it was her husband driving the car. I was careful when telling her that he had been taken to Bellevue, but she sounded like she was having a heart attack anyway. "He's okay," I lied. "EMS was taking good care of him when I left." She calmed down somewhat and said her son would take her over to the hospital. I told her that the car was parked at the precinct and she could pick up the keys from the desk sergeant. Fiore left the keys at the desk with a note instructing them to give them to the family.

We drove back out and parked in an empty parking lot on 37th Street. I sat smoking, listening to the distant sound of cars and trucks, the occasional pieces of conversation as people walked by. Each time a car drove down the street they ran over a manhole cover that made a kerplunk sound. Above us on the sixth floor the windows shone with a scarlet glow, and an oriental red lantern hung on the fire escape. It was a Korean geisha house. Straight ahead in between the buildings we had an amazing view of the Empire State Building, lit up for the holiday in red, white, and blue. Two fire trucks barreled down the street, horns blasting, sirens going. It was so loud my heart started pounding in my chest.

I read the paper for a while then watched the building, smoking another cigarette, a million things running through my head.

Fiore broke into my thoughts. "Got a lot on your mind, Tony?"

I shook my head. "Not much."

"Everything okay? Ever hear from that old girlfriend of yours?"

"Nope."

"Going down to the Jersey shore this weekend, right?"

I nodded and heard him chuckle.

"Are you leaving in the morning?"

"No," I said. "My family is coming over for a barbecue tomorrow, then I'll head down the shore tomorrow night or Friday morning."

"You have a big family?" he asked.

"Not really, one brother, one sister. My parents are divorced, my father's remarried. They're all coming tomorrow, so it should be interesting. It always is."

"Why, don't they get along?" he asked quietly.

I laughed. "Not really."

I pulled out and drove toward 6th Avenue. I didn't want to tell Fiore about my family or anything else for that matter. I tried to give myself something to look forward to about this weekend but couldn't. I didn't want to see my family, and I didn't want to go to the shore and drink too much.

I lit another cigarette and drove down to 8th Avenue and made a right, heading north. I passed Port Authority on my left and the triple-X stores with their constant parade of customers on my right.

I stopped at the light on 42nd Street, getting ready to head toward Times Square, and smiled. To the right my old pal John Wilson was dealing crack out of a potato chip bag. John and I went back a ways, and he always tried to be real cool with me. He used to try and give me free tapes and CDs, telling me he'd "take care of me" and get me anything I wanted. Now that really made me mad, him thinking I'd look the other way for some stolen CDs. I must have locked him up for drugs four times already, yet there he was, back on my streets. He was about six feet tall and fat. His dark hair was buzzed, with the tips bleached white. He wore a big white T-shirt with a cartoon on the front and red tropical print shorts, white socks and sneakers. His eyes were looking around each time someone put their hand inside his bag of potato chips and dropped money into his hand.

I pulled the car over and got out, nightstick in hand. He froze when he saw me, then he jumped. I could see him wondering if I saw him dealing. He switched gears and smiled.

"Hey, Officer Cavalucci, howz it goin'?" He was white but spoke with a Spanish twang.

"Hey!" I smiled. "You got some potato chips for me?"

He crumpled the top of the bag. "No, there's none left."

"Oh, come on John, you don't have any potato chips for your favorite officer?" I reached for the bag.

"No, sorry, there's no more."

I took the bag and looked inside at the multicolored caps to the crack vials. "Wow, multicolored potato chips! My favorite!"

John took off running toward 8th Avenue, heading north. I started to chase him, laughing as I went. His shoes were too big for his feet, and he almost lost both shoes as he tried to run. When I caught up to him, I kicked his right foot into his left foot and he went flying in the air. Whack! He hit the ground. His shoes came flying off, landing a couple of feet from his body. His hands and face were scraped, and he was bleeding all over. He started to cry when I put the cuffs on him. I turned around to see Fiore right behind me, one hand on his radio, the other on top of his gun.

We walked John over to the car and drove back toward the precinct. As I drove back he was crying like a baby in the backseat. Several minutes later an unmistakable odor filled the car.

"Did you go in your pants?" I yelled into the back.

"I think so." He continued sobbing.

"What? I can't believe you just crapped in your pants! You know what? Now you're gonna sit in it for the rest of the night."

A lot of perps would mess their pants, figuring the cops wouldn't want to deal with them and just let them go. If you pick someone up for crack and they crap in their pants, forget it, leave them. You can always go another block down and grab someone else for crack with cleaner underwear.

Fiore rolled down his window and actually started to gag. "Tony, let me out of the car!"

"You have kids, how can this bother you?" It was disgusting, but even I wasn't gagging.

"It's not the same, Tony. They're my kids." His eyes were tearing and his face was red.

I pulled the car over, and he got out, taking in big gulps of air. I didn't want to goof on him—he'd never said anything about me puking—so I dropped it.

"You see! Now my partner's gagging because you're so disgusting. You're gonna sit in it all night," I spat toward the back.

Fiore got back in, keeping his head out the window as I drove. I took John back to the precinct and put him in a cell. The guys in the cell were screaming at him. "Man, what did you do? Ah, that stinks! White boy crapped his pants!"

I left him handcuffed in the cell, stinking up the place. I wasn't taking the arrest, so I knew I'd have to get him cleaned up, but I was gonna let him sit in it while I did the paperwork.

Romano, a rookie, wanted the collar so he could stretch the overtime for the whole day and get fifteen and a half hours while staying in the precinct for the night of the Fourth. As I did the paperwork, the other perps were calling John names. John was talking about how he'd done time before and that it was no big deal.

I walked over to the cell. "No big deal? No big deal? You were crying like a little girl when I locked you up," I yelled into the cell.

"Officer, please, let me clean up."

"Okay, shut your mouth and follow me. I'm gonna take you outside, and I'm telling you right now, when I take the cuffs off you so you can wash yourself, if you run, the next place you'll wake up is Bellevue, you understand me?"

He nodded.

I took him outside where the guys in peddlers park their vendor carts. It was fenced in so he couldn't run anywhere. There was a short hose, and he had to stand right up against it while he washed himself. I gave him a plastic bag for the soiled underwear and brought him in to the men's room to wash his hands with soap. I left him with a warning. "If you ever pull a stunt like that with me again, you'll sit in it all night."

Fiore had been quiet through this whole thing, just staying close by in case I needed him. I didn't think he objected to the way I handled the situation, probably just some of my language, which I've edited here. That was another funny thing about Fiore—he didn't curse. All cops cursed; in fact, I cursed more at work than anywhere else. Not him, but we've never been in anything really hairy together yet. Time will tell.

We stayed inside until our meal, ordering turkey and cheese sandwiches from a deli. We went back out at 5:00 a.m.—a transformer had exploded, sending a manhole cover flying ten feet in the air and crashing into a parked car. We stayed there until Con Edison was on the scene. At 6:45 when we were getting ready to head back in, someone called a bomb threat in at the Empire State Building. Just in time to start off the Fourth of July festivities. A security guard said a suspicious-looking suitcase was left by the front entrance. The Empire State Building was in Charlie-Frank sector, so we went to back up O'Brien and McGovern. After a half hour of waiting for emergency services and the bomb squad to get there McGovern finally said, "Screw this" and walked over to open it up. The only things inside were some clothes, papers, deodorant and other toiletries. By the time I got back to the precinct I was so tired I could barely stand. I changed back into my shorts and shirt, wished Fiore a good weekend, and went out to my truck.

The heat and humidity were incredible. When the city gets this hot there's always an undercurrent of hostility. The weather had been cooking up for a week, and it was supposed to break a hundred degrees today. I could already hear sporadic fireworks as I drove home. The mayor's plan to rid the city of fireworks is futile. Every year they say the same thing, and every year there are plenty of fireworks. Thousands of people all over the city today would be drunk and armed with explosives. Now that's a scary thought. By tonight there will be so much smoke and litter from the fireworks, it'll be three days before the city cleans it up.

I was dreading spending the day with my family. I just

wasn't up to the drama of a family get-together and was already wishing it were over so I could go down the shore for the weekend.

The traffic was heavy, and it took me forty-five minutes to get home. When I pulled up in front of my house Denise and Sal Valente were carting a redwood picnic table into the yard. I walked around to find them setting up the deck for the party. I was tired and people were already here at 8:30 in the morning.

"Tony, I put your air conditioner on so it's cool in there and you won't hear us out here. I had the air on all night downstairs so if it gets too hot we can eat inside," Denise said. She was wearing a white Old Navy shirt with a flag on it and short blue shorts. Her hair was caught up in a red fabric thing and she had little Statues of Liberty hanging from her ears. Sal wore blue shorts, a white tank top, and a red baseball cap. What were these two up to?

"I'm going to bed. What time is everyone coming?" I asked.

"Two o'clock, but don't worry about the food. Sal and I made the salads last night. And except for what needs to be grilled, everything else is done."

I nodded and made my way inside. It was freezing in the house and even worse in my room. I put on a sweatshirt and sweatpants and crawled under the covers with my teeth chattering. I set my alarm for 2:00 and was asleep almost immediately.

They dropped two bombs on me that day. My alarm went off at 2:00, but I hit the snooze until 2:27. I heard the hum of my air conditioner and then the sound of voices below a minute or two later. I could hear Marie's big mouth telling Vinny to get another bag of ice for the cooler. I crossed to the bathroom. The temperature of the house was slightly warmer than my room. I showered and shaved, dressing in a black shirt and beige Dockers shorts. There was a pot of coffee brewing in the kitchen, and as I poured a cup, my grandmother came through the sliding doors.

"Tony! Come and give Grandma a kiss." She beamed as I crossed to kiss her, and she got me in one of those hug head-locks, choking me with her perfume. She was decked out in patriotic red shorts and a blue and white striped shirt.

"Everyone's here. Come out and get something to eat." She hugged me again, grabbed a bowl from the refrigerator, and went back out to the deck. Through the glass doors I could see all the boats out on the water. A lot of smaller boats came up to see the festivities, and two days ago one of them capsized. The currents under the Verrazano are strong and the wake of an aircraft carrier is no joke. I didn't get the whole story, just that an off-duty cop saved a two-year-old girl from the water when the boat tipped.

Out on the deck my mother was talking to Vinny. From where I stood in the kitchen I could see the lines of bitterness etched into her face. But she had lost some weight and looked better than she had in a long time. Marie and my dad were talking to Frank Bruno and his wife, and their daughter, Nicole, was sitting on a beach chair with a bored look on her face. Denise and Sal had set up the deck buffet style with the table next to the grill and chairs set up along the deck. A radio was tuned to the oldie station, and a doo-wop song was playing. Vinny was grill chef while Sal helped Denise at the table.

I went to the refrigerator for milk and found it stuffed in with bowls of potato and macaroni salad, hamburgers, and hot dogs. On the bottom shelf sat a watermelon cut into the shape of a basket with grapes, blueberries, strawberries, and other fruit inside. I grabbed the milk from the back of the top shelf and poured some in my coffee. I took my coffee out onto the deck and set it on the picnic table. The sun was strong—it had to be over ninety degrees. There was no shade, and we didn't have an umbrella, just a slight breeze coming off the water.

I went to kiss my mother hello, and she gave me her cheek and continued talking to Vinny without turning to acknowledge me. This was her way of letting me know she was angry at me and that she wanted me to try and figure out why. Forget that. I was tired of playing this game every time I saw her. Everyone else but Marie and Nicole greeted me with a kiss or a hug. I could feel the underlying tension and hoped something would break the ice and put everyone at ease.

"We sold the house," Marie said smugly, smiling first at me then my mother. I picked up my coffee and found a bug in it so I cracked open a beer instead. Denise and Sal walked into the yard. Denise looked upset, Sal looked concerned.

"Mom's looking for a fight today," Denise said to me.

"Why, what happened?" I asked.

She shrugged. "I guess the house being sold. The first person that looked at it bought it. They gave a tentative closing date of September 15. Marie loved telling Mom. I felt sorry for her, but when I tried to kiss her, she turned her face. I asked if she was all right, and she wouldn't answer. She's only talking to Vinny, her baby."

"Just ignore her, Denise. Let's just have a good time." I gave her an affectionate hug.

"Your mother's pretty cold," Sal added.

"You have no idea," Denise replied.

Things went pretty smooth while we ate. Vinny grilled burgers, hot dogs, steak, and sausage on the grill. There were peppers and onions, baked beans, potato and macaroni salad. My grandmother made a tomato salad with red onion and basil and a tray of baked ziti, just in case someone wanted hot food.

Once everyone was full, Grandma and I put the perishables back in the refrigerator.

Vinny came into the kitchen and asked that we come out onto the deck for a minute. I thought he wanted to point out a ship coming through the channel or something because he seemed pretty excited. Christie must have just arrived; she stood next to Vinny with her hands behind her back, smiling up at him.

Vinny beamed as he spoke. "Everyone, I want to announce that last night Christie and I got engaged."

Shouts and applause went up around the deck. My grandmother let out a cheer and started to cry. Christie pulled her left hand out and showed us a nice-sized diamond ring. I was hurt for a second because I couldn't believe Vinny hadn't told me before. I'd always thought that if one of us got engaged, the other would help pick out the ring. I didn't say anything, just gave him a bear hug and welcomed Christie to the family.

I was stupid enough to think that Vinny's engagement would be the thing to lighten up the party, but it was the very thing that started the war. Everything was okay at first—Vinny produced two bottles of champagne, and we all toasted the couple. My brother asked me to be his best man, and Christie asked Denise to be a bridesmaid. We heard my mother mutter, "Are you sure that's a good idea?" and I saw the look of pain pass over Denise's face. My father held up his glass and said, "A toast, to Vinny and Christie on their engagement and their future. May they be happy and healthy." My dad loved to play the father when people were watching.

"I'll drink to that," I said.

"You'll drink to anything," I heard my mother mutter. Aunt Patty leaned over and whispered something to her, and she made a face.

"Salute!" Grandma said loudly, trying to run interference.

I had to give Denise credit for not reacting. That is, until my mother said, "Vinny's younger than you, Denise. What are you going to do, live with Tony forever?"

"Mom, this is their moment. Can't we just let them enjoy it?" Denise said.

My mother saw Sal look at her and shake his head, so she threw Denise a dirty look. I grabbed another beer from the cooler and offered Denise one, but she shook her head.

"Have a drink Tony, that'll fix it," my mother said sarcastically.

I lifted my bottle to her. She was holding a red plastic cup that I knew was filled with wine, and she mock saluted me with it.

"That's enough, Marilyn," my father warned.

"Don't tell me what to do, Vin," my mother shot back.

For once Marie tried to avoid a fight, or so I thought. She started gushing with wedding advice, and a look of shock passed her face as she said, "Oh no! I have to get a mother-of-the-groom dress!" She barked out a laugh. "I'm too young for this!"

Denise closed her eyes, I shook my head, and my father looked like he wanted to crawl under the deck. Vinny got that look in his eyes that said, "Please don't do this," and Christie looked down at her hands.

My grandmother meant well, trying to smooth things over, when she said, "I've always prayed that I would live to see great-grandchildren, so don't make me wait too long!"

"If we waited for Tony or Denise to have them, we'd all be dead," my mother added.

We were all shocked when Sal addressed my mother. "What is wrong with you?"

"What did you say?" she answered indignantly.

"You heard me. What is wrong with you? Why do you treat

your own children like that? I've watched you all day—Vinny you hug and kiss, and Tony and Denise you turn your face from, insult them every chance you get. How could you treat them that way?" He looked hurt and confused. If it were anyone but Sal I would have decked him.

"Sal, don't worry about it," I said. "Just her way of showing affection."

"No, it's not," he said. "Denise has been upset since yesterday. She knew this would happen."

"Let me tell you something, mister." My mother advanced on him. "Just because you're sleeping with my daughter doesn't give you the right to criticize her family."

"Not that it's any of your business, but I'm not sleeping with your daughter." Sal turned to Denise. "Do you want to leave?"

She hesitated then nodded. He held out his hand, and they walked off the deck toward the front of the house. Denise turned around. "You coming, Tony?"

"No, I'll be leaving for the shore soon," I called back.

I had originally planned to leave the following morning after the barbecue, but after things got out of hand I decided to leave that night after the fireworks show.

It cooled off a little after the sun went down. I was stretched out on a lounge chair watching the water when Nicole sat down next to me. "So, Tony, I hear you have a house down the shore for the summer."

"No, a couple of my friends do," I said, not looking at her. "Where?"

"Manasquan."

She nodded. "How's work?"

"Fine."

"You want to walk over to Fort Wadsworth to watch the fireworks?" She tilted her head to the side and smiled. She was really pretty, light brown hair with green eyes, and used to getting her way.

"No." I smiled. "I think I'll stay here and watch them."

She pursed her lips together and nodded. "I won't ask you again, Tony," she said as she walked away.

"Fine with me," I mumbled.

I heard another voice at my side. "Hey." This time it was Aunt Patty. Her white hair was pulled into a girlish ponytail, her skin tan. "How's my favorite nephew?"

I leaned over and hugged her. "How's life with Mom?"

"Being here upsets her. She's usually not this bad." She smiled sadly. "I think it's still traumatic for her to see your father and Marie."

I nodded.

"I feel sorry for you and Denise, the way she treats you," she continued quietly, looking around to make sure no one heard her. "She really does love you both."

I snorted.

"You remind her so much of your father, and she has a lot of guilt about Denise." She surprised me when her eyes filled. "You used to have such a great family."

"That was a long time ago. You'd think we'd all be over it by now."

"Some people never get over it. What about you, are you okay? You're drinking a lot."

"Aunt Patty, it's a holiday, I'm having a couple of drinks. I'm fine."

She put her head down and nodded. "Selling the house may not be a bad thing, Tony. It's time for all of you to move on, especially your mom."

"I guess," I said sadly.

"If you ever need to talk, I'm always here."

"I know, thanks," I said.

As the time for the fireworks display got closer, the beach next to my house filled with people. They stood at the edge of the water, some sitting on the cement wall dividing my yard from the beach. The fireworks went up by the seaport in Manhattan, giving us a spectacular view. The show lasted close to an hour, and within minutes after it ended the beach crowd had dispersed.

I went upstairs and packed a bag, putting my gun in the bottom drawer. I'm not allowed to carry it in New Jersey, and I definitely didn't want it with me when I was drinking. My father, Marie, and Frank Bruno and his wife were still talking out on the deck with Christie and Vinny when I left. I said good night and walked out to my truck.

Traffic was light on the Garden State Parkway as I headed down the shore. The house Mike rented was on the waterway. It stood three stories high, white with blue trim. Mike rented it with five other people—three nurses from St. Vincent's hospital, a fireman, and Richie Patterson, who was a cop in the 120 precinct on Staten Island. Everyone was in their late twenties, early thirties, which is why the realtors rented it to them. The guys in their early twenties are known to destroy the rented beach houses, so the realtors prefer the older crowd. The houses on the block were pretty much the same, gravel front yards, boats in the back, the salty smell of the water permeating the air. Richie Patterson had a boat, a nice seventeen-foot Bow Rider that we all used.

I went to the house to drop off my truck. I knew everyone would be at the Osprey Hotel off Main Street. One of the nurses whose name I couldn't remember was sitting on the couch with a guy. I said hello and went upstairs to Mike's room. I put my bag in the closet and pulled out the top dresser drawer, leaving my shield and police ID underneath it. I didn't know everyone in the house, and even if I did I wouldn't chance losing my shield. I'd lose ten days vacation for it.

I walked the five blocks to the Osprey. I could hear the music long before I got there. There was a line of people outside the building, but I cut to the front and asked for Doug Wheeland, the manager of the place.

"Why do you want him?" a blond musclehead with a crew cut and sunburn asked as he folded his arms to beef up his biceps.

"He's a friend of mine—tell him it's Tony Cavalucci," I bellowed over the noise.

Doug loved cops, and he knew me from all the years I'd been to the shore. He emerged with the bouncer a few minutes later.

"Tony! Come on, man, Mike and Richie are inside, let me buy you a drink!" He shook my hand and slapped me on the back in a half hug. He was tall and lean, with blond sun-streaked hair and wrinkles around his eyes from all his years on the beach.

The Osprey was rocking. We passed through the first room, which had a live band, and into the second room, which had the big bar and a DJ. Beyond the big bar was a room with a small dance floor that was empty.

It was now midnight, and Mike and Richie had been at it for a few hours. Mike was pressed up against a sunburned blond, laughing into her ear. Richie was talking to a couple of guys I'd never met before. Doug bought me a beer, and we talked about going tubing on Richie's boat the following morning. Doug couldn't stay long because he had to watch the bar, but he promised to be at the house by 11:00 in the morning. I spent the next two hours drinking with Richie. At 2:00, when the bar closed, Mike was nowhere to be found, so Richie and I walked home together and sat up until 4:30 playing cards with Rob the fireman and Lisa the nurse.

I woke at 10:00, showered, and wore blue shorts for the

boat. I took a shirt but didn't put it on. In the kitchen some-one had made coffee, but I passed on the 7-Eleven muffins. I drank a cup of coffee and walked two blocks for a bacon, egg, and cheese on a bagel. When I got back to the house Mike and Richie were out back on the boat, and Doug pulled up a couple of minutes later.

Lisa the nurse and her ditzy friend came out on the boat with us. We took them out to open water. We took it easy on them, only spilling them from the tube once or twice each. It's a lot of fun. You attach a big inflated tube to the back of the boat as if you were waterskiing and whip around on the water with it. If you go fast enough, they bounce a few feet in the air when the tire hits the water. If you make a sharp turn the force of the turn pulls the tube out from under them. It's hysterical. The guys can usually hold on, the women end up in the water.

By 3:00 everyone was sunburned and laughing, and we made plans to go to the Osprey for happy hour. From 4:00 until 6:00 they served half-price Long Island iced tea and Jell-O shots. We got to the Osprey at 4:15, and by 6:30 I was numb. We went out for a pizza, and it tasted terrible but it absorbed some of the alcohol in my stomach.

We didn't go home after the pizza but back to the Osprey for more drinks. A friend of Richie's was talking to me. She kept bumping into me, laughing at everything I said. She was very tan, with black curly hair and a white tank top. She thought tubing sounded fun and asked if she could come out on the boat with us. I felt kind of detached from the whole thing, not happy or sad. I didn't feel anything. At one point I went outside—I was talking to a guy who worked as a schoolteacher during the year and a cop during the summer. It sounded great to me, part-time cop, part-time teacher. I must have been slurring, because he told me I might have had too much to drink and maybe I should go home. That was the last thing I remembered.

For the first time in my life I woke up and had no idea where I was. I had my shorts on but no shirt or shoes, and I was lying straight across a double bed. The house didn't look familiar, and no one was home. A note on the bed next to me said, "We went down to the beach, meet us there."

That wouldn't work, since I had no idea who wrote the note. I felt a moment of panic. I tried to remember how I got there, but nothing came to me. The house was hot and quiet. My head was pounding, my mouth was dry, and I smelled of sweat and booze. I saw my wallet and a pack of cigarettes on the dresser. My shirt and shoes were on the floor, and the alarm clock on the dresser said it was 11:14. I got dressed and went outside and walked to the corner. I found myself on Pine Avenue, about three blocks from where I was staying.

I walked back to Mike's house which was empty and messy. I packed up my gear, retrieving my shield and ID from under the drawer. I found a Coke in the fridge and some ham and cheese. I ate the sandwich at the table, hoping it would settle my stomach. There was a bottle of Advil on the counter, and I took two, downing them with the rest of my soda. I was having a hard time functioning, and I hoped nobody would come in so I didn't have to talk. I began to panic, and I gave in to the urge to run—I threw my bag in the truck and drove too fast toward the parkway, my heart pounding in sync with my head. I just had to get home.

It was so hot and muggy that the sweat was dripping down my face and back even with the air conditioner on high. I had at least an hour's drive, and I couldn't concentrate on anything. Different thoughts ran through my head. I wondered fleetingly what Joe Fiore would think of me if he knew I had blacked out. Depression settled in over me like a cloud. I had gotten deeper into something that was getting more and more difficult to climb out of.

How did I get to this? When did everything get so bad? I thought about how unhappy I was about everything and I didn't know how to change it. I felt so lonely.

My house was empty when I got home. Dishes were in the sink and the deck still showed signs of the barbecue. I cleaned out the sink and turned on the dishwasher and went up to take a shower. I felt somewhat better just being home. The shower woke me up a little, and I went back downstairs to clean up. Sal's picnic table was still there. I folded up the chairs and hosed down the deck. I scrubbed the grill with a wire brush and put all the beer bottles out in the recycle pail. I tried to watch TV but couldn't concentrate on anything, so I puttered around the quiet house, looking for something to catch my interest.

By 9:00 that night I was back up at Dave's Tavern, drinking beer and playing darts. The bar was empty except for a few neighborhood diehards like myself. Dave was trying to talk me into coming to the Sunday night turtle races, so I told him I would be there. At 1:00 I called it a night and walked home alone. Neither Vinny nor Denise were home, and I woke up at 8:00 the next morning to an empty house.

The Sunday *Staten Island Advance* was on my front steps, and I thought about looking through the classified section for an apartment but quickly dismissed the idea. I wasn't ready to deal with moving yet.

Since it was a holiday weekend, the neighborhood was quiet. The weather was still hot and humid, but we were supposed to get rain by Monday and a break in the humidity. I couldn't think of a thing to do around the house. I did my laundry the day before when I woke up, and the house was still neat from when I'd cleaned up.

I drove up to Montey's for peppers, eggs, and potatoes again. I told Montey about my house being sold, and he wanted to know if I'd be staying in the neighborhood. He looked sad about it. We've known each other a long time. My first job had been as a stock boy in his deli when I was fourteen. I'd worked there for two years. I loved my neighborhood, but without my house I didn't know if I would stay there. I mentally dismissed most of the neighborhoods on the Island—the north shore was too commercial, and the west shore was the dump. That left me the east and south shores, because I wouldn't go inland where there was no water. I needed to be near the water. I'd be lost without it.

I spent the rest of the afternoon on a lounge chair on the deck. I slept shirtless in the sun until a tanker blared its horn and woke me with a start. I jumped up, heart pounding, drenched with sweat. A second later I heard voices coming from the kitchen and went inside.

"Where have you been?" I barked at Denise, still annoyed from being startled awake.

She raised her eyebrows. "At Grandma's, *Dad,* if that's okay with you." She paused. "Why are you home? I thought you weren't coming back until tomorrow."

"I felt like coming home."

"Why?" She looked confused.

"Because I felt like it, *Mom,* if that's okay with you," I countered. "And what's with you and Sal Valente?"

"Nothing. We're friends." She sounded sincere enough, so I let it drop.

"Are you going to Dave's tonight?" I asked.

"No, I have to work tomorrow. Turtle races are always a late night."

It turned out she was right about the turtle races. I got to Dave's at 10:00, and the bar was packed with turtle gamblers.

Little turtles were put in a line, each with their own lane numbered one through twelve. You bet on your number while the DJ played Meatloaf, Southside Johnny, and other party music that the crowd knew exactly how to sing along to. It was a real upbeat crowd, getting into the music and the races. I won two drinks, then sat by myself at the end of the bar talking to Dave. A knockout girl who looked about fifteen but had the attitude of a seasoned player sauntered up to me wearing tight white shorts, white sandals, and a tight red shirt.

"Buy me a drink?" She smiled, her friends giggling behind her.

"Sure." I shrugged as I signaled Dave. "What are you drinking?"

"Iced tea." My eyebrows shot up. She couldn't have weighed more than ninety pounds. A couple of these and she'd be in a coma.

"Iced tea for the lady," I said to Dave.

When she picked up her drink, she took a sip, said "Thanks," and walked away. Her friends laughed.

I'm too old to fall for a stunt like that. I should have known better. Feeling more alone than I'd ever felt in my life, I picked up my money, left Dave a tip, and walked to an all-night newsstand. I bought two six-packs of Budweiser, then walked back home. I put one of the sixes on the kitchen table and the other in the refrigerator while I went upstairs for my gun. I felt better having it near me. I brought the gun and the six-pack out on the deck and sat down on the lounge chair. I started drinking big gulps, half a bottle at a time, with big belches in between while I stared out on the water.

I heard voices from the party on the deck. My mother's. *Have a drink Tony, that'll fix it.* Then my father's. *That's enough, Marilyn.* Then Marie. *We have a closing date of September 15.* I heard the guys at work laughing that I threw up. I heard

my old girlfriend Kim say, *At least with him I have a future.*
I looked up because I thought I heard Denise say, *Are you
coming, Tony?* I heard the rope straining against the pipe as
the body swayed.

I drank until I didn't hear anything else.

*T*he birds were chirping when I opened my eyes on the deck. It was just getting light out. There was a pounding in my head, and my mouth was dry and sticky. I walked into the kitchen, popped two Tylenol, and washed them down with a beer. I went upstairs to put my gun away, turned on my air conditioner, and climbed into bed.

I woke up again at 11:00 Monday morning to silence. I got up and shuffled through the rooms. The only evidence of anyone having been there was a pot of coffee, still lukewarm. I poured a cup and put it in the microwave, punching the timer for one minute. I added milk and sugar, but it was still too hot, so I went outside to check the weather. The sky was overcast, the air hot and thick. Thunderstorms were expected by nightfall, with temperatures in the mid-eighties.

I drank my coffee and smoked a cigarette at the kitchen table. I wondered what I was going to do that day. After showering and shaving I went down to the Shell station to get my car inspected. I ate a warm bagel with melted butter while waiting. When I finished the bagel I wanted another one, so I walked back across Bay Street, hoping there were still some warm ones left. Fortunately there were, and I ate this one with fresh coffee. After finishing the coffee, I retrieved my truck and drove down toward the ferry.

I drove to Olsen's Salvage Yard to pick up a new set of hubcaps for my truck. This is the second time I'd had them stolen and probably shouldn't bother replacing them anymore.

"New hubcaps again, Tony?" Danny Olsen smiled.

"Yeah." I shook his hand.

"Forty bucks for the four."

I gave him the forty bucks and talked with him a while. He reminded me I should leave one hubcap off because nobody's gonna bother stealing an incomplete set. I know this but you would think that parking my car half a block from the precinct would offer some protection.

I spent the rest of the day cleaning my guns and taking a nap. I woke at 8:00 and had dinner with Vinny and Denise. We grilled a London broil and ate it with zucchini, baked potatoes, and a salad. Vinny was excited about the wedding plans. He had booked St. Michael's, and he and Christie were going to a travel agent that night to talk honeymoons. Denise thought he should try a cruise; Christie wanted to go to Hawaii, but Vinny is afraid to fly. He asked what I thought, and I told him to take a cruise to Hawaii. He made a face.

I left for work at 10:30 and sped all the way up the west side after catching traffic on the Gowanus Expressway. I barely made it to roll call on time.

The Harper brothers hit on the Fourth of July. I found out at roll call that a grapnel hook was found still attached to a rope on the roof at 315 West 39th Street. The brothers entered the roof from inside the building, probably hiding out during the day on July 3, and got fifty grand in garments from one of the smaller name designers. The garments were due to be shipped out on

July 5. The inspector put the anticrime unit on it, but personally I doubted they'd hit again so soon.

Fiore and I started the night without any jobs, so we cruised slowly through our sector. Most cars, when they cover their sectors, drive the Avenues. I like to cover my sector by driving each street east to west between 34th and 40th Streets and 5th and 9th Avenue. Fiore and I were doing this until 11:45, when we stopped at a light. I noticed a transit police car stopped at the same light and I waved over to them. Over the radio I heard Central put over shots fired at a location which was right around the corner from us. I pulled the car up into the intersection and looked down the block. I didn't see anything going on, so Fiore put it over the radio that we were 84, on the scene.

The promised thunderstorm hit, and it started to rain fat drops on the windshield as I pulled in front of the building. We got out of the car and went to the front door. It was an all-glass front door on a gray marble entranceway. Black marble accented the door and the inside floor was black-and-white tile. A kid was lying on his back in the lobby. The door was locked so I pulled out my utility knife and pried the lock open. I jammed it with my memo book to keep it open. We went inside and took a look at the body. He was a light-skinned Hispanic male about eighteen years old, wearing jeans and a button-down cream-colored shirt with the first two buttons open. His eyes were open, staring lifelessly at the ceiling. As I was looking him over, Fiore called in the confirmed shooting, possible DOA, and went past me to a small hallway. The hallway was about five feet wide and ten feet deep before it angled left. He walked through until I couldn't see him anymore. I felt for a pulse on the victim's throat; there was none. The body was still slightly warm—he hadn't been dead long.

As I checked him over, the two transit cops that were next

to us at the light came in. I could hear the rain against the sidewalk and the swoosh of cars as they opened the doors. They were young, rookies, maybe twenty-two, twenty-three years old. One was Irish, the other Italian. They came over to look at the body when Fiore came back with his finger in front of his mouth, motioning me to keep quiet and follow him. As I turned back to the rookies I saw one of them bent down giving the guy mouth-to-mouth. I slapped him hard on the back of the head.

"What the—" He spun around toward me.

"He's dead, get away from him," I snapped quietly.

"But what if he . . . ?"

"He's dead and the shooter might still be here, so stay there and don't touch him."

He nodded nervously.

I went over to Fiore, and as I got around the corner there was a small elevator and a stairway door. I could hear footsteps on the floor above us and thought maybe the shooter was upstairs trying to hide or find another way out of the building. We put it over the radio that the possible shooter might be in the building and called for backup.

We pressed the button for the elevator, but it wasn't moving, and the door leading to the stairwell was locked. We went back to the foyer where the body was, and I started looking to see if there was any bullet hole. I told the rookies again not to touch anything, and I carefully picked up the victim's shirt by the corner so I wouldn't upset the crime scene. I couldn't see any blood or bullet hole, which was surprising. The other cars came flying up 38th Street and pulled in front of the building while one sped past us.

Soon Lieutenant Jim Farrell was on the scene. He was probably one of the most brilliant cops I had ever met. I doubted there was anyone in the department I respected more. He's around sixty years old with more than thirty-five years on the job. A rumpled-looking man, he had a friendly face with a wide, bulbous nose from all his years of drinking. His curly salt-and-pepper hair had a tendency to stick out on one side. He wore wire-framed glasses and had a huge potbelly that reminded me of Santa Claus. Tonight his white short-sleeved shirt adorned with lieutenant bars was coffee stained, and the waist of his pants disappeared under his stomach. His voice was gruff from the pipe he was constantly smoking, the mouth-piece chewed up. He always reminded me of an absentminded professor. He was also a frequent drinking partner of mine. Like me, he worked career midnights and has paid for it in his personal life. He's been to the farm to dry out a couple of times, but in the end the booze always gets the best of him. His wife ran off long ago, leaving him to raise a son and daughter alone. His daughter got into an abusive domestic situation, and his son has been in and out of rehab for drugs. He never remarried and is used frequently in the command to handle difficult and delicate issues.

He spotted a limousine pulled over halfway up the block. He had Mike Rooney shut the car and take the keys from the driver.

Someone opened the door to the stairwell, and Fiore grabbed the door and kept it open so we could go upstairs. We grabbed the guy as he came out. He was white, about thirty years old, bald and skinny. We had our guns drawn and put him up against the elevator, telling him not to move.

"Okay. Okay, no problem," he said, putting his hands up.

"Where are you coming from?" I asked in a hushed tone.

"From the second floor, at the after-hours club." His voice cracked.

"Did you see anyone go in there or up the stairs?" I said, still holding him.

"No, I didn't see anybody! I was in the bar!"

I brought him over to the transit cops and told the lou we had access up the stairs. We checked the stairs, finding we couldn't go up to the third floor. A steel-gated door with a push bar on the opposite side blocked the entrance. I turned and motioned with my finger toward the door on the second floor.

The after-hours club was located on the second floor. We announced to the dim, empty bar that we were police officers and told anyone inside to come out now. As we came in through the door there were some tables to the right bathed in a red glow from a colored lamp. In front of us was a bar that extended to the left and ended with two other tables. Long, dark curtains covered the windows, and people actually came out from behind them as we announced ourselves.

We asked what happened, and no one knew. They had all heard the shots downstairs, and they panicked and hid in case the gunman headed upstairs. Mostly men occupied the bar, including the bartender. McGovern and O'Brien came up to help with the search, so I left them upstairs with Fiore and went back down to talk to Lieutenant Farrell.

The limousine turned out to be a group of wannabe gangsters from Bensonhurst in Italian silk and a lot of gold. They told the lou they had been in the building in a brothel up on the sixth floor. When they had come down from the brothel a bunch of guys from Staten Island pulled a gun and an orange box cutter on their friend, who was now dead in the foyer.

The lou told me to put some gloves on and check the body without moving it too much. I looked it over and finally found a small entrance hole in the guy's chest. I hadn't seen the entrance wound at first because the skin had closed around it. The bullet must have killed him instantly because there was very little blood on him. I gingerly held up the corner of his shirt and I could see another entrance wound in the groin, down below his waist on his left side. I couldn't figure out why he had been shot there, but I didn't want to turn him over and mess up the evidence. It was hot in the vestibule, and I suddenly felt a desperate need to be out of there.

"Did anyone check the limo?" I asked the lou.

"No, go on out and take a look, Tony," he said quietly.

When I stepped back outside it was still raining. Steam was coming off the street and the cars as the heat came up, making the air thick and muggy. I walked about fifty feet to where the limo was parked. The vehicle wasn't new—it was black with black interior and shabby. It smelled of liquor, cigarettes, expensive cologne, and stale breath. I checked the seats and the floor, finding nothing, I stuck my hand into the backseat, and it moved a little. I pulled it out and found a half-inch-thick gold chain on the floor behind the seat. As I searched the rest of the limo I found an orange box cutter in the panel on the door. I put the chain and box cutter in my pocket and went back up to talk to the lieutenant.

"Lou," I said quietly as I pulled him to the side. "What did this kid get robbed for?"

"Supposedly a big, thick gold chain," he said, eyes darting over to the wise guys being held outside.

"Was it a gold chain like this?" I smiled as I pulled it from my pocket.

He chuckled.

"And what did they use to do the robbery with?" I asked, knowing the answer.

"An orange box cutter," he answered.

"Like this one here?" I held it up.

He smiled again. "Just hold on to that for now. I want you to show it to the detectives and tell them where you found it in the car."

"If the guys from Staten Island robbed this chain using a

gun and a box cutter, then why were the chain and the box cutter in the limo?" I asked him.

"The shot in the groin is on an angle, down, like he shot himself pulling out the gun. I figure he was the one with the gun and when he pulled it out he shot himself. While the victim was stunned, the other guy grabbed it and shot him with it."

That made sense to me. Their buddy got shot, and they all ran out. Then they came around with the limousine to see what had happened to him. If the sector car hadn't stopped them, they would have been long gone.

The detectives came to the scene and went up to the brothel, a Korean geisha house on the sixth floor. The madam at the brothel identified two groups of men approximately eighteen to twenty years old who came in separately. We didn't arrest anybody then; instead we brought them all back to the precinct for an investigation. The detectives had a rookie sit on the body until crime scene workers and the coroner finished up there. Fiore and I went back to the precinct to explain to the detectives what we'd found. Then the detectives let the Brooklyn men tell their story, and they said the Staten Island wannabes took their friend's gold chain and shot him. When the detectives showed them the gold chain and the box cutter I found in their car they started turning over on each other. By early the next morning, the Staten Island guys were coming in with their parents to tell their side of things.

The way it went down was the Brooklyn guys waited downstairs in the lobby for the Staten Island guys to come out of the geisha house. The dead kid used the box cutter to rob the gold chain from one of the Staten Island wannabes, but the guy resisted. When he pulled out the gun and shot himself, the Staten Island guy got spooked and grabbed the gun and shot him in the chest. The gangs apparently knew each other.

With the exception of the dead kid, both groups of men were

Italian. They grew up fascinated by violence and corruption. They idolized guys like John Gotti and Carlo Gambino. They imitated their heroes in their mannerisms and speech, foolishly thinking that they could take what they wanted, killing for it if they felt like it. It threw me that the dead guy was Hispanic—he could never be a made man in the mob because of it. I couldn't figure out why he was their trigger guy. Maybe he was from the neighborhood and managed to finagle his way in, but he wasn't Italian—he shouldn't have been there. The thing that bothered me most was when he was shot they all ran, leaving him to die alone on the cold floor of that building. In the end the Brooklyn men were charged with robbery, and it was determined that the Staten Island man had acted in self-defense.

It was a long and exhausting night. Fiore and I didn't say much to each other. I must have looked funny because he asked a couple of times if I was feeling okay. I caught him looking at me strangely and wondered if what I was feeling showed on my face. I couldn't wait to finish up so I could head over to the bar—between my weekend and the dead guy, I really wanted a drink.

I vouchered the chain and the box cutter and waited for the detectives to finish their questioning before I went home. I went downstairs to the lounge to close my eyes for a half hour when Fiore asked to talk to me. As we walked out of the lounge, I asked, "What's up, Joe?"

"Tony, are you sure you're okay? I don't like the way you look."

"I'm fine," I said. "Just tired."

"I want to give you my home number and my cell phone number. If you need to talk, anytime, I want you to call me." He paused and took a breath as if trying to figure out what to say next. "I'll be honest with you, Tony, I'm concerned about you and I've been praying for you. I think you got a lot going on inside. You don't talk much, and that's not good. I just want you to know I'm here, and if there's something you want to talk about, it'll stay right here, between us."

I nodded. "Thanks, Joe, I appreciate that," I said, having no intention of telling him anything. Just then Mike Rooney stopped me before he left and said to meet him over at the bar.

"It's been a rough night, Tony, kind of depressing, dontcha think?" Joe asked once Rooney was out of earshot.

I nodded.

"I could stay awhile, we could go get some breakfast and talk if you'd rather do that." His eyes followed Rooney as he left the lounge.

"I'm tired. I'll just stop and see Mike for a minute and then I'm gonna head home," I said casually.

He nodded, looking concerned. "Okay, I'll see ya tonight."

"Yeah, I'll see ya tonight. Thanks, Joe." We shook hands.

I napped for about an hour, finished with the detectives, then changed into a pair of shorts and a T-shirt. My uniform was damp from sweat, so I put it in my bag so I could wash it when I got home. I signed out at 9:00 and drove my car to 9th Avenue so I wouldn't have to walk back over to the precinct after I'd been drinking.

Rooney, McGovern, O'Brien, and Garcia had already been at it for an hour by the time I got there. I bought a beer and walked to the back, where they were playing darts, laughing and joking. O'Brien and McGovern left by 10:00, Garcia left at 10:30, and Mike Rooney drank steadily with me until noon. I tried to get him to talk about the dead guy, but other than a few remarks about "goombahs" and "wise guys," he really wasn't interested. We walked outside together and stood out front in the rain and humidity, talking about our softball game against the 46th precinct that Wednesday.

The rain had cooled things very little, and the clouded sky

added to my dark mood. There was no traffic on the way home, and even the lower lanes on the bridge were clear. I stopped at Montey's deli for a six-pack and a meatball hero and got home by 12:40.

There were two messages when I got home, one from a title company about the house and the other from my partner John Conte. Normally I would have called him back, but I just couldn't work up the enthusiasm. I didn't feel like talking about the job, and he would want to know what was going on. John was kind of clueless—things like the shooting he would just chalk up to stupid bent noses and be on his way. The way he saw it, if they wanted to live that way, they paid the price. I agreed with him on that, but lately I couldn't shake it off like before.

I went downstairs to wash my uniform and opened the doors to the deck while I ate my sandwich. I put the six-pack on the kitchen table and cracked open a beer. When I finished the sandwich, I drank another two beers in quick succession, hoping some numbness would seep into my brain. The beers I'd had at the bar were slow and steady so I had an even buzz on. Now everything I drank was coming down on me.

I'd been feeling so alone and couldn't seem to escape it. My mind kept going back to the dead guy. His friends were there when he was doing the robbery, but once he got shot and needed them, they left. From there, my mind went to my family and Vinny leaving and how much I would miss him. Now that I knew my house was sold, it didn't feel like home anymore. In a few months it would belong to someone else, and I had nowhere to go. I couldn't get a place with Denise; we were too old for that. It was time she moved on, anyway. I felt old and tired and, for the first time in my life, hopeless. I hadn't been looking to get drunk, but now I was. I opened another beer, relieved that I no longer felt guilty about drinking it.

My gun was digging into my hip, so I pulled off my belt and took off the holster and laid it on the table, staring at it. I drank my last beer, and I was exhausted from the booze and lack of sleep. I decided to close my eyes for a second before I went up to bed.

I woke up in a dark and empty room. I couldn't tell where I was and felt like I had when I woke up in that strange house down the shore. My heart pounded so hard I could feel my pulse throbbing in my neck and echoing in my ears. I broke out in a sweat as I strained my ears for sounds that would give me a clue as to where I was. As my eyes adjusted I realized that the light was dim from a red lightbulb on the far wall. The room was small, maybe eight by eight with no furniture except a small table in the middle of the room. I checked for a door but there was none—no windows and no doors. I walked over to the table and saw my Glock 9-millimeter. It was loaded, still in the holster, just the way I'd left it when I'd closed my eyes. Fifteen rounds in the clip, one in the chamber. That's when I realized where I was. Alone in a room with no windows and no doors, and the only way out was my gun.

I woke with a start. I was at my kitchen table with my gun staring at me, along with the empty beer bottles and the wrapper from my sandwich. My hands were shaking, my shirt was damp, and my heart was racing in my chest. I looked at the clock; it was 2:20. I tried to remember how long I had been sitting there but couldn't. The house was silent—the only sound was the soft sound of the rain as it hit the grass outside. I picked up my gun and stared at it. Depression was becoming so familiar, I couldn't shake it off anymore. Every day something happened to make it worse.

A room with no windows and no doors. That's how I felt.

I picked up my gun and went upstairs to bed.

*F*iore would later tell me a story about two houses, the house on the rock and the house on the sand. That night at work, my house built on the sand collapsed.

I woke up at 9:30 on that Tuesday night. No sound came from downstairs, so I showered and shaved before going to the kitchen. A note from Denise on the table told me that she had left dinner. Sal had grilled swordfish and she left a plate of it in the refrigerator. Along with the fish were tiny red potatoes, heavy on the garlic, with parsley and olive oil, and a corn on the cob. I went to the basement and put my uniform into the dryer. I took my baseball bag out and put it by the front door for my game against the four-six precinct in the morning. I popped two Tylenol and guzzled them with my soda before eating dinner. My stomach was a little queasy, but I managed to clean my plate. I left late, 10:40, but at least my uniform was dry.

The sky was still a little cloudy, but the rain had cooled things. There was even a breeze in the night air. I got to roll call two minutes after the "fall in" order. Fiore must have gotten in on time—he was in the muster room drinking a cup of coffee when I came in. I nodded over to him as Sergeant Hanrahan called attention to the roll call. He gave the color of the day, orange, and he gave out the sectors, then the foot posts, then the details, and then ended with a message from the platoon commander.

"The platoon commander will begin giving out minor violations to anyone late to roll call," he said, his eyes scanning the room and resting on me.

I smiled sadly. I was so sick of this. I didn't care anymore about the job or all the crap that went with it. I wished I could feel the old rebellion rise up in me. Normally I would have planned to be late for the rest of the week, but it just didn't matter anymore.

Fiore caught my eye, and I felt guilty for a minute. Would it bother him later, knowing that he had worked with me the night before and didn't realize anything was wrong? I quickly dismissed the thought. I dealt with it, so would he.

Panic seized me as I realized what I was thinking, and I fought the urge to run out of the muster room. I stood outside smoking a cigarette to calm my nerves. I had grabbed my radio and waited for Fiore while he talked to the sarge.

The night was busy with alarms. We had four that were 90U, unfounded alarm, premise secure. Then we answered five in a row that were no entry. We stopped for sandwiches at 3:00; we both got turkey with cheese, lettuce, tomato, and mayo and ate them in the car. I'd wanted to get something else in my stomach. I kept burping up the garlic from the potatoes I ate for dinner.

We had a 5:00 meal. Since we picked up sandwiches earlier we both slept in the lounge for an hour, and by 6:00 we were driving to the Sunrise Deli on 40th Street to get some coffee. The sun was up and the streets were starting to fill up with people moving to get to work. The air was clear but already hot, almost eighty degrees.

We went up to 42nd Street and made a right, heading down to 7th when a woman in a beige cotton suit ran up to the car and said, "I think someone's jumping off the roof up there." Our eyes followed her pointed finger to a hotel above us. We saw a body up there, hanging over and getting ready to jump. We pulled the car out of the way so he wouldn't land on it and parked it across the street. The hotel had an entrance on 42nd Street, not a main entrance, maybe a service entrance, that we walked toward. Both Fiore and I were trying to count the windows as we crossed the street. I counted fifteen, he counted sixteen. The building had about thirty-five stories—it turned out the jumper was on the seventeenth floor.

Fiore called Central, telling them there was a possible jumper and that we were checking it out. We grabbed the guy at the desk to ride up with us. On the elevator ride calls were coming in to Central about the jumper. The hotel was old and shabby, one of those forty-dollar-a-night jobs with musty rugs and ancient furniture. Nothing you'd find in the tour books.

We got off on the fifteenth floor and knocked on a door. The man who answered didn't have a ledge, but he said there was a ledge two floors up. We looked out his window and could see the jumper two flights up. We ran back up the stairs instead of waiting for the elevator.

The desk attendant didn't have keys, so we kicked one of the doors open. The lock on the window was tied with a thin wire, which we had to unravel to get the window open. For a second I thought that maybe the jumper put it there so we couldn't get out there to him. But I realized he couldn't get the wire on from outside the window. Apparently whoever was staying in that room had put the wire on so no one on the outside landing could get in.

From the window I could see the jumper hanging out there. I would have broken the window, but I didn't want to startle the guy any further. I started cursing as I pulled at the wire.

"What's with all the suicides lately? I thought everyone likes to kill themselves around the holidays. You know, give the family something to remember for the years to come," I rambled, yanking on the wire with hard jerks.

"Tony, want me to get that?" Fiore asked quietly.

"I got it!" I snapped as the last of it came free.

We climbed out of the window onto the ledge only to find a black iron fence five feet from us. We walked toward the jumper, hearing his groaning as soon as we stepped outside.

He was hanging at a bizarre angle—his back was toward the street and his legs were toward the building in a stretched-out position. What was this guy doing? As we approached I saw that he was impaled on top of a black iron fence about three feet high that went around the walkway outside. One spike of the fence was through his left leg, his hamstring actually, the point of it showing through his pants. Another spike was in his left side, through his ribs. His left arm was moving spastically; his right arm was still. My stomach felt sick for a second looking at him, but I shook it off.

Fiore rushed out to grab him, and he screamed and ended with a high-pitched moan. I was sure that if Fiore had realized he was impaled, he wouldn't have grabbed him like that. The jumper's head was lolling back and forth as Fiore called back Central, asking for an ambulance and emergency services. We didn't want to move him; Fiore loosened his grip but continued to hold the man while I sent the desk clerk back downstairs to meet emergency services. I told him to make sure he found out exactly where we were because I had no idea. The building came out in steps, with the lower floors out further and thinned as it neared the top. He must have jumped from higher up, unaware that he'd only fall a few floors.

I held his right leg loosely. He was trying to ease the pressure on his left leg, but as he pulled back he would cry out from the pain in his right side. He was white, late twenties or early thirties with shaggy brown hair and a lanky build. His eyes were green and clouded with pain. I smelled alcohol on him, along with sweat. I was worried that he was going into shock, so I tried to get him talking.

"What happened?" I asked.

"Leave me alone," he murmured.

"What happened?" I asked again.

"Hang on, buddy," Fiore said in a quiet, reassuring voice.

"Let me die," he moaned. "I can't even die right." He had a slightly Southern accent. He wouldn't be the first guy to take a trip to New York to kill himself. They like the anonymity that comes with the city.

"Hey, take it easy. Buddy, look at me," Fiore said quietly. "Why do you want to kill yourself?"

"'Cause I don't want to live." He sighed. "Try to throw myself off the building, and the friggin' wind blows me back. Didn't know the building came out this far. Never could do anything right, anyway."

"I'm glad you didn't do this right," Fiore said. "This won't help anything, only make it worse."

"Leave me alone and let me die," he muttered.

"Talk to me, buddy. What's going on? You're not from New York. What are you doing here?"

"What do you care?" His skin was getting chalky.

"Where's your family?" Fiore prompted.

"Back home. Lost my job, can't pay child support. Haven't seen my family."

"Where's home?" Fiore asked.

"Maryland," he said with a groan.

"What about your parents? This is gonna hurt them."

"Like they care. Nobody cares." He started to cry, a low, mournful sound.

"There are people who love you, people who will be hurt if you die; you have to think about them," Fiore said as if the guy didn't want him to shut up. "You divorced from your wife?"

"Left me. Says I'm a drunk. No one will notice if I'm gone. No one cares. Even God hates me, won't let me die. Don't want to do this anymore."

"Do what?" Fiore asked.

"Live," he said, looking Fiore in the eye.

I heard the wind, the traffic moving as the world went on below us. Horns blew, the exhaust roared from the back of a bus, I could hear a radio playing, and the bass vibrating up seventeen floors. Standing on that building I felt with clarity everything he was feeling. He didn't want to feel it either. I felt sorry for him, sorry that he had to jump off buildings without having the capability to end it in one second like I could. I stared at him, fascinated, understanding his logic. I was so sick of this job, sick of seeing this crap every day. I wallowed in garbage every night and I was tired of it. I had no wife, no family, no one who loved me. How long did I want to keep doing this? Not one more day, just like him.

"Listen to me," Fiore continued. "God doesn't want you to die. He doesn't want this for you. He loves you."

"No one loves me," he moaned. "Can't do nothin' right, never could."

I could see it was a struggle for him to talk. He must have been in agony. The fence was keeping the bleeding to a minimum, but emergency service would have to cut the fence and take it with them.

"God loves you," Fiore said.

"God hates me."

"No, he doesn't, he loves you."

"Then why am I here?" the man moaned.

"Listen to me!" Fiore said urgently. "Look at me."

The man's eyes focused on Fiore.

"You need to understand that you really don't want to die," Fiore said.

"Yes, I do," he said.

"No, you just don't want to hurt anymore. Do you think God doesn't know your pain? That he hasn't been right beside you all this time waiting for you to come to him? He knows what you're feeling; he knows what brought you to this place and time. He knows that you think you're always gonna feel this way and that you . . ."

Fiore put his head down as if trying to concentrate. He pulled his head up as realization crept into his face. He spun around toward me. "Tony, what are you thinking?" he asked quietly.

I stared at him, wondering if he could read my mind.

"Tony!" he said a little louder.

I took a step back away from him as my heart started to hammer in my chest.

Fiore seemed torn between me and the guy on the fence. I don't know how, but he knew what I was thinking. We stared at each other as the sergeant and other officers entered the landing.

I backed away from them as Fiore kept speaking quietly to the jumper, whose name was Russ. He came up from Baltimore the day before by bus, planning to throw himself off the Empire State Building. Did he really think he'd be the first guy to try to jump off there? They've seen his kind before.

I caught bits and pieces of the conversation as Fiore continued to talk to him. I heard him say at one point, "Jesus paid such a high price for you, he doesn't want you to die this way. When he died on the cross it was to set you free from all the pain you feel and draw you to him. Take the step, come on." Fiore didn't care that the sergeant was there; he just talked on and on about God. How God loved this guy and wanted to save him and did this guy want to accept Jesus in his heart. The jumper, Russ, was grabbing Fiore's hand, crying and nodding as they spoke. Everyone else looked uncomfortable as this was going on, and when emergency services arrived, Russ asked Fiore to stay with him while they cut him out.

The paramedics worked on him first. They set up an IV and started taking his blood pressure while emergency services took out their gear. Fiore was rubbing Russ's shoulder, repeating, "It's all right, it's gonna be all right."

He started to cry again while emergency services put a harness around him. They attached it to the fence on either side of him so he wouldn't fall off when they cut him out. Then they put harnesses on themselves and hooked on to the fence so no one would go over. They wrapped a blanket around his skin so the sparks wouldn't hit him and used a small circular saw with a carbide bit to cut him out. They would remove the metal spikes in surgery once they got him to the hospital.

Rooney, Garcia, McGovern, and O'Brien watched with the sarge while they cut him out. I had stepped away from the spectacle to smoke a cigarette. The emergency workers put Russ onto the stretcher, and the sarge told Fiore and me that we would be going to the hospital. Someone from the day tour would relieve us, and we could do our paperwork when we got to Bellevue. Russ from Baltimore would be treated medically first then transferred to psych.

We took the elevator down with the EMTs. Fiore would ride in the ambulance and I would take the sector car down to Bellevue. I took 34th Street to the FDR drive and made a right, driving along the service road of the FDR into the back of Bellevue to the emergency room. The *beep-beep* of the ambulance backing in met me when I pulled in and parked the car.

They took him right into surgery. I was waiting outside the ER at triage when Fiore came out. He got right to the point.

"Do you want to kill yourself, Tony?" he asked quietly.

I didn't answer, just put my head down, not confirming or denying. I walked outside through the automatic doors and lit a cigarette, trying to come up with something to say but couldn't think of anything. I was ashamed and scared but knew in my gut that Fiore wouldn't see that as a weakness. I knew I had to go back and face him. I finished my cigarette and went back in. Fiore was still standing where I left him.

"Tony, do you have any guns at home?" he asked.

I shrugged. "Sure."

"What do you have?"

"A two-inch Smith and Wesson five shot, my off-duty, why?"

"You have guns in your locker?"

"Yeah, a Ruger, three-inch six shot. Why?" I dreaded what was coming.

"I don't know what to do about this. I don't know if I should go to the sergeant." He looked confused.

"I never said I wanted to kill myself," I pointed out as rationally as I could.

"I know. The Holy Spirit told me."

Could that really happen? Fiore was serious.

"Listen, Joe, don't worry about it, I'm fine," I said.

"You're not fine! You're thinking about killing yourself! You spit out the stats on cops killing themselves like it's your phone number. You drink too much. You have personal problems. Don't tell me not to worry about it!" He wasn't yelling but he was right up in my face. He took a deep breath. "Should I go to the sergeant?" he asked quietly.

"No!" Then quieter, "No way." If he went to the sergeant, they would take my guns away and I would be labeled for the rest of my life.

"I don't want to betray you, and I know how the department is with stuff like this. You'll be marked. At the same time, I can't go home today knowing you feel this way," he said, somewhat calmer.

I don't know why I didn't try to deny it. Maybe I knew he wouldn't believe me. I tried another tactic. "I just had a bad weekend, but I'm feeling okay now. Don't worry—"

"No, I'm not leaving you alone so you can go home and blow your head off. No way."

"I—I don't know what I'm gonna do," I stammered.

He held up his hand and put his head down for a minute. He looked up at me, still holding up his hand. "I'll tell you what, this is what we're gonna do," he said. "When we get done this morning I'm not leaving you alone. However you want to do this—we stay at the precinct, you come home with me, or I go home with you. If I don't think it's straightened out, I'm going to the boss."

"I don't need a babysitter," I said. "If I was serious enough, there's nothing anyone could do to stop me, and you know it."

"Don't you think I know that?" he said quietly. "What about that guy in the laundry room? His girlfriend knew what he was thinking and she couldn't stop him. He had someone who loved him, someone he trusted enough to say he wanted to kill himself, and it still didn't help. I don't know what's going on in your life, but I know that you're lonely and hurting. If you had anything better to do, you wouldn't be in the bar with Rooney every day."

"So what if I go to the bar? So do O'Brien and McGovern, and—"

"I'm talking about *you*, Tony. You're gonna talk to me. If you don't talk to me, and if I don't think this is getting straightened out, I'm going to the sergeant. In fact, we're going to your house so you can give me your off-duty, and when we get to the precinct you can give me the one you have now and whatever's in your locker."

I don't know why I wasn't mad at him. Maybe because I knew he was sincerely trying to help me, not because he had to, but because he cared about me.

"Joe, I won't lie to you and tell you that I haven't been thinking about eating my gun," I started quietly. "For a minute up on that roof I thought about it. I don't feel that right now; the thought comes and goes." This was true—lately I've been thinking about it more and more, but I had my good moments too.

"But Tony, that thought will grow bigger and bigger if you don't deal with it. Unless things change in your life, this isn't going to go away. What about Tommy Moffit? No one knew he was gonna kill himself that morning; he seemed like everything was fine. A fight with his wife set him off—things that normally wouldn't trigger suicide are out of proportion when you're depressed. Alcohol makes it worse because it numbs you, the consequences don't seem as big." He was talking with his hands now, balling them into fists and putting them out in front of him with his fingers stretched open. He ran his hands through his hair and closed his eyes. He looked as tired as I felt.

"Go home, Joe. You're tired and you have a family," I said quietly. "I'm sure your wife wants you home."

"Don't worry about my wife. I'm going home with you or I'm telling the sarge. It's your call."

I shrugged, defeated. "I guess we're going to my house."

By now it was almost 8:00. We didn't get out of Bellevue until 9:00. On the drive back to the precinct Fiore didn't talk, just kept his head down. When we went downstairs to change, Fiore took my Glock and Ruger and locked them in his locker. He had called his wife on his cell phone from the hospital, telling her he wouldn't be home and would call her later. Now as I drove down West Street I didn't know what to say.

"Tony, tell me what's been going on in your life. Is this about your girlfriend?" he asked.

"Honestly, no."

"Tell me about her. What was she like?" he asked seriously. "You said she ran off on you, and that has to bother you."

I took a deep breath. "It wasn't any great love. It was more like someone to pass the time with. I couldn't see myself marrying her, and I definitely couldn't see her having kids," I said sarcastically. I wished I could explain it better. "She was beautiful, she worked on Wall Street at the exchange. She liked money. She never understood why I was a cop; she always said I could do better. I guess being around hotshot stockbrokers gave her a thirst for the high life. I went to the Jersey shore, she went to the Hamptons. We were different." I shrugged.

"If you were so different and couldn't see yourself marrying her, why were you with her?"

I wasn't going to tell him it was about sex. I had a feeling that wouldn't be a good enough reason for him. It was more that I had someone there with me, so that I wouldn't be alone.

"Have you ever been in love?" he asked.

I thought for a minute. Aside from Marie Elena Carlino in high school I couldn't think of anyone else that ever rocked me. Marie Elena is married now, had three kids and weighs about two hundred pounds. She's still pretty, and I see her once in a while at Montey's Deli. But I don't think I ever really loved her.

"No, probably not," I answered.

He nodded. "So what about your family?"

"What about them?" I asked cautiously.

"You tell me," he said. "What's going on there?"

Surprisingly, I told him. About my father and how he stopped being my father when he met Marie and how much I missed him. I told him about Marie and how I thought she wanted to destroy my family, how she hated Denise and me and loved tormenting my mother. I told him about how much my mother drank and how bitter she was and that I didn't think she loved me anymore. I told him about my house and that I had to move.

"Tony, not to hurt your feelings, but living with your sister and brother at thirty-two years old is not exactly healthy. You should be married now, having kids, not in the bars drinking your life away."

"I know that, but I don't want to live alone," I said. "Working nights, I barely see anyone as it is."

"Maybe you should work days."

I shook my head. I didn't see any reason to work days. I liked my tour—more money, less hassle.

"How much are you drinking?" he asked.

I paused, wondering if I should be honest. Why not? If he knew I was thinking of shooting myself, I might as well tell him the whole thing.

"I drink every day. Last weekend after a barbecue with my family I went down the shore. I drank so much I blacked out." I looked at him. "I woke up in someone else's house, a woman. I don't know who she was or what happened. She left me a note to meet her at the beach, but I had no idea what she looked like."

Fiore nodded for me to continue.

"I came home because it scared me. I wound up just drinking at Dave's, the bar on my corner, for the rest of the weekend."

"I don't want you to drink today," he said.

"I don't know if I can do that," I said honestly. "It's been so long since I went a day without drinking, I don't know what will happen."

"You'll get a headache, be irritable, and maybe shake a little, but you'll be fine. We'll work it off."

"Work it off?" I said dryly.

"Trust me—jog, walk, lift weights, whatever. Don't you lift weights?" he asked.

I nodded. "Usually." John and I used to work out on our meal.

I haven't lifted in a couple of weeks. I used to bench press about 250, but I couldn't do that much anymore. Realistically I could do about 200 pounds. John and I used to do chest and biceps together, alternating the following day with legs and shoulders, then a workout with back and triceps.

"You have weights at home?" he asked.

"No, I work out at the precinct."

We decided to walk. I was too tired to work out anyway, and I smoked too much to jog. So we walked—a lot. And we talked. I can't remember ever talking so much to another person in my whole life. And Fiore didn't talk about himself, just asked me questions and let me tell him what had been going on to make me so depressed. For once I was truthful—no smoke screens or evasions. I didn't really know him that well, but I told him things I'd never told anyone.

We started off at my house. He took my off-duty and put it in his bag and zipped it. I made some coffee, and we drank it outside on the deck. The water was smooth as glass, the sun reflecting off the tiny ripples. He loved the house. He loved the view of the bridge and Manhattan and said he understood why I didn't want to leave.

I showed him Fort Wadsworth and a ferry leaving St. George. He had never been anywhere on Staten Island, he'd only driven through it on his way to Jersey. I got quiet and depressed again.

"It's time to move on," he said. "Put it behind you like a man and move on. If there's one thing I've learned, God always has something better for us. Sometimes we can't see it, but you have to trust him."

I nodded. "Joe, I don't know if I can do this without a drink," I said again.

He stared at me for a minute, and I thought he was going to give in.

"Let's go." He stood from the lounge chair.

"Go where?"

"I don't know," he said. "Let's just keep moving. Is there any-where you want to go? Besides the bar, I mean." He smiled.

I shrugged. "I guess the boardwalk in South Beach. We can drive there and—"

"No, we're gonna walk there."

"It's far, at least a mile from here. Why don't we drive there and then walk up and down it as many times as you want."

He shook his head.

"It's about three miles long!" I burst out.

"Come on, a mile there and another three miles one way will give you eight miles total. You'll be too tired to drink." He got up and started walking toward the front of the house. He stopped when he realized I wasn't following.

"What are you doing?" he asked.

"It's hot out. At least let me change my shirt and grab some water," I said irritably.

"Go ahead," he called back. "I'll wait for you right here."

I put on a tank top and swallowed two Tylenol because I was getting a headache. We walked up to Montey's, and I introduced him to Fiore and bought two bottles of water. The morning sun was cooking up, and the boardwalk had absolutely no shade. We walked Bay Street to the Coast Guard gate of Fort Wads-worth. We cut through the fort, and I took Fiore to the top of the bluff directly under the bridge and showed him the view. If he wanted to walk, we might as well take the scenic route. We walked down to the beach behind the officers' housing and walked along the sand until we reached the boardwalk. We had to climb over the fence to get up on the boardwalk, and entered it by the beach club.

The beach club was a longtime trouble spot that had great pizza and lots of fights. Every weekend underage kids with phony

IDs would drink themselves into oblivion, then beat each other bloody until the cops locked them up. I knew this because I used to hang out there when I was a kid. I get pizza there once in a while, but never on a Friday night.

We walked the boardwalk and bought two more bottles of water from a hot dog vendor. I would have gotten a dirty water dog, but they weren't ready yet. Once we were back on the board-walk we started to talk again.

"What bothers you about the job?" Fiore asked. "I know it's not the only reason you're depressed, but it has to play a part. Are you upset because your partner got hurt?"

"No. I mean, yeah, I'm sorry he got hurt. But no, I don't miss him as much as I thought I would. John was a good guy, and we were good friends, but the fact that I'm not working with him isn't why I'm depressed."

The truth was, I liked working with Fiore. He was smart and interesting and never wanted to argue. For someone who was so set in his ways about God he wasn't judgmental. Take last night with me. Anyone else would have just taken my word that I was okay and forgot about it. I never would have expected him to come to my house with me to talk it out.

"So what bothers you about the job?" he asked again.

I blew out a breath. "The money—they pay us nothing. They never want to give us a raise." During our last contract the city gave us a raise proposal that launched a massive "Zeros for Heroes" bumper sticker campaign by the PBA. They actually wanted to give us a five-year contract with a zero percent raise the first two years.

"I mean, some bosses are good guys, but the ones who aren't and the brass, they don't care about us. As long as they get their numbers for the COMSTAT meetings, they just use us. The public hates us, the press hates us, and no matter what we do, they find fault with it."

Fiore nodded, so I continued.

"Everything is negative, I mean, what do we deal with? Drunks, drug addicts, the sewer of humanity night after night, and it never ends. Who's beating up someone, who's stabbing someone, who's robbing someone, who's jumping off a building, it just goes on and on."

"You're right about all of that. But at some point all cops go through this. Jesus tells a story in the Bible in the book of Matthew about a wise man and a foolish man. And Jesus says that everyone who hears his word and does it, he compares him to a wise man who built his house upon the rock. The rains came, and the floods and the winds beat against the house, but it didn't fall because it was built on a rock. But everyone who hears his word and doesn't obey he compares to a foolish man who built his house on the sand. The same rains came, and the floods and the wind beat against the house, and the house fell." He put his hands out in front of him to make his point. "It was the same storm that hit both houses. Do you know what I mean?" He squinted. "Do you know what I mean?" he said again.

"So I guess I'm the foolish man," I said dryly.

He chuckled. "No, I just don't think you've really heard the Word. The man who builds his house on the Word of God, his house can withstand the storm. The man who doesn't build it on God's Word has no foundation to anchor him in that storm. Is your house built on the Word of God?"

"Probably not," I said. Then, "No."

"I think now would be a good time to start."

I nodded. "I know what you're saying, but I honestly don't know if I could be like you."

"God doesn't want you to be like me, Tony. He made each of us unique. If he wanted us all to be the same, we'd be machines, not people. Everything that is good about you, he put inside you to glorify him."

"What about the bad stuff?" I asked.

He shrugged. "We get taught that, from our families or out in the world. He wants us to be separate from all that, to serve him."

I shook my head. "Until I met you, I thought religion was for weak or gullible people. I hate those television evangelists who always ask for money. I don't think you're either of those things, but I do think it's easier for you to live that way because you're married."

"I've struggled with the same things you have, Tony. I may have been raised going to church, but I had to struggle with not partying and sleeping around too," Fiore said.

"But you're settled with the person you love. You're not alone," I said.

"I understand what you're saying, but a life with God is a life of blessing, and you'll never be alone. Right now you can only see life the way you've lived it without God, and you see how that's turned out. But if you really commit yourself to God, you'll never want to live any other way. You have a decision to make. The Bible tells us in Deuteronomy 19 that God has set before us life and death—if you choose him, you choose life."

I wondered briefly how my life would have turned out if I never followed the crowd, if I walked away instead of proving I could do more shots of booze than the next guy. If I didn't have to have the best-looking girlfriend, just the nicest, would I be married now with a family? I didn't have it in me to choose right when I was younger. I hoped I had it in me now.

We walked the boardwalk through South Beach and into Midland Beach, where the boardwalk turns to a wide cobblestone path. At the turn of the century South Beach was a resort town, and the boardwalk had rides and concessions. After the concessions closed and what was left of the rides moved to a small amusement park, the boardwalk deteriorated. It was a magnet for drug dealers and vagrants, with a pretty big homeless population.

About ten years ago the borough president restored these three miles of beach, turning the burnt-out remains of the old boardwalk into a seaside attraction. Local bands played here on the weekends, and parks department festivities had become the norm. At one entrance a fountain billowed with water while dolphins in motion soared at different heights. It would have been beautiful except one of the dolphins had its backside sticking up while its face was buried in the cement. I guess it was supposed to look like he was diving in the water; instead it looked like he had smashed into the cement and gotten stuck there.

It was now past lunchtime, and we had walked over four

miles. We ended up in Miller Field, an old World War I airfield that the Parks Department now uses for sports leagues and picnic grounds. There is a roller hockey rink and huge playground. The old hangars are still there, and also a small row of houses for the park rangers. We sat down on one of the picnic tables by the ranger station, but Fiore got up and said we needed to keep moving or he'd fall asleep.

Summer sunbathers were out en masse on this hot summer day, and the beach was full when we turned around and headed back toward the Verrazano Bridge. The beach concession stands were open, and we bought more water to fight off the dehydration. Fiore wanted to get a couple of hot dogs, but the guy on the South Beach part of the boardwalk had better dogs. I was sweaty and my feet were swollen, but I'd still walk another mile for a better hot dog. I tried to keep talking but yawned every other word, and then Fiore caught it and he yawned every other word.

"Stop!" I moaned.

"Stop what?" He yawned

"Stop yawning." I yawned.

We stopped talking so we had the energy to make it home. I suggested catching a bus that ran along Father Capodanno Boulevard. The bus would leave us by the bridge, but Fiore said the walking would do me good. I thought about running away and jumping on the bus, but I didn't want to hear Fiore, plus I didn't know if he could find his way back to my house.

We stopped at the South Beach hot dog cart. We each got two dogs with mustard and sauerkraut, and black cherry sodas. We ate standing next to the cart. I smoked a cigarette before walking again, putting the butt in my soda can. By the time we got back to my house it was 1:30 and I was too tired to stand. So was Fiore. I gave him my room, turning on the air conditioner. Then I turned on Denise's air conditioner and crawled into her bed.

I fell into such a deep sleep that I didn't hear Denise come in the room after work. I woke up at 8:00. I used the bathroom and brushed my teeth, then went down to the kitchen to make some coffee. Denise was at the kitchen table, reading the paper.

"Everything okay?" she asked as I came in. She looked confused.

"Sure."

"Who's that guy upstairs in your room?"

"He's my new partner," I said as I busied myself with the coffeemaker.

"Why is he here?"

"We worked late, and it was easier for him to sleep here," I said as casually as I could.

She nodded. "He's cute."

"He's married," I warned.

"Okay!" She laughed. "I didn't go that far into the room to see if he was wearing a ring!"

I smiled. "He's a good guy."

"That's good. Are you hungry?" she asked, looking a little funny.

"Starving." The last things I ate were the hot dogs, and I couldn't remember what I had before that. I popped two Tylenol and poured a cup of coffee. I heard Fiore moving around upstairs and poured him a cup.

His hair was a little flat and his eyes puffy but he smiled as he came in. "Hey, Tony." He shook my hand and pulled me in for a hug. "How you doing, buddy?"

I moved away, embarrassed. "Joe, this is my sister, Denise," I said, my face red.

He smiled and shook her hand. "Hey, Denise."

"Hi, Joe." She smiled back.

"I can't get a signal in the house, so I'm going to go outside to call my wife," he said, holding his cell phone as he went out onto the deck.

"I waited for you to eat. I was about to order pizza, that sound good?" Denise asked.

"Yeah, but order from Giuseppe, the fresh mozzy and tomato basil pie."

"Pickup or deliver?"

"Deliver," I said. I wanted to shower and shave before I ate. Fiore came in from the deck just then, and I asked if pizza was good for dinner. Denise ordered two pies, the fresh mozzarella with basil and a plain pie with mushrooms. Fiore drank his coffee and went up to shower first. It was then that I realized I had forgotten to go to my softball game. I didn't know what I was going to say to the guys. They'd want to know why I hadn't gone over to the field when I got back from Bellevue. I put my head down and groaned.

"What's the matter, Tony?" Denise asked from the table.

"Nothing, I just forgot to do something."

She said something else, but I was already halfway up the stairs to my room. I got some clean clothes and pulled my electric razor out of my top drawer. I shaved in front of my mirror while waiting for Fiore to finish in the shower. He came out of the bathroom with his hair still damp; I guess he didn't blow-dry it. I showered and dressed quickly, aggravated that there were no more Q-Tips and that I had to use tissue to dry my ears.

I was a little cranky, but other than that I had no big signs of detoxing. I put my bag together for work, panicking for a second that I couldn't find my gun. I realized that I had given it over to Fiore and started to feel depressed again. I took a breath to calm myself and went back downstairs as the doorbell rang for the pizza.

Denise sensed that something was going on and did her

best to keep the conversation going smooth during dinner. She asked Fiore about his family and asked to see pictures. She asked where he lived and talked about a friend of hers who lived in Smithtown, which Fiore said was near him. Fiore was friendly and talkative and one of the few guys I knew who wasn't knocked out by Denise's looks. I could tell Denise liked him—she wasn't attracted to him, but liked him as a person.

That night I started to learn about God. On the ride into work Fiore told me about salvation, about believing that Jesus is the Son of God. He said that Jesus died on the cross for my sins and was raised from the dead. He said that anyone who called upon the name of the Lord would be saved.

"Do you believe that Jesus is the Son of God?" he asked.

"I know I've been taught that, but I don't know what I believe. I know they say that he was crucified by Pontius Pilate, died and was buried and on the third day rose again." I could still recite it from memory, but the words were foreign to me.

"The most important part of the prayer of salvation is that you believe it. I want you to be saved, but I don't want you to say something you don't believe. Why don't you tell me what you really believe about God?"

"Honestly, I think he's mean." I looked over at Fiore to see if he'd be shocked by that, but he just smiled. "I mean, he has all this power and yet no control over what goes on here."

"It's interesting that you see it that way. You've actually got a better grip on this than most people." He looked impressed. I had no idea what he meant.

"How?" I asked.

Fiore had a Bible in his lap, a black leather one that looked pretty worn out. He opened it and started flipping pages. "If you go to the book of Genesis, the first book in the Bible, you'll learn why it seems like God has no control here. When God created Adam and Eve and put them in the Garden of Eden, he gave them authority over the earth. When Adam disobeyed God and ate of the tree after he was told not to, he gave up his authority, and Satan took control. This separated man from God. When Jesus went to the cross, he was the sacrifice for our sin. He put us back in right standing with God and built the bridge to put us back in fellowship with him. Like Adam was before the fall. Jesus's death at Calvary gave us a choice to accept the righteousness he bought for us. When we accept Jesus, Satan no longer has dominion over us. In Philippians 3, I think it's verse 20," he said as he turned there, "it says our citizenship is in heaven."

"What about purgatory?" I asked.

He looked confused.

"You know, the place between heaven and hell where you're in limbo," I said.

"I have no idea . . . wait . . ." He thought a minute. "Do you mean Abraham's bosom?" he asked.

I shrugged. He started reading something about Lazarus, a poor man who had sores that a dog licked while he sat outside some rich man's house. He said when Lazarus died the angels carried him to Abraham's bosom. They comforted him while the rich guy went to hell and could see Lazarus from there. He was tormented and wanted Lazarus to go and tell his family to believe. By the time I got to the precinct I was listening so intently to this story, I barely noticed the ride in.

We changed into our uniforms, and he reached into his locker and gave me my Glock. As I put it in my holster he stuck out his hand for me to shake.

"Congratulations, Tony." He smiled as I shook his hand. "You just got through your first day without a drink."

"Oh yeah." I shook my head. "I almost forgot." It's funny, but I felt better than I had in a long time.

The night wasn't crazy, but it was busier than I wanted it to be. We had two car accidents, one on 8th and 34th involving a cabby and a bus, the other was in front of Macy's. That one had injuries and we had to wait for an ambulance. We answered two alarms. We talked on the way to jobs and on the way back. We talked while we searched a building, walking down the stairs. Fiore said he wanted to start by telling me about the love of God. When we got back to the RMP, he read me John 3:16–17. He read it one way and then read from what he called an amplified Bible—he said that kind of Bible goes in depth and explains things. I liked what he read so I wrote the verse down on a page in my memo book so I could read it later.

"For God so greatly loved and dearly prized the world that he (even) gave up His only begotten (unique) Son, so that whoever believes in (trusts, clings to, relies on) Him shall not perish—come to destruction, be lost—but have eternal (everlasting) life.

"For God did not send the Son into the world in order to judge—to reject, to condemn, to pass sentence on—the world; but that the world might find salvation *and* be made safe and sound through Him."

I liked that. I had always thought that God was sitting up there waiting to damn me to hell for all the stuff I did. I never looked at it that he didn't come to judge us. I liked how that sounded—"made safe and sound through Him." But then it brought another slew of questions from me.

"But Joe, isn't it a sin that I haven't gone to church since 1983? Can't I go to hell for that?" I asked him as he filled out another unnecessary alarm form.

He looked up from his writing and thought about that. "I don't think it's a sin not to go to church," he answered. "I mean, if the only reason you go to church is so you don't go to hell, you're wrong to begin with."

163

"Why would I be wrong? I'm supposed to go to church. If I don't go, then I'm sinning." At least that's what I always thought.

"Tony, I never go to church because I have to; I want to go," he explained. "I go because I love God and I love to hear his Word." He sighed. "I want you to come to church with me. No, don't say anything yet," he said as I started to object. "Not this Sunday. Next week, on July 21st. My wife and I are dedicating our daughter that Sunday, and I was going to invite you anyway. We're off that Sunday, so you don't have to take the day off. It's an early service, 9:00, and then we'll be having people back at the house for a barbecue. The barbecue starts at 1:00, but you could help me set up for it, put the tables up outside and set up the volleyball net."

"What's dedicating your daughter mean?" I asked.

"You'll see," was all he said. I hoped it wasn't some strange ritual with weird sacrifices. After everything he'd done for me in the past twenty-four hours I couldn't say no to anything he asked me.

"I'll go," I said. "Just give me directions to your house."

"I've been thinking about that," he said. "Maybe you should come home with me in the morning. I don't think it's a good idea to leave you alone just yet. I thought we'd finish out the week with tomorrow, and Friday morning you come home with me."

"I don't want to go to your house. I feel funny," I said.

"Why? I went to your house and didn't feel funny. Besides, my wife wants to meet you." He smiled. I wondered how much he'd told his wife. "You'll like her. She's nice and she cooks good."

"Why not." It wasn't like I had anything else to do. At least with Fiore I'd forget about going out with Rooney in the morning.

I was on my second day of not drinking, and something

inside me wanted to see it through. I couldn't explain it, but I had something to prove to myself about the drinking. And if I went home with Fiore, I wouldn't be at the bar. I had to keep busy this weekend. The Jersey shore was out; too much partying there. Dave's Tavern was out for the same reason. I guessed I could always walk the boardwalk until I passed out from fatigue again.

We stopped at the McDonalds on 7th Avenue across from the needle and button statue that lets everyone know they're in the garment district. It was almost 2:00, and there wasn't much left to eat. They had no fries, so I got two Big Macs, minus the onions, a chicken sandwich, and two apple pies. Fiore had a double cheeseburger, a chicken sandwich, and one apple pie. We parked the car in the empty lot eating and talking.

"Joe, my grandmother gives me medallions to wear under my uniform. Do they keep me safe?" I asked.

"The Word of God keeps you safe. Psalm 91 tells us about God's protection." He opened his Bible between bites and started to read it to me.

"I think you read that to me at court when you told me about the shield of faith," I said.

He smiled. "You remember that?"

I nodded. "I liked that about the Roman soldiers with their wood shields. I have to tell you, I never heard stuff like this." I shrugged. "It's interesting."

"I know."

He told me about God's protection again as we ate. I liked what he said about "the secret place of the most high." It sounded like a good place to be.

We answered two more jobs before heading inside to take our meal. One was a larceny in progress in which the complainant didn't want to do a report. The other was an alarm on 5th Avenue that came up secure. We slept through our meal, heading back out at 6:00 to finish out the tour. We had no jobs, and Fiore dozed in the car. I didn't want to bother him. I'm sure he was tired from all the walking.

After our tour I took the Long Island Railroad for the first time in my life. I hoped Fiore didn't want to hoof another eight miles today—I really wasn't up for it. The sun was bright, with temperatures in the low eighties, just right. We caught the train at Penn Station at 8:20. There's a 7:50 train, but that's when we get out. I guess Fiore didn't believe in cutting out a little early to catch the train. Joe has a pass to ride for free but I didn't. We argued over who would pay when the ticket guy came, but Fiore won. I didn't even find out how much it was. I know it's not cheap—when cops had to pay for it, they drove in.

The Long Island Railroad was totally different from the city trains. The seats were cushioned, a far cry from the hard plastic seats on the city trains. These were more like airplane seats only they didn't recline. The seats were in rows, three to the left and two to the right, instead of lining the sides of the train so strap hangers could stand in the middle. I heard there was a bar car, which we didn't go in.

The train was pretty empty. No skells came in to ask for money. Passengers were reading, sleeping, or listening to music with headphones. There was no screech of the wheels like the subways but instead a constant low hum with an occasional blare of the horn as we passed an intersection or approached a station.

We got off at the Ronkonkoma station where Fiore had parked his car. His car was a piece of crap, a navy blue 1984 Honda Accord with body rot and a hole in the floor of the front passenger side.

"Are you crazy? I can see the ground!" I yelled over the noise from the muffler.

"I'm usually alone when I drive this," he yelled back. "I have a new minivan at home that Donna drives."

I smoked a cigarette in the car. I didn't want to smoke around his family and didn't know when I'd get my next one. He rolled down his window, but that just let the exhaust into the car.

Fiore lived on a cul-de-sac that held about ten houses. It was nice, real suburbs. The houses were all similar, split-levels and center hall colonials, some more elaborate than others. Fiore lived in one of the middle homes, a split-level that was nice but more modest than the rest. The lawn was mowed but not landscaped like some of the others. You could tell Fiore had done it himself. It didn't have those twisty green trees or the drooping show trees. But it did have flowers planted in front and along the walk and a lamppost that had a hanging basket of flowers on each spike that came out the side. A white Plymouth Voyager was parked in the driveway; the back bumper had a fish symbol with JESUS in the middle. A small bicycle lay on its side near the front door, as if a kid dropped it in a hurry and tore into the house.

The front door was open; the screen door was one of those full glass panel kind. Maybe it's me, but I didn't think three kids and a full glass panel storm door was a good idea.

"Daddy!" A little dark-haired boy came racing outside.

"Josh! I missed you, buddy. Give Daddy a hug. Oh, you are getting so big." Fiore picked him up. "Josh, this is my friend Tony. He's my partner at work." He put the boy back down.

"Nice to meet you, Tony," Josh said seriously as he shook my hand.

"You too, Josh," I said.

He was a cute kid. He had big brown eyes, a bandage shaped like a crayon on his right knee, and red Kool-Aid on his shirt.

"Steven's here," Josh said.

"Oh yeah? You two wanna wrestle me again?" Fiore tickled

him. He went into this tickle-wrestle thing with the kid, growling and acting like an idiot. I guess that's what fathers do.

Fiore's wife Donna came to the door holding a little baby. She was prettier in person than she was in her picture and not as chubby. She was wearing beige pants that came to just below her knees. Denise wears them too, but I forget what they're called. She wore a long shirt that came to mid-thigh and beige open-toed shoes. Her dark hair was pulled back in one of those clips that looks like it has teeth. She wore no makeup that I could see and had short nails.

Fiore gave her a predatory look, and I wondered if coming here was a good idea. She smiled a sly smile back as he came in for a kiss. He nuzzled her neck and then scooped the baby out of her arm and started kissing it and making goo-goo noises. "Where's my pretty girl? Give Daddy a smile!" and stuff like that. I felt uncomfortable in the middle of such a family reunion, but Fiore didn't seem to notice.

Finally Donna said she had made coffee and asked us if we wanted breakfast.

"Please, we're starving," Fiore said as I started to refuse.

The small foyer was open, to the left a staircase going up, to the right a staircase going down. We walked upstairs into a bright kitchen, decorated in all light blue and white. Off to the left was a living room with a brick fireplace and picture frames of all styles and sizes. Over the mantle was a seascape painting, and the sofa was dark green leather with a matching chair and ottoman. The coffee table was covered in action figures, some standing, some laying down. A space guy had a string tied to his hand and another action figure dangled along the side of the table from it. A basket of laundry was on the couch, with a folded pile of clothes next to it.

I stepped into the kitchen, unsure what to do next. Donna filled a mug of coffee and placed it on the table.

"Tony, sit down," she said. "Stop looking like you want to bolt out of here. Joe's told me a lot about you. I'm glad you're here." She smiled.

"Thanks," I said, sitting down.

"Joey get to camp on time?" Fiore asked.

"Just about. I got there by ten after nine," she said.

"My oldest son, Joey, is in hockey camp," he explained. "Donna has to drive him into Seaford every morning; it's pretty far from here."

I nodded.

"Michele dropped Steven off. She's setting up for Vacation Bible School next week," Donna said.

"Where is he?" Fiore asked.

"He's changing—he spilled a glass of juice, and his clothes were soaked."

A little blond-haired boy came running into the kitchen and jumped on Joe.

"Little Stevie, my man!" Fiore yelled, slapping him a high five.

"Who's that?" the boy asked, looking at me.

"This is Tony, my partner. Shake his hand, buddy."

"Are you a cop too?" Stevie asked, shaking my hand.

"That's right, I work with Joe," I said.

The kid was cute, big dark green eyes, freckles across his nose. "Do you have a gun?" he asked.

"We all have guns," I said.

"You ever shoot anybody?" he asked seriously.

"How old are you?" I asked, chuckling.

"Four and a half. How old are you?"

"Thirty-two." I smiled.

He nodded. "You're almost as old as my mom. She's thirty-three."

"I'm sure she'll appreciate you telling me that," I said just as seriously.

"Did you ever shoot anybody?" he asked again.

"Go get Josh," Fiore said, changing the subject. "As soon as Tony and I finish eating we'll come and dunk you in the pool."

"No, you won't!" Stevie said and went clamoring down the stairs, calling for Josh.

We drank our coffee, and Donna cooked up breakfast. She made pancakes, which were delicious, with bacon on the side. I tried to help her clean off the table, but she shooed me out of the room.

We went downstairs, through a family room, and out a set of sliding glass doors to the backyard. A screened-in area had a set of lawn furniture, and there was a pool in the backyard. It wasn't an inground pool, but it was a pretty big round one. Josh and Stevie came running outside, ready for us to go in with them. We spent the next hour in the pool, with Fiore throwing them up in the air. Then we took turns throwing them to each other while they laughed hysterically. We had worked them up into a frenzy and played monkey-in-the-middle with a Nerf ball to calm them down some. It was fun. I don't see kids much, but I was having a good time with these two.

It was getting late, and Fiore said he had to get some sleep. Stevie seemed to take a liking to me and asked if we could play again later. I told him I wasn't sure what I'd be doing later, but I'd try. We dried off and went back inside.

The house had three bedrooms upstairs, and the downstairs had a small bedroom off the family room, where I stayed. The room had a small bathroom with a stall shower that I could use after I woke up. I went to sleep by noon, and if Fiore's family made any noise I never heard it. It was still light out when I woke up—my watch said 6:30.

In my two days of not drinking I found I was sleeping less but waking up rested. I jumped in the shower, hearing muted noises from upstairs. I didn't have my razor and looked scruffy, but there was nothing I could do about it. I put on my clean shirt and my shorts that I wore to work. I followed the sounds up to the landing, where I saw a woman talking animatedly about something.

She looked tall from where I stood. Her light brown hair was pulled back in a ponytail, and I saw some blonde streaks running through it. She was wearing a navy blue tank top and beige walking shorts. Her legs looked great until I walked up a couple of steps and saw she was wearing men's construction boots with thick white socks. She turned as she heard me come up, and I saw a flicker of something in a pair of big brown eyes.

I nodded to her as I entered the kitchen. Joe was sitting at the kitchen table in shorts and a white undershirt with his baby asleep on his shoulder. His wife was stirring something in a pot, and Josh, Stevie, and I guess Joey were sitting at the table talking. Joey came around and shook my hand and politely said hello.

"Coffee, Tony?" Donna asked.

"Please," I said. "I didn't know what to do with the towel, so I put it back over the rack."

"Don't worry about it. I'll get it later." She came to the table with two cups, indicating a place for me to sit and planting a kiss on Fiore as she put the other cup in front of him.

"Tony, this is my friend Michele, Stevie's mom." She turned to the kids. "Okay, you guys, go inside while the adults have their coffee." They scampered off toward the back of the house.

I turned and shook Michele's hand. "Hi."

She smiled. "Hi."

She was pretty in that Ivory soap kind of way. No makeup that I could see. I was used to women with long, fake nails and lots of war paint. She put her hands back in her pockets so I couldn't see her nails, but my guess would be short, no polish.

"Michele is working the Vacation Bible School at our church next week, and she was just telling us about the theme."

Michele seemed a little flustered by my appearance, which made me hope that no one had mentioned why I was there. I pictured Fiore's wife whispering something like "Joe's new partner is here—he's suicidal, and Joe's been staying with him so he doesn't blow his head off." Add paranoia to my list of psychopathologies.

Michele was saying that the Vacation Bible School theme this year was God's promises. She said they had been working on a twenty-foot wooden ark with painted animals in it. They also had a rainbow of balloons in every color over the ark that they would unveil on the first day. Fiore and his wife were oohing and aahing over the whole thing; I just nodded and said it sounded great.

She sounded smart—I noticed she didn't leave all the vowels off the ends of her words like most New Yorkers do. She looked at all three of us as she talked about the ark, as if I knew something about it. I remembered the story of Noah, but I'd never seen it done with a twenty-foot ark. It sounded like the kids would like it.

Eventually she said she had to get going and called for Stevie. Donna asked her to stay, but she said she had promised Stevie they would go to McDonald's for dinner. Stevie slapped me a high five, and Michele shook my hand again as they left.

"Nice meeting you." She smiled. Pretty eyes, but those boots had to go.

"Same here." I smiled as I watched her go down the stairs.

"Tony, are you coming out for the baby's dedication?" Donna asked when Michele had gone.

"Sure, thanks for asking me," I said. I wondered how this whole dedication thing worked. Was it like a christening where you buy the kid a savings bond or give money? I didn't know who to ask. Maybe Denise could ask her church lady friend for me and find out if I needed to wear a suit.

I was trying to figure out how much I should put in the envelope when Donna started getting ready for dinner. She put plates out and called the boys to set the table. Fiore put the baby in a swing in the dining room and wound it up real good. He faced the baby where she could see the table and came back to take out the cups and fill them with ice. He added soda to the big glasses and Kool-Aid to the small plastic ones.

Dinner was like a scene from *Little House on the Prairie* except that we ate macaroni and meatballs. Joe sat at the head of the table and said grace like I'd never heard. Everyone else's head was bowed solemnly. I can't remember exactly what he said, but he thanked the Lord for letting them have me over for dinner and thanked him for his family and for Jesus. It was a humble, heartfelt prayer, and I felt myself getting choked up. Lack of booze must have been making me emotional. After grace everyone dug in. I had to give Donna credit—she made a good gravy. She even made us meatball heros with the leftovers.

After dinner we played whiffle ball outside with Josh and Joey. Donna had cleaned up, put the baby out in a stroller with a net over it, and sat on the front steps to watch us play. We played until the sun started going down and went back inside while Donna got the kids cleaned up. When Joe went downstairs to set them up in the family room with a videotape, Donna and I sat at the kitchen table drinking coffee.

"Joe tells me he's been telling you about the Lord," she said.

I nodded, feeling embarrassed again.

"It's funny—I used to feel uncomfortable when he witnessed to me. I couldn't stand him!" She shook her head, laughing at the memory. "I was so messed up at the time, out there in the world living all wrong." There was that "out in the world" stuff again. What world did they live in?

"I'm glad he was patient, you know?" she continued. "He saw something in me that I couldn't. I'm glad he didn't write me off."

I couldn't picture her "living wrong," whatever that meant. I knew she was trying to tell me that she knew how I felt. Who knows, maybe she was a boozer in her old life.

"I guess he told you about me," I said.

"He tells me everything." She smiled. "And whatever he tells me stays here. He really likes you, Tony, and I know he's concerned. I won't make you uncomfortable by talking to you about it, but I want you to know that I've been there."

"How?" I asked.

"It's a long story. I'll tell you about it someday when we have the time, but let's just say I was at my ugliest when I met Joe."

"How did you meet him?" I asked.

"A neighbor brought me to church one night for a service and introduced us. I had a bad attitude." She shrugged. "Joe was so nice. I remember wondering if he'd be that nice if he knew how messed up I really was. But every week I showed up at church, back for more. I'm just thankful the Lord got hold of me and showed me the truth."

Joe came upstairs, and the subject changed to the baby's party. I broke down and asked how the whole thing worked.

"Do I wear a suit?" I asked.

"You don't have to, Tony. Wear whatever you want," Donna said.

"Wear a suit," Fiore said. "But bring something to change into. The party's in the yard and your suit will get too hot."

Donna packed our sandwiches and two sodas in a paper bag, adding napkins. Josh and Joey came upstairs and shook my hand before going to bed. Donna gave me a kiss on the cheek and a big hug before I left. I could see why Fiore liked her so much—she was sweet and open and honest. From what I've seen with the guys at work, most men love their wives; they just don't like them.

"Am I blessed or what?" Fiore yelled over the roar of the muffler as we drove westbound on the Long Island Expressway in his deathtrap mobile. I had lit a cigarette and was taking deep drags on it.

"You're definitely blessed," I yelled back. "I like your wife."

"Me too," he yelled.

"Does she have any sisters?"

Fiore laughed. "Don't worry, we're already praying for God to send you a wife."

"A wife? How about a girlfriend?" I yelled.

"Nope, a wife is what you need."

"Can you pray that she's about five-four, blonde hair and—"

"To use your word, Tony, don't be a meatball. You've picked enough women. Let God do it this time. Trust me, he's never wrong. You need a praying, believing wife."

I noticed he didn't mention a good-looking wife.

10

On the train Joe took out a Bible for me that Donna had bought after picking Joey up from hockey camp that afternoon. It was now Thursday night—we would work tonight and Friday night, be off Saturday and Sunday, and be back to work Monday night for a midnight tour. I was a little uneasy about going home in the morning, but Joe said he would be coming home with me again. I argued with him about it, but he wouldn't budge.

"No way, Tony. Donna and I talked about it and I'm coming home with you," he said emphatically.

"Joe, go home to your family. They need you."

"I know that, but one day isn't gonna hurt them. Besides, Donna misses me when I'm gone, and not seeing each other for two days makes for a nice weekend." He wiggled his eyebrows. "I want to go to that boardwalk again. That guy in South Beach has good hot dogs." He laughed when I groaned.

When we boarded the train, Fiore took out his Bible. We started in the first chapter of John, about how in the beginning was the Word and the Word was with God and the Word was God. I never would have thought I would be so fascinated by the Bible. I ran my hands over the surface of my new Bible, touched that Donna had bought it for me. We read through the first chapter of John, then Joe pulled out a worn-out, soft-covered Amplified Bible. He said I should read it with my Bible, to explain the verses better.

"Keep it with you. Read it first in your Bible, then in the Amplified. I always find it easier that way. If you don't, then just read your Bible."

All that Bible reading went out the window the minute I got to work. I had a fight with Mike Rooney at roll call. He started with me the minute I walked into the muster room with Fiore. He had taken off the night before, so I hadn't seen him.

"What's the matter, you were too sick to come to the game yesterday?" he bellowed from across the room. "Were you puking too much?"

Nervous chuckles could be heard throughout the room. I ignored him as I drank the coffee Fiore gave me.

"So what was it, Tony?" Rooney continued. "Too many meatballs? Too tired? Tell me what was so important that you left us with only nine guys for the playoffs?" He strutted over toward me.

"It's none of your business," I said, my voice deadly.

"None of my business? You make us lose the playoffs 'cause you don't show up, and it's none of my business?" he yelled, charging at me.

"I had something I had to take care of," I said, putting down my coffee. "You got a problem with that?"

"You don't have to explain yourself to him, Tony," Fiore said quietly.

"Oh, so now Fiore's fighting your battles for you?"

Whatever he was going to say next died on his lips as I ran at him and put him up against the wall. He was taller by about three inches and outweighed me by thirty pounds, but I was strong and I was mad. Papers flew from the corkboard on the wall as he smashed into it. I heard the *oomph* as his back connected to the cement.

"Cut it out, Mike!" O'Brien yelled to Rooney as he pulled us apart. "He made every game this season."

"Not the most important game of the season!" Rooney spat. "You know what, Tony? Don't bother coming back next year—we don't need you playing for us."

"You don't know when to shut your mouth, Mike," Fiore said quietly but with intensity.

"You got a problem too, Joe?" Mike turned toward Fiore.

"Shut up, Mike," O'Brien said, still holding him.

Fiore had me by the arm. We had knocked over a garbage pail and one of the cork bulletin boards was hanging from one side, spilling paper and notices onto the floor. Rooney and I kept eyeing each other, breathing heavily, when the sarge called attention to the roll call. We took our places without another word. The sarge didn't comment on what was going on. Rooney was seething throughout roll call and kept throwing looks at me. I stared him down each time until he looked away. There were no jokes tonight, and we filed out without talking.

The night was pretty slow. Fiore and I spent most of our time in the parking lot on 37th Street reading the Bible in between jobs. I started stepping out of the car to smoke; Fiore seemed to sneeze from it. We drank coffee and talked about how things were going for me.

"How do you feel now?" Fiore asked.

"I feel better. A little shaky, but okay," I said.

"Are you sure?"

I nodded. "I'm sure."

The most exciting thing we had was a stabbing on 34th Street. It wound up being a drunk and disorderly with a stab wound in the subway. Since it happened in the subway, Transit handled it.

We ate our sandwiches during our meal, sleeping for a half hour afterward. Rooney ignored me in the locker room in the morning, mumbling under his breath as he walked past me. I had calmed down and was sorry I fought with him. I really liked him, and I let him down by not coming to the game. I could never tell him why I didn't go to the game—he wouldn't understand.

I finished changing and gave Fiore my gun again. The morning was cool and sunny as we walked over to where I'd parked my truck. There was no traffic on the West Side, a lane was closed in the tunnel but cars were moving steady. We got to my place in twenty-eight minutes—or at least to Montey's. Potato, egg, and peppers were on the menu, and Fiore loved it so much I had to go back and get him another one.

Fiore the drill sergeant had me walk the eight miles again. To give him credit, he walked it with me without complaint. We finished earlier this time, by 11:30. We sat on one of the benches, eating our hot dogs, and slowed our pace after that. I wasn't as exhausted as I was last time, just a good tired.

"Maybe you should walk this over the weekend," Fiore said, breaking into my thoughts.

"I was just thinking the same thing," I said. "Trying to think of what will keep me busy over the weekend. It'll be me and all the old ladies taking their daily stroll." I chuckled. "I should probably try to start jogging."

"Make a list," he said. "Wash your car, walk this every day, avoid your friends or any family you would drink with. Drive out to my house if you want."

I wouldn't do that; I had imposed on him enough already. Maybe I would go to the movies, cut the grass—I'd think of something.

We got back to my house by 12:15. Fiore slept in my room again, and I took Denise's room. I woke up at 7:00, before the alarm that I had set for 7:30. I brushed my teeth and went downstairs. Denise was sitting on the couch watching TV with the sound muted.

"Tony, what's up?" she asked. "Why is your partner here again? Why didn't you come home yesterday?"

I decided to be at least semi-honest with her. "I stopped drinking. He's just trying to give me a hand with it."

"Really? No drinking at all?" She looked shocked.

"Nope." I shook my head.

"Ever again?" she asked.

"I don't know, but this is my third day and I'm glad."

"Is it hard?"

"Not as hard as I thought," I said honestly.

When she saw that Fiore was here again, she had picked up steaks and potatoes. We put the potatoes on the grill in foil as Denise marinated eggplant and zucchini to grill with the steak. I woke Fiore up at 8:00, and we ate with Denise out on the deck.

"Grandma wants us to come for dinner on Saturday to celebrate Vinny's engagement," she said between bites.

"Who's going?" I asked.

"The usual suspects, minus Mom, of course."

I didn't know what to say. If I went, there would be booze there and my family—not the combination for staying sober. On the other hand, if I didn't show up it would cause an uproar. Not going to the engagement dinner for my brother, who I was the best man for, would be a definite no-no.

"We'll see," I said.

"Tony, you have to go," she said, her voice rising. "Vinny will bug if you don't. I'll bug if you don't. You can't leave me alone with Marie."

Fiore didn't say a word through the exchange, just continued to eat. When we were on the Verrazano Bridge, heading into work, he brought it up.

"Do you have to go?" he asked. He was Italian—he knew about the family etiquette.

I nodded. "Yeah."

"Is it hard not to drink at family gatherings?"

"It's hard not to drink *before* family gatherings," I said.

He chuckled. "Don't stay long. Don't get sucked into the strife."

"That's easier said than done," I said.

"I'm sure it is."

"Everyone is going to give a toast. *I'll* have to give a toast."

"Just lift your glass. You don't have to drink it," he said.

Until I decided to stop drinking, I had never realized how much booze played a part in my life. When we got to the precinct I found out I had won a basket of cheer on a raffle I didn't remember buying a ticket for. It was from Garcia's kid's school, and the basket sat on the desk filled with every liquor imaginable. I laughed when I saw it. Fiore laughed too. I picked up the basket and brought it down to the locker room and put it in front of Mike Rooney's locker. He came up behind me as I went to walk away.

"What's this?" he asked, stone-faced.

"A peace offering." I held out my hand. "I'm sorry about the game."

"Why can't you tell me what happened?" he asked, looking hurt.

"Mike, it's got nothing to do with you," I said honestly.

"Why haven't you been in the bar?"

"I really don't want to talk about it."

He hesitated then shook my hand. "I don't know why you

can't tell me, but you know where to find me if you want to talk," he said.

I was glad he wasn't mad anymore. I liked Rooney.

I was anxious about the weekend, especially the party. I wrestled with the thought of going back to Fiore's house, but it was time to face myself alone. I decided to wash my truck, cut the grass, do the laundry and—if it got bad enough—go to the movies. I'd let everyone wonder who the weirdo was sitting in the back of the theater alone.

Friday nights were usually busy, and this was no exception. We had a 10-11 (alarm) and a possible 31 (burglary in progress) on West 30th. Holmes was on the scene, but the search came up negative. We had a confirmed break-in and conducted a search but came up with negative results again. Then we were called back to do a search of the premises next door that came back negative. In between jobs and while searching the buildings, I hit Fiore with questions.

"So who wrote the Bible?" I asked.

"A lot of people."

"Yeah, like who?" I raised my eyebrows.

"Well, Moses wrote the first five books of the Old Testament. The other Old Testament books were written by the prophets."

"Who wrote Isaiah? That's a big one." I noticed that as I was flipping through the pages.

"Isaiah wrote it," he said as if he were talking to an idiot.

"Okay, Einstein, who wrote Revelation?" I asked sarcastically.

"John."

I should have realized he'd know that.

"In fact, John wrote a few books," he went on. "The Gospel

of John that we've been reading, and First, Second, and Third John."

"So all the apostles wrote the Gospels."

"No, Matthew and John were apostles, Mark I'm not sure of, and Luke was a physician."

"A doctor?" I asked. "Why was a doctor writing a book in the Bible?"

"He wrote two books, Luke and the book of Acts, which is about the early church after Jesus was raised from the dead and went to heaven. It's one of my favorites," he said.

"How could a doctor write part of the Bible? Wouldn't you have to be a priest or at least an apostle or something?"

"Just keep reading John," he said. "Worry about the doctor later."

When I was getting ready to leave Saturday morning I could see that Fiore was debating bringing me home with him again.

"Are you gonna be okay? Tell me the truth," he said.

"I'm okay. I'm not saying I'm fine, but I can hold my own this weekend."

He shook my hand and pulled me in for a hug. I wasn't used to men hugging me. I mean, my father would hug me, but not with so much enthusiasm. I gave Fiore my gun, and he locked it up and then walked me out to my car.

"If you have any trouble this weekend, I want you to call me." He gave me a piece of paper with his address and phone number. "Any time, day or night, I mean it! And if things get too crazy at home, take the ride out—we'll be happy to have you."

"Go home to your family, Joe, I'll be fine."

It turns out I was fine. Not that it was easy, but I got through it.

As I drove home I made plans to do constructive things for

the weekend, only to find Mike Ellis on my doorstep. He had a case of beer and plans for the weekend.

"Tony, what happened last week?" he said. "You took off without saying good-bye. I hope she was worth it." He chuckled.

I laughed, sidestepping the question. Let him think what he wanted. He handed me a beer, and I shook my head.

"Too early for me," I said.

He made a face. "Since when?"

"I'm tired, Mike. I really have to get some sleep."

There was an uncomfortable silence.

"Well, since you're so tired, I guess I'll head down the shore. You're welcome to come if you feel like it," he said as we shook hands.

"Thanks, Mike, but I have a lot to do this weekend."

"Maybe another time."

"You bet," I said, not meaning it.

I did some laundry, separating the dark colors and putting my uniform in with them. I was hungry, so I had a bowl of Fruity Pebbles that Denise had bought and went to sleep by 9:30. I woke up at 4:15 and found Denise sunbathing out on the deck. I made a cup of coffee and went outside, squinting in the sunlight.

"We have to be at Grandma's by 7:00," she said.

I nodded then went to the shed for the lawnmower. I started in the front of the house where we had the least amount of grass and worked my way to the back, cutting in even rows. I had shorts on, so some of the grass shot out and stuck to my ankles. The mosquitoes were coming out of the grass as I cut, and I wished I'd put on bug spray. The West Nile–infected mosquitoes were all they talked about on the news. Denise was yelling something over the roar of the lawn mower, and I finally shut it off to hear her.

"Use the bug spray!" She tossed me the can of Off. I sprayed it on, and the smell of it reminded me of camping. I looked at my watch: 4:50. Time was really moving here in this life without drinking. I wondered if I'd live in slow motion for the rest of my life.

I emptied the mower bag around the shrubs and trees that needed to be pruned and threw the rest of the grass in the garbage. I got the weed whacker out to do the edging and the weeds, but that only took me fifteen minutes.

Having finished all possible yard work, I went downstairs to put my dark clothes in the dryer and my whites in the washing machine. I took a shower, shaved, and put on jeans and a white golf shirt. It was only 5:30 and I had an hour and a half to kill before dinner. Denise came up to shower and change.

"Do I need a gift for this dinner tonight?" I asked.

"No, Christie's parents are throwing a formal engagement party. I don't know when it is, but she'll let us know. I think she said they're having it at the marina. Hey, do you want to ride over with me? You know, show a united front?"

"Against who?" I asked.

"Against Dad and Marie," she said dryly.

I sighed. "I don't want to fight tonight, Denise."

"I forgot, you're not drinking. How many days is it?"

"Four," I said tiredly.

"You have to drink tonight, at least champagne," she said.

"No, I don't," I said.

"You're not going to have champagne? Not toast to Vinny?" Her voice was rising.

"I'll raise my glass," I said. "I just won't drink it."

"You're not an alcoholic, Tony. Is your new partner filling your head with all this stuff, making you think you have a problem you don't have?" She was upset now.

"I'll see you at Grandma's," I said, grabbing my keys and walking out.

"Fine," she called after me.

I got in my truck and drove the back roads to Grandma's. I was starving so I stopped in the Italian deli next to a gas station for two rice balls to munch on while I headed to the Hallmark store.

My hands were greasy from the rice balls, so it was impossible for me to pick up the cards. I couldn't find one for a brother, so I just got a standard "Congratulations on Your Engagement" card. I wanted to get something for my grandmother, so I went over to the candy counter to look for something that wouldn't break what was left of her teeth. They had a selection of Godiva chocolates, so I bought her a box of truffles, which they put in a gold bag with tissue paper.

It was now only 6:00 on the longest freaking day of my life, and I had only been awake for two hours. I didn't know what to do for an hour. I contemplated walking on the boardwalk, but that would take too long. I could stop and eat, but then I wouldn't be hungry for Grandma's dinner. I sat in my truck next to Carvel, smoking a cigarette to pass the time. Having used up eight minutes, I drummed my fingers on my steering wheel, sweating from sitting there with the windows closed. I started the truck and drove to Grandma's. Her apartment was only a mile away, and I was forty minutes early. I parked in 4A again and scanned the parking lot for other cars. It looked like I would be the first one there. I crossed the lot to the front door and rang the bell for 1C. She buzzed me in and assaulted me with a hug and kiss while kicking the door shut behind me.

She made the food buffet style—trays were set up on the dining room table with plastic cutlery and paper plates with wedding bells on them. There was penne with a red sauce, veal with mushrooms, stuffed chicken with roasted vegetables, and a tray of potato croquettes. A tossed salad was in the middle next to a smaller tomato and onion salad. Two bottles of merlot, a bottle of valpolicella, and two bottles of asti spumante lined the back of the table. She had a dozen of those plastic champagne glasses that come apart as you drink out of them.

"It smells delicious," I said. "You look great." She was wearing a black dress with big gold buttons, gold shoes, and gold earrings. The outfit was a little tacky, but I figured if she could still cook a meal for ten people and dress for it, she deserved the compliment.

The door buzzed again. I looked at the TV, but it was off. I turned it on and flipped through it so I could see the lobby station. My stomach sank when I saw my father and Marie in the foyer. Just what I needed, alone time with them.

I managed to block out Marie's incessant chatter. It was funny how I did it. I just kept repeating over and over in my mind the first verse of John 1: *In the beginning was the Word, and the Word was with God, and the Word was God*. It helped. I was so intent on doing it that I didn't hear her talking.

"So did you find an apartment yet, Tony?" She smiled sweetly. What a snake. I looked at my father to see his reaction to her, but his eyes had already glazed over.

"Actually, no, but I talked to a lawyer. He told me if I didn't move out, I could really make your life difficult." I smiled. "Did you know I could live in the house until you got a court order to get me out? It could really make it hard to sell."

That shut her up. It wasn't true and it was mean, but I really couldn't stand her. The door buzzed again, and Denise, Vinny, and Christie all came in together. Denise walked past me to kiss Grandma hello. I hugged Vinny. I hadn't seen him all week. I kissed Christie, stopping to admire her ring again.

The dinner was okay. I even managed to get through the toast by lifting the glass to my mouth and pretending to drink out of it. Think of the irony when you have to pretend you *are* drinking so your family won't get mad. I realized I must have drunk a lot in the past, because everyone offered me a drink—Grandma, Vinny, my father, even Christie. I didn't want to decline them all, so I took them sporadically then waited till no one was looking and poured them down the sink. Denise ignored me. It's funny, she hates when my mother does that, but now she was doing the same thing.

I squirmed through till about 10:00 and then said I had plans for the night.

"Be careful," my father said emphatically, giving me a sly wink. I guess he figured I'd be out getting wasted, picking up women. I didn't want to disappoint him, so I winked back and he laughed. "I mean it, Tony, don't do nothin' crazy." I wondered if he'd think walking eight miles on the boardwalk alone in the dark with no gun was crazy, but that's exactly what I did.

I parked my car at my house because I didn't want it to get broken into at the boardwalk. I walked up to Bay Street and thought about crossing the street before I had to pass Dave's. But it was too late to do that because Dave was standing out front with two guys and waved me over.

"Tony, let me buy you a drink." He hooked his arm around my neck.

"Not right now, Dave, I have to go somewhere," I said almost frantically. I pictured the bar and could just about taste a cold one. I started walking away. "I'll see you around," I called back.

"Wait! Where are you going?" he asked.

"That way." I pointed in the general direction of the beach as I turned away.

When he yelled out, "Come on, let me buy you a drink," I covered my ears with my hands singing "I can't hear you" as I broke into a jog. By the time I reached the Coast Guard base I was sucking wind.

I slowed my pace, walking to the boardwalk. A surprising

number of people were out running and walking and doing all kinds of things. I never realized how busy the boardwalk kept the cops here. I saw two guys dealing what I guessed was crack out of the parking lot. They were sitting in a silver Mustang GT, and cars would pull up next to them, pass money, and grab something before driving away.

The night was cool, with a light breeze blowing off the water. The farther I got from the bridge, the more I could see the stars. By the time I got to Miller Field, it was midnight. I walked the two and a half miles back to South Beach again and sat by the dolphin fountain. It was still too early to go home, so I walked some more. I estimated I walked about twelve miles that night, but I didn't drink and that was what I wanted. My resolve grew stronger inside me on that walk—I wasn't out of the woods yet, but at least I had found a path. I finally got home at 3:30. I was exhausted and fell asleep almost immediately.

Denise knocked on my door at 8:00 the next morning. Now that I couldn't blow my head off and leave the body for her to find, she was really getting on my nerves. In fact, if Fiore did leave me the gun I probably would have shot her. I told her to get lost. Okay, so maybe I was a little irritable from not drinking.

Now she had the stereo blasting. I couldn't get back to sleep, so I picked up my new Bible to read. I was still reading the book of John. In the second chapter I read how Jesus broke up the temple. People were using it like it was a flea market, and he was mad. He tossed the tables and ran everyone out of there. I always remembered the "turn the other cheek" thing about Jesus, but I guess he got his point across when he had to.

I was now on the fourth chapter, and I got up to the part about the woman at the well and the living water. I pulled out the Amplified version to understand it better. It said the water that Jesus gives will become a spring of water, flowing continually within him into eternal life. I'd have to ask Fiore about that one. I read on, not understanding a lot of it but feeling comforted anyway.

I eventually fell back to sleep and woke up again at 11:45. The stereo was off, and it didn't sound like anyone was home. For once I was glad to be home alone. I was about to get in the shower when the phone rang. I went down to the kitchen to pick up the cordless on the fourth ring.

"Tony, it's Joe."

"Hey, Joe," I was glad that he was thinking of me.

"How's it going?"

"I'm fine, but my legs hurt a little from running away from all the booze this weekend."

"I had a feeling it'd be coming at you from every direction," he said quietly. "Between the basket of cheer from Garcia's kid's school and the family party, I knew the devil would come to steal the seed."

"Huh?"

"Never mind. How are you holding up?" he asked.

"I'm okay. Walked the boardwalk twice last night."

I heard him laugh.

"With no gun to protect me."

"Donna and I have been praying for you."

"Thanks, buddy. I mean it, thanks for everything," I said. "Hey, I was reading John again."

"Yeah?" He sounded thrilled. "Glad to hear it, stay at it. Listen, I won't keep you, just wanted to see how you were."

"I'll be fine. I'll see you tomorrow night."

"I'll get the coffee," he said as he hung up.

I went back up to shower and shave, then went to Montey's for a ham, egg, and cheese on a roll and a cup of coffee. I ate it at the kitchen table while reading the paper. The weather was cool, low eighties, and getting cooler in the evening. I planned to wash my truck and then watch the Yankee game. The Yanks were playing Boston at Fenway, and rival games were always good. Both our New York teams were looking good so far. Piazza had a seventeen-game hitting streak going; he was having some year. The Yanks were doing great as always; Paul O'Neill had an eleven-game hitting streak and Bernie Williams had a ten-game streak.

I wish I could say that my weekend had some excitement to it. The truth was I climbed the walls until I left my house at 10:00 Monday night. The Yanks were humiliated by Boston seven to four. I shut it off in the eighth inning. The only bright spot on Sunday was Denise asking me to go to Dave's for turtle races. Now that she wanted a drinking partner she was talking to me.

"Get away from me," I said as I turned the kitchen hose on her. "You're not talking to me, remember?" I directed a spray of water across the room.

"You psycho!" she yelled as she ran out the front door.

*T*he next week flew by as I got used to life without booze. After the first few days, I wasn't as obsessed with calculating "I haven't had a drink in four days, six hours, and twenty-seven minutes" as I had been.

I spent Monday morning fishing under the bridge off the rocks by the Coast Guard base. I had bought a strip of squid and some live killeys at the bait shop on Sand Lane. The fluke on the Staten Island side of the bridge are nice, bigger than those on the Brooklyn side. I don't know why, maybe the Brooklyn side is fished out. I had caught two doormat-sized fluke that my grandmother loved. I picked her up after work at her bus stop that day to give them to her. She insisted on cooking them for me, so I went back to her apartment while she cleaned and filleted them, fried them in breadcrumbs, and squeezed lemon over them. She made a side order of linguine with garlic and oil and a salad.

The day was sunny and about eighty-five degrees with a warm breeze blowing. At least we had a break from the intense heat we've had over the past few weeks. The morning was quiet—the only sound besides the sea and the gulls was the occasional rumble of a truck overhead on the bridge. I caught a bluefish that was at least eight pounds. He bent my pole almost to my toes, and it took a good fifteen minutes to tire him out. I forgot how much I loved fishing.

I fished for a few hours, then packed up and walked around to the beach. The tide was going out. When I was a kid I would spend hours here, looking under the seaweed-covered rocks for crab or eel. There's a rock jetty and it's amazing what you could find when the tide goes out. Mussels, clams, and small fish would get trapped, not able to get back out to sea. I would have waded in the water, but it didn't look too good. There was a lot of garbage strewn along the shore. Apparently the barge that transported the garbage from the other boroughs spilled trash out as it went. There was also a lot of Coney Island whitefish, so there was no way I was taking off my shoes and putting my feet in the water.

I didn't jog that morning. I had gotten into a routine of jogging on the boardwalk when I got home in the morning. It was really a walk/jog, but I was jogging more now. Eventually, when I quit smoking, I wanted to start running. The biggest thing I dealt with was not the exercise but the boredom and the knowledge that I had come to a crossroad in my life and had some decisions to make. Fiore made a commitment to God sound so easy. I'll admit there was a tug—the more I learned, the more I wanted to know.

Fiore and I fell into a routine at work of talking about God. We talked going to and from jobs and if possible while we were on them. In between we would read the Bible. I drove him crazy with my questions, and he was worried that he wasn't teaching me the right thing.

"You need to go to church," he said. "I'm not a pastor, and I don't want to teach you the wrong thing."

"I'm going to your church this week," I said.

"If you're interested in learning about God, you need to go to church every week," he said. "If you want to be taught."

"I haven't gone to church in twenty years. What difference is a week gonna make?"

He rolled his eyes. "I've been thinking that we should just stick to the basics about salvation," he said seriously. He put out his thumb. "John 3:16." He held out his index finger. "Romans 10:9–10." He put out his middle finger. "And Romans 8:2. Write them down. I'll read them now, but I want you to go home and study them. Remember what John 3:16 tells us?"

"About how much God loves us?"

"That's right! You remember!" He was grinning like crazy. "For God so loved the world, that he gave his only begotten Son, that whoever believes in him should not perish, but have everlasting life."

I nodded, remembering the verse.

"Think about that, Tony, he loved the *world*. You and I see the world all the time, and it's not loveable. All the skells, all the perps, the rapists, the child molesters, all the good and bad. Jesus died for them and for us."

I let that sink in. I had a hard time tolerating the sight of perps like that.

Then Fiore really shocked me. "We're supposed to love everyone like that too. He said we should love one another like he loved us."

I thought about that for a minute.

"But let's not get off track," Fiore said as he flipped through pages. "Okay, in Romans 10:9–10 it says: 'If you confess with your mouth the Lord Jesus and believe in your heart that God has raised Him from the dead, you will be saved. For with the heart one believes to righteousness, and with the mouth confession is made to salvation.' That's the prayer of salvation. Have you thought about saying the prayer of salvation?"

I nodded. "I just want to think about it a little more. I don't want to say it unless I really mean it."

He agreed. "Have you been praying and talking to the Lord?" he asked.

"Is that what you call him, *Lord*?"

"I call him Lord. Sometimes I talk to Jesus. The Bible calls God a lot of different things, but let's just stick to God the Father, Jesus, and the Holy Spirit. Just talk to him. He loves you, Tony, and he's waiting for you to come to him. I think by now you know he exists, don't you?"

"Yeah, I do," I said. I couldn't explain it, but I knew God was reaching out to me and using Joe Fiore to do it.

Joe and I really had become good friends in such a short period of time. Honestly I've never had a friend like him. On my first night back after Vinny's party, when I told Fiore I still didn't drink, I thought he was gonna cry. He hugged me and called Donna to tell her. I wished he'd stop hugging me like that—I didn't know what the guys would say if they saw it. I didn't want to say anything to him and hurt his feelings. He really let me know he was standing by me, whether I drank or not. It made no difference.

My being on the wagon was challenged almost a week after the night it began. Fiore and I took a job for a dispute at a triple-X place on 8th Avenue south of 41st. The job came over at about 1:30 a.m. It was out of our sector, but sector Henry was busy.

We got out of the car and proceeded to the establishment. As we approached it and walked past some phone booths, a white male in his late twenties wearing shorts and a muscle shirt hawked up some phlegm and spit it at us as we passed. He was built like a bull, six feet tall, probably about 275 pounds. I didn't know it at the time, but he was the guy we had gotten the call about.

I heard the sound as he coughed it up and then felt it hit the back of my head. I turned around and looked in the direction it came from and saw the bull standing there. He was all muscle, swaggering with a hip-hop walk. His hands swayed back and forth, with his thumb and pinky out, the rest of the fingers folded in. He wore a baseball cap turned to the side and bopped to an internal beat.

"Did you just spit on me?" I asked, stunned.

"Officer, he did spit on you," a middle-aged man said as he walked out of the store.

This being a porn place, his word was questionable.

The bull ignored me and pretended to be surprised when I went to grab him. "What are you doing?" he yelled. "What's going on?"

A white, male hippie-looking guy in his early forties with round wire-rimmed glasses wearing leather sandals, khaki shorts, and a white shirt stopped to watch.

When I put the spitter up against the window of the triple-X place to lock him up for disorderly conduct, he went berserk. As I tried to pull his arm behind his back, he pulled his arm out and pushed off the glass to turn around and grab us. At that point I grabbed him by his left shoulder. Fiore grabbed him by his right shoulder, and we put him up against the window of the store. As we attempted to cuff him, his right hand was up against the window. I had his left hand down, close to his waist. Just as I got the cuffs onto his left wrist, he swung his right arm around, catching Fiore with the force of his body and knocking him into me. I was bent down, with his left arm by my stomach as Fiore hit me. My left shoulder went right through the window.

The sound of shattering glass echoed around us. I moved my head out of the way so I wouldn't get hit with it. That's when I saw the hippie filming us, hoping to get some police brutality on tape so he could sell it to the news. He moved in with his camera, close enough to distract us.

Glass was on my shoulders and in my hair as I still held the cuff in my hand. Fiore grabbed the spitter by his right arm and shoulder and pulled him to the ground. Because he was so big, I started to go down with him. I had to let go of the cuff. I heard the *whack* as he hit the pavement, landing facedown. I dropped on his back and grabbed his arm in a hurry. He started making roaring noises, straining with all his might to get up.

As I was on his back I held his left arm down, with the cuff in my right hand. The metal link between the cuffs was in my right hand so that I had a grip on his wrist and he couldn't pull his arm away. As I was doing that, I looked up because there was a camera in my face on the left side. We were by the curb now, rolling on the filthy sidewalk while this idiot was filming me. I put my left arm up. "Get out of here! What are you doing?" I asked, appalled. "I'm trying to cuff this guy."

Now that the spitter was pinned on the ground we could cuff him. Fiore had his right arm. I pushed with my knee into the guy's back and pulled his left arm up so he had no leverage to stand. Fiore pulled his right arm up to the middle of his back, and we cuffed the guy. Immediately he started kicking and screaming again, trying to get up. Judging by the way he acted, he was on something, and it wasn't just alcohol.

"That's him, Officer," came a voice from behind us. I turned around to see a short, middle-aged man coming out of the triple-X store. The camera was in my face again as I turned. I said, "Get out of here!" holding up my hand. When the hippie didn't move, I said, "If you don't step back, you'll be locked up for obstructing."

"I know my rights," he sneered. "This is a public sidewalk, and you can't stop me from filming."

"Then get away from me!" I barked out.

The manager of the porn place started telling us the cuffed guy had been breaking up the store. The cameraman came up again, this time on my right side. I turned to my left so I could listen to the store manager. I was holding onto the perp's left arm with my other hand, pushing down on his left shoulder. I mentally tried to calm myself down because I felt myself starting to explode.

Fiore stepped in front of the guy with the camera, pushing him back. "Listen, I am only going to tell you this one more time—get back or you're getting locked up for obstructing." Fiore was angry. This was our second warning for the guy to step back—on the third he'd get locked up. He knew this and backed off just enough.

Fiore had called for backup, nonemergency, once we had the EDP cuffed. Since this was an EDP, we would need the sergeant at the scene and an ambulance to take the perp to Bellevue. The guy was on something, and we didn't want him going into heart failure from exerting himself during the psychosis. As it was, he was getting a burst of energy every twenty seconds and fighting and screaming all over again. When he stopped fighting he would take in deep panting breaths until he got his next rush of strength. I was exhausted from grappling with him.

ESU arrived first, then the ambulance and Sergeant Hanrahan were on the scene. They wrapped the perp in a mesh blanket, keeping his arms and legs close to him so he couldn't hurt himself or anyone else. The mesh would keep him from overheating. They put him on his stomach with his head to the side on the gurney because he was biting and spitting.

Once he was in the ambulance I noticed that my hands and face were cut from the falling glass. Nothing serious, but the ambulance worker took a look at me. The cameraman didn't bother filming the blood on me—he was filming the perp wrapped in the mesh blanket being taken into the ambulance.

"Hey!" I yelled. "The show's over. Now get out of here."

He took his time putting away his camera, mumbling that I couldn't tell him what to do. Fiore could see how angry I was, and he went over to the guy and said, "You had your two warnings. Get out of here now or I'm locking you up."

The cameraman moved away—he knew the third warning would mean an arrest. He'd done this before. The department had had problems like this before. If I had taken his camera and locked him up for obstructing, I would be the one under scrutiny. If push came to shove, the brass would feed me to the wolves. It would look like he was locked up to cover a brutality conspiracy he caught on film.

While the perp was in the ambulance, Fiore spoke to the store manager. Now the spitter would be a collar, not just an EDP. Fiore would take the collar so it didn't look like I took his spitting personally and locked him up for it. The complainant at the store wanted to press charges anyway.

Fiore went by ambulance to Bellevue, and I followed in the RMP. The hospital shot the perp up with tranquilizers and took off the mesh blanket. They tied him down with sheets to the gurney and put him in a room. The hospital had his wallet and gave us his name and pertinent information needed to process the arrest. Fiore went to the station to start the paperwork. I stayed at Bellevue until 7:00, when someone relieved me. I saw Fiore when I got back to the precinct. I was still angry about the guy with the camera.

"I should have locked him up," I said, pacing. I don't know why I was letting it get to me. It's not like it hadn't happened before.

"Let it go, Tony," he said. "It doesn't matter. Stop a minute and pray, just talk to the Lord and ask him to help you."

I didn't want to talk to the Lord. I wanted to drink until I wasn't so mad that I wanted to break something. By the time I'd changed into shorts and a T-shirt, I'd decided to meet Rooney at the bar. Fiore took my gun again, which made me mad, and I stomped away from him without saying good-bye.

I sat in my truck outside the bar, debating about going inside. I hadn't had a drink in a week, and I knew that if I went in there, I'd be turning back somehow. I decided to pray and see if it worked.

Father, in the name of Jesus, I prayed silently, remembering how Fiore said to do it. *I want to have a drink so bad. I'm so mad at that guy with the camera.* I sighed. *I don't know what to do.*

Two things hit me right then. One was I wanted the drink to control my emotions for me. And two, Jesus died for scum like the guy with the camera.

I didn't go in the bar. I went home. I was still angry, but not in a rage.

Traffic was clear until the Verrazano Bridge. The upper level was closed. The cars on the lower level were backed up, bumper to bumper. I got so aggravated I drove on the left shoulder, swung around through the cones, and took the upper level anyway. At midspan I saw about six workers standing in a circle talking. One of them yelled out, "Hey this level is closed, can't you see we're working here?"

Yeah, they looked like they were working.

I called out, "I'm sorry, I didn't realize it was closed." Then I added, "Sorry about that." He flipped me the bird as I drove off.

I drove straight to the South Beach parking lot and parked my car near the dolphin fountain. I pounded the boardwalk as much as I could, running off my frustration in the hot sun. I stopped at the hot dog vendor and bought a bottle of water and two hot dogs with mustard and sauerkraut. I finished them off and went for a third, eating while I drove home. By then the urge to drink had lessened. I slept the rest of the day. I decided I'd better buy a speed bag to take out my frustrations on.

I was bored out of my mind. I stayed away from Dave's bar, driving home on the service road and coming up the back way. I avoided Denise at home. She still wasn't talking to me so that wasn't too hard. She'd been spending a lot of time over at Sal Valente's house.

Wednesday night there was a water main break at 38th Street and 8th Avenue, so Fiore and I spent our tour directing traffic off of 8th Avenue. The break happened at 10:30, toward the end of the four-to-twelve tour. When Fiore and I got there to relieve Rice and Beans, the DEP and the fire department were already there, along with the yellow trucks that handle the water main breaks. Halogen lights and pumps were set up to illuminate the area while they worked. The water must have risen up onto the sidewalks, because they were still wet when we got there. I could hear the generator from the pump working, a constant buzzing filling the air. They had to open up the street to get to the pipe, then shut the main valve to fix the break.

The midnight foot posts took the side streets and stopped any traffic from getting to 8th Avenue. We worked there all night.

I slept Thursday away, too tired for my daily jog. I woke up at 5:30, took a shower, and shaved. I had dinner at Alfredo's Restaurant. Vinny had left me a note saying that he would be there with Mike, but when I got there they were gone. His note said they would be there at 7:30, but I guess they changed their minds. I ate alone—linguine and white clam sauce with a salad and a Coke. I went back home to get my gear and watched TV until 10:20. I drove straight through the city without traffic, taking thirty-three minutes to reach the precinct.

Fiore and I spent a good part of Thursday night in the

parking lot on 37th Street between 5th and 6th Avenue. The Empire State Building was lit up in all blue, and I watched it through the buildings as we talked.

"How are you feeling, Tony?" Fiore asked.

"Honestly? A lot better," I said.

He looked doubtful. "What about the depression?" he asked. "Do you still feel overwhelmed?"

"No, not like that. I'm sober now, so I'm dealing with things a little better."

He nodded. "Are you still reading your Bible?"

"Every day. I like reading it," I said. I just wished I understood more of it. The Amplified Bible helped—it explained a lot of the words. I found when I read I felt peaceful, not so alone anymore.

We got called to three alarms that night. They were all locked down, premises secure. At 3:16 Central put a call over for shots fired.

"South David," Central called.

"South David," Fiore responded.

"I have a 10–10 shots fired at West 40th and Broadway."

"South David going," Fiore answered. We heard the other sectors respond.

On the ride there Fiore asked, "Is there a callback?" Sometimes the 911 caller leaves a number so Central can call back for more information.

"No callback," Central responded.

We pulled up to an open courtyard on the south part of 40th Street. It was empty and quiet. Fiore radioed us 84 and asked if Central knew where the call came from.

"A pay phone in Port Authority," Central responded.

We gave it back 90X, unfounded.

We stopped for coffee at the Sunrise Deli and drove back to the 37th Street parking lot to drink it.

"Donna said she told you about before she got saved," Fiore said casually.

"She just said she wasn't living right," I answered. I was standing outside the RMP smoking a cigarette, drinking my coffee.

He chuckled. "She doesn't tell many people."

"Tell them what?" I asked, looking in the car.

He shrugged. "When she first came to church she had that big hair, black eyeliner thing going on. She was wearing a short skirt and those high spike heels." He smiled and shook his head. "She had such an attitude."

"So how'd you hook up with her?" I asked.

"She was partying a lot—she told me later she was all messed up. I knew it. I didn't get involved with her until I knew her commitment to God was real. I liked her from the first time I met her. We were friends, but she was seeing some guy in a band. She used to go to all the clubs with him. At first she just came to our midweek service; then when her boyfriend left she started coming on Sunday."

"Were you a cop then?" I forgot how long he said he'd been married.

"Yeah, I had about two years on."

"She told me she was obnoxious then," I said. "Was she?"

He shrugged. "A little, but she was still sweet." He smiled.

It was funny how they each saw it in a different way.

We got a call for a dispute at the New Yorker Hotel on 8th Avenue between 34th and 35th Streets The dispute was between a cabbie and a passenger. The cabbie said the guy didn't pay, the passenger said he did. I could tell the passenger was handicapped. He was a male white, about thirty years old, thin and sickly looking, coughing and limping dramatically. I thought he was faking it until I saw the sores on his arms. He was dressed in worn jeans and carried an old briefcase.

The cabbie said the fare was to the New Yorker Hotel. When they got to the New Yorker, the passenger changed his mind. Now he wanted to go up to Port Authority to see if any of his friends were there. The cabbie said no, you wanted the New Yorker, you're at the New Yorker. He had another fare from the New Yorker that he didn't want to lose. The man with the briefcase said he asked to go to Port Authority, not the New Yorker Hotel. He said he paid the cabbie. The cabbie said he only paid him three bucks for a nine-dollar fare.

I asked for the crib sheet, which would give me the pickup and destination for each fare. Sure enough, the fare was to the New Yorker Hotel. I figured it would be—a cabbie wouldn't call us unless someone ripped him off. They want to get right out to their next fare. Standing here talking to me, he'd be losing money.

As I questioned him, the passenger coughed and gasped for breath. I looked him in the eye. "Now, listen to me. The bottom line is he took you here like you asked. If you don't pay him, I'm locking you up for theft of service."

Suddenly the limp and the cough were gone as the passenger tossed a few rolled-up bills on the trunk of the cab. I'm sure he knew by the tone of my voice that I wasn't joking. I don't think he faked the sores on his arms, just played it up to make me feel sorry for him. I didn't. The cabbie counted out the bills. I doubt he got a tip. He thanked us and took off.

I left the precinct by 8:00 Friday morning and reached my front door by 8:45. I used the bathroom and grabbed a bottle of water for my run.

I parked at the dolphin fountain. I walked and jogged the three and a half miles and was wide awake by the time I got home. I drove up to Bay Street at 11:00 and got a haircut. If lightning was gonna strike when I went to church on Sunday, I wanted to look nice. I stopped for a bagel and coffee, eating at the kitchen table. I turned the air conditioner on high and put on a pair of sweats to sleep in. I was asleep by noon, setting my clock for 7:30.

Vinny was home when I got up. I showered and shaved and we ordered out for sandwiches. Meatball for him, eggplant parm for me. He had taken the day off from work so he could fill out some bridal registry. They went to Fortunoff's at the Woodbridge Mall, and he and Christie picked out china. This way everyone could give Fortunoff's their name and see what to buy them. He was describing his china to me, telling me it was bone with flowers on it. Like I cared. I was giving him money. Let him buy his own dishes.

Friday night was our last tour before we swung out. Fiore was all excited about his baby's thing on Sunday. He asked me to be on time. He said there might be some traffic in the morning and suggested I leave early just in case.

The night was busy; Fridays usually were. But it didn't get interesting until 3:30 when we got a call in Charlie Frank sector.

"South David," Central called.

"South David," Fiore responded.

"I have a 10–10 at 330 West 30th Street, apartment 5 Frank." A 10–10 is a call for help.

It was the third call to this address in the past few weeks. Every time we answered it was the same thing. A little old man claimed that a woman went into his apartment, and he asked us to get her out. We parked outside the building and rang the bell for apartment 5F. The guy buzzed us in, and we took the elevator to the fifth floor and rang the bell to the apartment.

From within the apartment came a "Who is it?" We identified ourselves as police officers, and a short, skinny old man answered the door. He had to be at least eighty years old. He had thinning white hair and was wearing light blue boxer shorts and a buttoned white shirt. His knobby knees could be seen above his black nylon socks, and he wore no shoes. He had bushy eyebrows and hair growing out of his nose.

"Officers, come in. I want you to get this woman out of here." He pointed behind him. He had a slight accent and a raspy voice.

The apartment was a shabby studio. We walked into a tiny kitchen area that held a wooden table with two chairs. Beyond the kitchen was a sleeping area. It was so small that the bed came right to the edge of the kitchen. To the right of the kitchen was a closet-sized room with a reclining chair and a TV set. Off the sitting room was an ancient bathroom.

I could see a woman in her mid-twenties standing behind him. She was thin with long, straggly dark hair, olive skin, and brown eyes. She was wearing purple satin underwear.

"Who is she?" I asked.

"I don't know, but she doesn't belong in my apartment," he said emphatically.

"Well, how'd she get in your apartment?" I asked.

"I don't know," he said.

"What do you mean you don't know?" I made a "who are you kidding?" face.

"I was sleeping right over there." He pointed to the bed. "I woke up and she was there."

"So what you're trying to tell me is that you were sound asleep and woke up to a woman in your apartment in her underwear?" I asked, laughing.

"Yes!" He nodded dramatically.

"Now why do I find that hard to believe? How did she get into your apartment? Did she climb up five flights on the fire escape just to see you in your boxers?" I asked.

"I don't know, Officer, but I want her out of here," he demanded.

The woman wasn't saying a word. She stepped back into the

area by the bed and came out a minute later with a dress on. It was tight and black with thin straps. I saw his black pants draped over the foot of the bed. As he babbled on, he was oblivious to her in the background. Fiore and I watched her reach over to the pants, trying to pull the wallet out of them.

"Are those your pants over there on the bed?" I asked, knowing he'd catch her with them.

"Yes, those are mine!" He dove for the pants, trying to grab them out of her hands. They wrestled with the pants for a minute until he pulled them away. She still held his wallet in her hand, and I saw her take some bills out of it. This was getting comical. I looked at Fiore to see his reaction. His face was serious.

"Give the wallet back," I told her.

"He owes me money," she said quietly, handing him the wallet. Her left hand was clenched by her side.

He counted what was in his wallet. "She robbed me!"

"What's in your hand?" I asked, amazed that she took the money right in front of us.

"Nothing," she said, clenching her fist tighter.

"Open your hand."

"No."

This went back and forth between us for a couple of minutes until I grabbed her wrist and said, "Listen, you can either give me what's in your hand or I'm gonna take it out and we can lock you up. What do you want to do?"

She didn't answer, so I pried her hand open and found forty dollars in it.

"I want her arrested, Officer," the old man said. "She tried to take my money!"

"You want me to arrest her?" I said. "Are you trying to tell me she doesn't belong here? You didn't let her into the apartment?"

"I didn't let her in," he said.

"Then how did she get in? I'm finding it hard to believe that you're sound asleep and wake up to find a woman in purple underwear in your apartment. How old are you? Stuff like that never happens to me!"

"Officer, he knows how I got here," the woman interrupted quietly. "He let me in. He picked me up on 8th Avenue and took me here,"

I pulled her over to the sitting room, and Fiore stayed talking to the old man.

"What's going on?" I asked her.

"Listen, I come here all the time. He picks me up, I'm a regular of his. Sometimes," she shrugged her shoulders, "he don't wanna pay."

"So why do you keep coming back?"

"Usually he's okay and pays me. But sometimes he won't pay." She shrugged again.

"Well, he's gonna have you locked up," I said.

"Why?" She looked surprised.

"First of all, I saw you take money out of his pants. Secondly, he's saying you were in his apartment unlawfully."

"But he brought me here!" she said.

"I understand that." I paused. "What I can do is have you sign an affidavit and get him for patronizing a prostitute. I lock him up too, and he won't be doing this anymore."

She thought a minute and nodded. "Okay, I'll sign."

She picked up her pocketbook, and I went through it. I gave it back to her, and she put it on her shoulder before I cuffed her.

"Thank you, Officer! I just want her out of here!" the old man burst out.

"Do me a favor and put your pants on," I told him.

"Why?" he asked suspiciously.

"Because I don't want to talk to you in your underwear

209

anymore. Put your shoes on while you're at it, I need you to come to the precinct with us."

He argued back and forth until he got dressed.

"Okay, now it's time to turn around," I said. "We're arresting you too."

"Why?" he yelled.

"For patronizing a prostitute. According to her, you do this all the time. You bring her back to your apartment and pay her for sexual favors. She's willing to sign an affidavit stating so."

"That's not true!" he wailed.

"Well, she said it's not true that she came into your apartment illegally," I added.

As I cuffed him his pants fell down. I looked around for a belt but couldn't find one. I gathered the back of his pants and put them in his cuffed hands. He jumped around and stood on his toes to avoid being taken out of the apartment. Then he screamed, "You dogs!"

"Dogs? What is that supposed to mean? Listen, this is the third time somebody's had to come to your apartment because you want to pick up a prostitute and don't feel like paying her afterward. You think we're here to take care of your dirty work. Well, that's not gonna happen anymore 'cause what we're gonna do now is lock you up. I guarantee you won't be calling me again to get rid of a prostitute for you."

"That's not what happened!" he screamed.

He became frantic as we brought him out of the apartment. He called us dogs the whole ride downstairs. Fiore looked straight ahead, not saying a word. As we put them in the RMP I said, "Watch your head, Pops." I put them both in the backseat with Fiore between them.

I drove them back to the precinct. When we got to the stairs at the front door, the old man tried to dig in his heels. Again. The desk sergeant gave me a look and said, "Okay, what is this?" The old man carried on the whole time, calling us dogs and other choice words.

I motioned to the sarge to come over to the side as Fiore filled out the pedigree sheet on both of them.

"Sarge, this is the third call we've gotten on this guy. Charlie had the other two. Every time this guy has a pros in his house, he thinks he's gonna call us to get rid of her so he doesn't have to pay."

He laughed. "What are you locking him up for?"

"Patronizing a prostitute. She wants to sign an affidavit," I said.

"Okay." He nodded. "Put them in the back and keep them separated. I'll let the lou know what's going on."

It turned out the guy was married and lived in Brooklyn. The place on West 30th Street was his love nest where he took prostitutes. Apparently he was some kind of community leader in Brooklyn, and if word got out he was arrested for patronizing a prostitute, he'd be ruined. Personally I doubted if anyone would believe he could patronize a prostitute, but hey, what do I know?

The lieutenant came back out with him and told us to put him back in the cell. He was quiet now, no longer calling us dogs.

"Tony, this is what I want you to do," the lou said. "I explained to him the reason we locked him up. He won't be doing this anymore. He's mortified, and he doesn't want any of this to get out. We'll void his arrest, and he'll drop the charges against her. We'll hold on to the affidavit from her and the one he signed in my office. I explained to him that if he ever calls again on something like this, we'll lock him up for this affidavit and the next one. I told him we have enough going on here, and we don't need him calling us because he doesn't feel like paying a pros."

"No problem, I'll void it out," I said.

We drove the old man back to his apartment. The old man didn't say anything on the ride back, not even thank you. I said, "Good night, Pops" as he got out of the car and barked as he walked up the steps to his apartment.

I turned to Fiore. "What does he mean by calling us dogs?"

"What difference does it make?" he answered. "He's just lost."

I tried to press him about that, but he told me to forget it.

We slept through our meal. We stopped to eat when we went back out at 5:30, bacon and egg on a roll. The rest of the night went without incident. I shook Joe's hand before I left the precinct, saying I would see him the following morning. I went right to sleep when I got home. I had a lot to do that night.

I woke up at 4:00 p.m. on Saturday. I had decided to shop for a new suit, so I put off eating until I got to the mall. Macy's at the mall was having a suit sale, so I bought one there, a gray single-breasted, two-button job in an athletic build. The pants were a little long, but other than that it fit good. I picked out a conservative maroon tie, a new short-sleeve Charter Club dress shirt, and a pair of gray dress socks to match the suit.

I walked through the mall to the center food court and ordered a Philly cheesesteak and a Coke. The mall was crowded with families and teenagers, and I had a hard time finding a table.

I found a sporting goods store next to the Gap and bought a speed bag and a pair of unpadded gloves to go with it. After leaving the mall, I drove to my grandmother's apartment so I could drop off my pants to be hemmed.

"Who is it?" the intercom asked suspiciously.

"Grandma, it's me, Tony," I said.

She buzzed me in and was out in the hall as I turned the corner.

"Is everything okay?" she asked. I guess I never visited her on a Saturday night before, unless it was for dinner.

"It's fine," I said as she got me in a hug.

It was only 8:00, and she was already in her pajamas. She had the Yankee game on. She's madly in love with Derek Jeter and had the TV on so loud I could hear it in the lobby. She had me try on the suit pants so she could pin them, and she hemmed them while we watched the game. Then she pressed them, using a wet paper bag to make a sharp crease in the new hem. I wound up staying at her house for the whole game. She fell asleep in the seventh inning, snoring loud enough to make me laugh. I lowered the sound and watched the rest of the game, then shut off the TV and locked the door when I left.

Life got exciting again the day of Fiore's baby's party. Let's face it, if the highlight of my weekend was watching the Yankee game with my grandmother, there isn't much to tell. I thought I'd talk to Fiore about getting me some tickets to a Yankee game. Someone in his family had season tickets, and there's always some afternoon game that they won't travel up to the Bronx for. If I gave Grandma some notice, she could get the day off from work. I shook my head—now I was making dates to take my grandmother to Yankee Stadium. I had to get a life.

The morning of Fiore's party I was up by 7:00. I showered and shaved, putting on cologne and my Movado watch that I'd bought for two hundred bucks in St. Maarten a couple of years ago. I didn't want to sweat on my new suit so I blasted the air conditioner in my truck. I stopped on Bay Street for a cup of coffee and a buttered bagel which I ate in my truck before hitting the road.

Fiore had given me directions printed out on his computer. There was a map with typed directions, and they were pretty easy to follow. When I exited off the Long Island Expressway, I saw a silver Toyota Camry pulled over on the right. A woman in a beige sleeveless dress was attempting to change a tire while a little blond-haired boy stood on the side. I pulled over in back of her and put my flashers on.

"Need a hand?" I asked as I approached.

She was pushing so hard to turn the lug nut she lost her balance and slammed the lug wrench into her shoulder.

"Tony!" It was Stevie, the kid from Fiore's house.

"Hey, Steve, howz it goin', buddy?" I asked as he high-fived me. "You guys going to church?"

"Yup," Stevie said. "But we got a flat."

"Want some help?" I asked his mother.

"Yes, thanks." She smiled and looked flustered as she rubbed her shoulder. She stood up to give me access to the tire. Her high heels gave her a couple of inches, so she was almost as tall as I was. Everything about her screamed class. The only jewelry she wore was a string of pearls around her neck. She wore her hair down, shoulder-length with some blonde highlights—I couldn't tell if they were natural or not. She had no stockings on, and without the hiking boots, she had great legs.

"I really appreciate this," she said with a smile. She had intelligent eyes. I hadn't noticed that before.

"Mom, please let me stay upstairs with you in church," Stevie said.

"Steven, it's only for an hour. You're supposed to be downstairs with the other kids for Sunday school," she answered.

"Did you ever have a flat tire?" he asked me.

"Sure, plenty of times." I messed his hair.

"You're gonna get dirty," he said.

"I won't get dirty." I took off my jacket and went to put it in my truck, but she held out her hand to take it. It was getting hot—the temperature was supposed to reach the high eighties, and it felt close to that already.

"Do you live around here?" I asked.

"In Manorville," Steven answered. "Where do you live?"

"Staten Island."

"You're far from home," the woman said. I couldn't remember her name.

"Not that far. It took me about an hour and fifteen minutes to get here," I said.

I pulled three of the lug nuts off and was wrestling with the fourth when Steven asked, "Are you married, Tony?"

"Nope," I said as the nut came loose.

"Neither is my mom."

"Steven!" his mom said.

I smiled and filed the information away. He was a cute kid, asking me questions as I pulled the tire off.

She shook her head. "I'm sorry."

"No problem," I said, going around to the trunk to pull out the donut. "Are you going to Joe's house for the baby's party?"

She nodded. "For a little while."

"The spare will hold for a little while, but you'll have to get the flat fixed," I said. I placed the flat in the trunk and looked it over for nails. "You should be okay today, just get it fixed tomorrow." I looked at my watch. It was already 9:45, and church started at 10:00.

She took her pocketbook out of the car as I slammed the trunk. She tried to give me money for changing the tire.

"Don't insult me," I said.

"Sorry. I really appreciate this." She held out her hand.

My hand was covered with dirt, so I held it out and raised my eyebrows. "I don't want to get your hand dirty."

"Wait, let me get you something." She reached in her car and pulled out a box of those wet wipe things and gave me two. After I cleaned my hand I held it out.

"Thanks," I said.

"Michele." She shook my hand.

"I remember," I said with a smile.

"Sure you did." She smiled back. "Thanks again."

"Thanks, Tony," Steven said, pumping my hand and smiling. "Now we won't be late." As they got in their car, I heard him ask again, "Mom, can I stay upstairs with you?"

I stood there like an idiot watching her drive away. I did forget her name. I like women who wear shoes, not construction boots. Now that I'd seen her dressed like a woman, I was rethinking things. She looked hot today, not like she was hiking in the woods, munching on granola.

The church was about a quarter of a mile down, and when I got there, a cop was directing traffic outside. He waved me in, and a parking attendant asked if I'd been there before. When I said no, he directed me to a spot in front of the church. I laughed when I saw the name, House on the Rock. It was a new building, unlike any church I'd ever been to. It was a two-story white structure, no steeple or anything, with glass doors in the front.

I walked up four steps and reached for the door when someone opened it from inside. A line of people with name tags shook my hand and said good morning, then directed me inside to a huge room packed with people singing to a live band. One of the ushers looked around and found a seat in the midsection near the back on the aisle and escorted me over. I would have preferred to stand, but he took off to seat the next person before I got a chance to tell him.

The man and woman next to me shook my hand and went back to their singing. The woman had her hands raised, and the man sang along with the band. There was a screen in the front next to the altar that gave the words to the song. I felt stupid standing there but didn't know what else to do. I looked around for Fiore and Donna but didn't see them.

As the music slowed, an acoustic guitar played some chords while a man came up to pray. He thanked the Lord for the congregation. He prayed for the needs of the church, then said "Praise you, bless you, thank you" and some other things and told everyone to sit down. A woman went up and talked about tithing, asking if anyone needed an envelope. She gave some Scripture about giving ten percent of your money, and I felt some cynicism rise up in my chest. Sure, here they were asking for money. But these people didn't seem to mind—when the basket came around they were real happy putting their envelopes in. I hadn't been to church in so long I didn't know what to give, so I threw in a twenty, hoping that would cover it.

As the church quieted down I heard a kid call out, "Hey, there's Tony!"

Half the congregation turned to look as little Stevie ran down the aisle toward me.

"Hey, buddy," I whispered.

Michele followed behind him, looking mortified. "Steven!" she whispered. "Get back here!"

"Please, Mom?" he pleaded. "I'll be quiet. Can I sit with Tony?"

"No, you can't sit with Tony!" she whispered, exasperated. "You don't even know him."

"Yes, I do, I met him *twice*." His whisper was like a bullhorn.

The pastor started to preach, and Michele crouched down in the aisle, throwing glances back over her shoulder toward the altar and the pastor. Maybe she was worried he would get mad that she was out of her seat.

Stevie climbed up on my lap. I don't know who was more shocked, me or Michele.

"It's okay, leave him here," I said.

"No! I don't even know you," she whispered.

Just then Fiore came up behind me, crouching next to my seat.

"Hey, Tony," he whispered, looking puzzled. "Hey, Michele," he said, kissing her cheek and giving Stevie a silent high five.

"Stevie wants to sit with me," I said, smiling.

Michele shook her head. "I don't like him going to people he doesn't know." She was almost apologetic. "No offense, Tony."

"None taken."

"Please, Mom?" Stevie begged again.

I guess she didn't want to sit there and argue about it. She gave Stevie a stern look and went back over to her seat, throwing worried glances my way. Fiore shook my hand and went back to his seat.

Stevie settled down in my lap as the preacher asked if there were any first-time visitors. I didn't raise my hand but saw Fiore pointing me out to one of the ushers. He'd pay for that.

They came over and gave me a booklet with a pen and a tape in it. The usher asked me to fill out the card and give it to him before the service was over.

They dedicated Fiore's daughter at the beginning of the service. Fiore and Donna were all choked up as they promised to raise her according to the Word. The pastor prayed for the baby and then for Fiore and Donna. It was nice. The baby wore a christening outfit, all white silk. Another woman and man, who I guess were the godparents, held her. It was nice seeing that they don't assault the baby with water, like during a baptism. The babies always cry.

In the meantime Stevie started twirling his hair. He farted, vibrating my leg with it.

"I farted," he whispered, giggling.

"I know," I said dryly.

It stunk. I thought about pointing to the top of his head and waving my hand in front of my face so no one thought it was me. I didn't see anyone looking or gasping for breath. As the smell faded, I settled in, holding Stevie as he twirled his hair. I wondered who his father was and why he wasn't with them. Then the sermon caught my attention, and I stopped wondering.

It was about someone named Gideon. The name sounded familiar, but other than that I never heard the story. The pastor said that Israel had been hiding from the Midianites. And this guy Gideon was cutting wheat in a winepress, which the pastor said was like playing golf in a closet. Everyone laughed, but it flew over my head. He said Gideon was hiding because these Midianite guys would steal their food. An angel came to him, saying, "The Lord is with you, mighty man of valor." The funny thing was the guy was a wimp, complaining to the angel about all the bad stuff that happened to Israel (he sounded like me a couple of weeks ago). The preacher said that this guy would go on to save Israel. Then the preacher brought the whole thing around to everyday life. He said that in 2 Peter 1:3, the Bible says God has given us all things pertaining to life and godliness. We can win our battles if we see things through the eyes of faith instead of through our own eyes. To do something that we know we can do doesn't take any faith.

I was impressed. I had never heard it put that way before. People were saying amen while the pastor was talking. At the end of the service he asked everyone to bow his or her head.

I put my head down, surprised to see that Stevie had fallen asleep. I listened as the pastor gave an invitation to walk to the throne of God to anyone who had never made Jesus Christ the Lord of his life.

I bowed my head as a guitar started playing softly. The preacher talked about Calvary and how Jesus died to pay the price for our sin. He said that if there was only one person on earth, he still would have done it. Just for you, he said. *Just for me.* There was expectancy in the air, and a feeling of peace came over me. I put my head down and repeated in my head the words he'd said out loud. That I was a sinner, that I believed that Jesus is the Son of God, that he died for me, and that God raised him from the dead. I asked Jesus to come into my heart and be Lord in my life.

Then the pastor asked the congregation to say it out loud. I joined my voice with the others, crossing the bridge to salvation.

I was wiping at the corners of my eyes as church ended. I picked Stevie up as I stood, turning him into my shoulder as his mother came toward me.

"He's sleeping," I said.

"I can't believe he went to you like that." She paused, embarrassed. "It's nothing personal, but I don't want him to go to strangers. I know that you're a friend of Joe's, but you're still a stranger."

She had a point. I didn't know what to tell her. It's not like he went anywhere with me; she was there the whole time.

"So talk to him. Tell him not to go anywhere with a stranger," I said. "You were right there," I pointed out.

Donna and Fiore came over with the kids just then. Donna was beaming when she saw me and kissed my cheek. "Hey, Tony! I'm so glad you came."

"I got a flat on the way, and he stopped to change it for me," Michele said.

Donna smiled at me. "You're such a gentleman."

I bowed.

"What time is the party?" Michele asked Donna.

For some reason I was happy she and Stevie would be there.

"Well, it's at 2:00, but Tony's coming back with us now. Joe's family and my sister are already here," Donna said. "Don't go back to Manorville, come over now."

"Are you sure?" Michele looked doubtful. "The party doesn't start until 2:00."

"You probably shouldn't drive too much on that donut," I pointed out.

"Are you sure you don't mind?" Michele turned to Donna.

"Not at all," Donna said, smiling at me.

Fiore pulled me over to the side. "You look good with a kid."

"He farted on me," I said.

"They do that." He smiled. "Michele's not married, in case you were interested."

"I might be interested," I said. "Where's Steven's father?"

"He's not around," he said. "You'll have to ask Michele about it; it's up to her what she wants to tell you. Good kid, though. He plays with Josh. Needs a father."

"The father's not around at all?" I asked.

"No."

I nodded.

Her name was Michele Dugan. Her father was Irish, her mother Italian. She lived in Manorville in a two-bedroom house that she bought by herself. She grew up on Long Island.

She was thirty-three, a year older than me, and she taught fifth grade. I found all this out when she helped me set up the tables and chairs in Fiore's backyard while Donna and Fiore got the food together.

"I like your church," I told her as we put plastic tablecloths over the tables.

"Pastor John is great. The children's church is great too, but Steven's been giving me a hard time about going. I think he's going through a little separation anxiety."

I nodded, having no idea what she meant.

"Do you work over the summer?" I asked.

"I'm working the Vacation Bible School at the church for the next two weeks, then I'm off until the third week of August."

I had a week off in August.

Fiore had about fifty people there that day. I met his parents, Lou and Connie. They were both friendly, outgoing people like Fiore. His father was a big man with a potbelly and dark eyes and looked to be in his sixties. His mother was short and round, with pretty green eyes and red hair and looked much younger than her husband.

At one point I stepped into the middle of an argument between Fiore's dad and his Uncle Frank about the 1955 World Series between the Yankees and the Brooklyn Dodgers.

"Tony, tell my brother where game seven of the series was played," Fiore's dad implored.

I smiled. "My guess would be either Yankee Stadium or Ebbets Field."

"They won the last game at Yankee Stadium," Fiore's dad said emphatically. "It went nine innings, and the score was two nothing for the bums."

"What was the starting lineup for the Dodgers?" I asked, baiting him.

"Don't get him started," Fiore's mother mumbled.

"Never mind, Connie. Come here and sit down, Tony, let me tell you. Johnny Padres was pitching—"

"Are you sure it was Johnny Padres?" Uncle Frank asked with a twinkle in his eye.

"It was Johnny Padres," Lou said emphatically. "Pee Wee Reese was on short, Gil Hodges was on first, Junior Gilliam on second, and Jackie Robinson was on third. Roy Campanella was catching, and Carl Furillo was in right field. Duke Snyder played center field, and Sandy Amoros played left field."

"Pretty good." I applauded. "When did they move to Los Angeles?"

"Broke my heart, dem bums. The last time they played in Brooklyn was in 1958."

"How many World Series did they win?" I asked, knowing the answer.

"Only one, but there has never been a team like them, before or after," he said sadly.

I wasn't gonna argue.

Fiore's brother and sister were there too, their kids playing with Fiore's. They all lived close by and went to House on the Rock. They were humble people, not ashamed about praying openly and giving thanks for the food and their family. I felt a little jealous. Well, not jealous exactly, just a yearning for a family like that.

Donna's mother and sister were there, looking kind of uncomfortable but still nice. They weren't saved, Donna told me later, and she and Joe continued to pray for them.

Joe finally caught me alone by the downstairs bathroom.

"So what did you think of the church?" he asked.

"It's different than anything I've ever seen," I said honestly. "But I liked it."

"That's great." He nodded but didn't say anything more.

Fiore was busy with his family, so I spent most of the day

with Michele and Stevie. Michele called him Steven, but by the end of the day he asked her to call him Stevie like I did.

I played with Stevie and talked to Michele. I threw Stevie around the pool. Once I tossed him so high I scared myself.

"Hey, buddy, you were flying!" I said, my heart pounding as I picked him up out of the water.

Michele's face was frozen in horror.

"Wasn't that fun?" I asked him excitedly. "Sorry!" I called to her.

Stevie nodded nervously. "Yeah, but don't throw me that high anymore."

"Okay," I laughed.

Next we played volleyball with Fiore and the other kids at the party, then I watched as they tossed water balloons and drew on the sidewalk with chalk.

I found out by the end of the day that Michele was a very honest and up-front person. Since I'm a cop, people lie to me all the time. For no reason, they just lie. I probably shouldn't have asked her about Stevie's father, but we'd been talking for three hours and I wanted to know.

"I wasn't saved when I got pregnant." She looked at me to see my reaction. I nodded for her to continue. With my track record, I wasn't saying a word.

"He was a lawyer," she continued.

"That should've been your first clue," I threw in.

She laughed. "Anyway, we'd been dating, and I didn't know he was seeing someone else. When I told him I was pregnant, he said he wanted nothing to do with it. I didn't hear from him again until after Steven was born. He signed something terminating any rights to Steven and was married not long after that."

"Sounds like a great guy," I said dryly. "So how do you know Donna?" I asked, changing the subject. We had filled our plates with food again and had gone back to sit at a table. That was another thing I liked about her—she wasn't afraid to eat in front of me. I always hate taking someone out to dinner so they could pick on a salad. But Michele ate like an ironworker. She matched me burger for burger (two), bypassed the hot dogs, and went straight to the sausage and peppers. In between, she had macaroni and potato salad, and I'd bet money she was having cake.

"Good appetite," I commented.

She turned, chewing and swallowing like a lady, and said, "I hadn't eaten yet today."

"You probably won't have to eat tomorrow."

She narrowed her eyes. "What were you saying?"

I smiled. "Where'd you meet Donna?"

"I met her at church. Josh and Steven are in children's church together. How long have you known Joe?" she asked.

"He's been at the precinct a while, but we just started working together about a month ago." Was that all it was?

"He's great. So is Donna."

I agreed.

"So what about you? I know this was your first time at our church, but is there a place you go to in Staten Island?"

"I haven't been to church since I was twelve."

"What kept you away all this time?" she asked softly.

I told her a lot of it, probably because she was being so straightforward with me. She didn't even blink when I told her about the drinking. We talked a little about the job and some of the problems that go with it.

"Are you having a difficult time with the drinking?" she asked.

I shook my head. "No, it's funny—it's not as hard as I thought it would be."

She nodded. "Have you ever been married?"

"No."

Stevie ran over to me then and jumped up into my arms. I let out a growl and tickled him as he laughed hysterically. She got a funny look on her face watching us and then looked away when she realized I was staring at her.

"I'd like to take you out to dinner," I said as Stevie ran off.

Her face was serious as she said, "I'd like that."

"How about tomorrow?"

"Tomorrow?"

"That way you won't have time to change your mind."

"Don't you work at night?" She looked nervous.

"Not tomorrow night."

She thought a minute then said, "Okay, tomorrow."

"Think of a place to go, and tell me how to get to your house. Maybe you should give me your number too, in case I get lost on the Long Island Expressway."

I got home by 10:30 that night, having smoked four cigarettes on the ride home to make up for what I'd missed all day. Denise was sitting on the couch in her pajamas, watching TV, when I came in. She smiled at me. Either she was up to something or our fight was over.

"Hey," I said as I hung my suit in the front closet. "No turtle races tonight?"

"No, I want to get to work on time tomorrow. Where have you been?" She yawned and stretched.

"Long Island. Fiore's baby was . . ." I couldn't think of the word.

"Baptized?"

"Yeah, something like that. I went to the church and the party afterward."

She nodded.

"I met someone today," I said.

She sat up. "A woman?"

"Yeah, a nice woman. Different than what you're used to seeing me with."

"How so?"

"Real nails, not anorexic. She has a little boy, Stevie."

"How old is he?" Denise loved kids.

"Four, and he's really cute. He sat on my lap at church. I'm going out with his mom tomorrow."

"Still not drinking?" she asked.

I shook my head. "No more for me. I'm going to start going to church too, out by Fiore." I looked at her to see her reaction.

She looked sad. "Just don't change so much that you don't like me anymore."

"Denise, I could never not like you. I love you, you're my sister. You know, drinking and hating Marie aren't the only things we have in common, although I'm gonna have to stop hating Marie."

"Why?" She looked appalled.

"Because I'm sure it's in the rule book somewhere." I sighed, not looking forward to that one. "Don't worry about that now. But you and me, we'll always be close."

"I love you too," she said, crossing the room to hug me. "But I'm scared. Everything is changing."

I drove back out to Long Island the following night. Michele lived farther out than Fiore in a small, older ranch, white with blue trim. It had a tiny porch with white lattice on the bottom around the front. Flowers lined a front walkway, and a vine with purple flowers climbed the lattice up to the front porch.

Stevie answered my knock and told me his mom would be right there. I was dressed casually, beige Dockers, black silk T-shirt, and black shoes. Michele came in wearing a sleeveless black cotton dress and black heeled sandals. Her hair was down around her shoulders. She looked beautiful.

We dropped Stevie off at a friend's house and headed to a restaurant called the Happy Crab. We were able to sit outside and eat next to the water. From where we sat I could see Fire Island in the distance. I had the lobster special, which was spelled *labster* on the menu. Michele got the seafood fradiavlo. I was a little clumsy breaking open one of the lobster claws and shot it across the table onto the floor. If Michele hadn't been there I would have wiped it off and ate it. Instead I picked it up and put it on the table next to my plate.

We were both a little nervous at first, and the conversation would slow until we started talking about God. I told Michele about what Fiore was showing me in the Bible, and she told me about a book she was reading about walking in love.

"It's such a challenge for me," she said. "It has to be worse for you and Joe with what you do every day."

"For the most part, Joe does it," I said. I told her about the only time I saw him lose his temper, when I dragged the skell out of traffic. "He was mad that the guy got scraped up," I explained.

"It must be devastating to be homeless," she said with feeling.

"Yeah, but a lot of them bring it on themselves," I said.

"I guess you can't feel sorry for everyone you come across."

"Nope," I said. "Some people you can't help but feel sorry for. Fiore amazes me the way he prays for everyone. I've started to do that recently, but I'm not as humble as Joe. I still have a temper that I'm trying to keep under control."

"How do you handle being a cop?" She searched my eyes. "Is that what you always wanted to be?"

I shrugged. "My father was a cop," I said, as if that explained it. "It runs in families sometimes. I started off thinking the job was one way, you know, us against the bad guys and we're cleaning up the streets. Then once you're there a while you realize it's like shoveling sh—uh, crap against the tide with a pitchfork."

She smiled.

"Then when you get used to the idea about the pitchfork and the tide, you learn that your enemies aren't always the bad guys on the street. They're the press and the higher-ups, race bailers and the politicians. Sometimes they can do a lot more than the bad guys can."

"And now?" she asked.

"Now I don't know how I feel about the job," I said honestly.

We went to other topics from there: her job, sushi (she liked it), baseball (she was a Mets fan), and the upcoming presidential election. She was a good conversationalist; she traveled a lot before she had Stevie, and she told me about a trip she took to Europe the year she graduated from college. She said that Italy was her favorite place and that the art in Florence was the most beautiful in the world.

We finished our dinner and drove west on Montauk Highway to get ice cream. We found an old-fashioned ice cream parlor and walked around, eating our cones and holding hands. It wasn't like any other date I've ever been on, no game-playing or attitude, just a good time.

Things got a little sticky when I was driving her home.

"Tony, I just want to let you know ahead of time—I mean, I don't know what you're expecting—" She stopped and put her hair behind her ears, which I realized was a nervous gesture of hers.

"Say what's on your mind," I said.

"It's just that I have a commitment to God that I'm going to honor—" She broke off again.

"Are we talking about sex here?" I was confused.

She shrugged and nodded.

"Listen, I haven't had this good of a time with a woman since . . . I don't know, probably never." I meant it.

She looked doubtful.

"Anyway, you're the one who brought it up. You must have sex on your mind."

She actually blushed. "I did not bring up sex."

"Well, for my part, I figured this would be one of those holding-hands-only dates. Getting lucky with you is probably a kiss on your front porch."

"I don't believe in luck," she said haughtily.

She did kiss me good night on her porch—not one of those groping, rubbing, hair-pulling kisses that leave you gasping for air. It was a sweet kiss, full of promise and expectation. I tasted it all the way home.

For our first night back, a police corruption scandal hit the papers. Apparently, four Queens cops on the four-to-twelve were getting free meals from a restaurant on Queens Boulevard and ran a plate for the owner. I'm not saying that what they did was right, but it didn't have to hit the front page. The scandal in itself wasn't so bad, but it came at a bad time. The NYPD had been so publicized for scandals in recent years that it still hadn't recovered. The boss was concerned both for morale and public reaction as he sent us out that night.

"Make sure you do everything by the book," he said. "I'm concerned about public backlash, and I don't want anyone getting hurt out there. Try to be patient. I know you're not doing anything wrong. I want you to be safe and be able to sign out in the morning. Don't get sucked into anything."

There was none of the usual joking in the muster room, and morale was low as the platoon filed out. A cloud seemed to settle on the already hot and humid night. It's amazing how the press can crucify us. I'd like to see any other administration have as little corruption as we do. The numbers speak for themselves. We have a department of over thirty thousand officers. If one percent of the cops were guilty of corruption, it would be over three hundred officers. If the department gets thirty cops on real corruption a year, it's been a bad year. I know some of the scandals have been horrendous, but most of them are not. The press targets the department and exploits the news out of there because the city loves to read about us.

This was weighing on my mind as I walked over to Vince Puletti to sign out my radio.

"I hear you're on the wagon," he said as he belched.

"Nice," I remarked at the burp, ignoring the question.

"I'm taking Pepcid. Stomach's been bothering me." He looked a little chalky as I signed for my radio.

"Maybe you should see a doctor," I said.

He waved me away. "Ah, what do they know, anyway?"

Fiore was smiling when we got in the car.

"So?" he beamed.

I played dumb. "So what?"

"How'd it go with Michele?"

"It was nice."

"Nice? That's it?" He looked disappointed.

"It was a great time," I said honestly.

His eyebrows shot up.

"Not like that—it was just good, clean fun like all us boy scouts have."

He was squinting at me to see if I meant it. "So? Are you going to see her again?"

"You bet."

"Good for you, Tony. God has good taste in women, huh?"

"So far," I agreed.

"But she's not blonde, five foot four, and . . . what else did you want?" He counted each attribute on his fingers.

"You're a meatball," I said.

He was still staring at me.

"What?" I asked.

"Nothing. I didn't get a chance to talk to you about church, that's all," he said.

"If I tell you I said the prayer of salvation, I don't want you hugging me," I said. If any of the guys saw me and Fiore hugging in the RMP, our careers would be over.

"Did you say it?" he asked.

"Yeah, I did."

"Praise God," was all he said.

We had no air-conditioning in the car, and it was eighty degrees and muggy with no breeze. We started off the night with four alarms to answer. We had a 30 (robbery in progress) with negative results on canvass. At 2:00 we were heading toward the Sunrise Deli and got a call for another robbery in progress with multiple alarms.

When we hear multiple alarms, that tells us it is legit. Multiple alarms mean someone is running through the premises, setting off the alarms. The building was right on the corner of 37th and 6th—Steinway Jewelers. It had a glass front with metal grating that allowed a passerby to see into the display window. We pulled up in front. There was a metal door on the right that looked to be an entrance to a side stairwell. Next to the metal door was a glass door, leading to an alcove with an elevator. Looking through the window we could see the display cases broken and a pair of legs disappearing through a hole in the wall. The hole was about two feet wide, four to five feet off the floor. We couldn't get in without breaking the glass, and then we'd have the metal grate to get through.

Fiore called in and confirmed it, saying there were burglars and that they were going up to the second floor. All units in the command were on their way.

I was trying to work the glass door open when the Holmes security guard pulled up. Holmes sent a young guy this time. He looked to be about twenty years old, Hispanic, with a military haircut. He was medium build, very polite and professional.

The security guard unlocked the gate and let us into the premises. The store was hot—the air conditioner had been off for a while. Fiore and I went through the hole in the wall and came out the other side into a stairwell. Part of the wall was on the floor of the jewelry store, but most of it was in the stairwell. Dust and pieces of concrete stuck to me as I climbed through and ran up the stairs. Fiore was behind me as I reached the second floor. I had my flashlight out, trying to find my way in the dark stairwell. The second floor door was locked, and I continued up to the third floor, only to find that locked as well. By the time I reached the fourth floor I was sweating and winded.

I stepped in and heard outside noise, traffic, wind, and voices from below. The entire fourth floor was under construction. The room was open, and stacks of Sheetrock and plywood on palettes were spread throughout the room. Four big pillars, huge boxes, and lots of debris gave the burglars a lot of places to hide. We walked as quietly as possible, with our guns out and ears tuned. We walked towards the back, checking the room as we went. In the back where the alley was, we found a piece of rope hanging out of the building.

I figured they must have climbed down the rope, gone through the parking lot in back of the building, and exited on 38th Street. We could see that the gate was bent where they ran through. I was sure they had bent the gate before they started, and practiced getting through it. They were probably long gone in a car somewhere.

We had a sector canvass the area. We told them the burglars probably went out into the parking lot and cut through. The sector went around to check the alleyway on the other side of the parking lot towards 5th Avenue. They circled the blocks to see if there were any cars with people sitting in them, but came up negative.

When we got back downstairs, Lieutenant Farrell was on the scene. He was chomping on his pipe, smiling. He loved this stuff. He looked like the old war dog that he is, comfortable in his element and seeing things that most people don't. I was coughing up dust and smoking a cigarette when he came over to me.

"I haven't seen these guys for a while," he said congenially.

"Who?" He was talking over my head here.

"The hole in the wall gang," he said as if I should know. "They hit a few months ago up in the North precinct. That time they got out with a bunch of Rolexes worth about half a mil."

"Any idea who they are?" I asked.

"I have my theories. It's the same MO, smash and grab." He put the pipe tip between the space in his front teeth.

"So this is the second time they've hit?" I asked.

"This year. Last year they hit twice in the North, once in the South." His eyes were constantly moving, scanning the damage as he spoke to me. "Let's go take a look," he said. I followed him to the back of the store.

The hole in the wall gang, as they were now called, got away with between sixty and eighty thousand dollars in jewelry, mostly in watches, bracelets, chains, and other gold jewelry. The diamonds and other precious gems were locked away in the safe. We had found the elevator on the fourth floor in the hallway and took it back down to the jewelers. I jammed my nightstick into the door of the vestibule leading to the elevator. We would have to go back up and get the rope for evidence, and we didn't want to climb through the hole in the wall again.

The owner was called to assess the extent of the damage. The gang smashed and grabbed the display cases, leaving the store in ruin. They took a shot at the safe but ran out of time. There was definitely more than one guy, and the place was scoped out before they hit. These burglars were pretty quick—once they broke through that wall, the alarms were tripped, and they were in and out in a few minutes. If we didn't show up that fast, they would have sawed through the safe. A handheld circular grinder with a carbide tip was found with the rope.

They had strategically turned all the cameras so none of this was caught on tape. There was one other camera, connected to the owner's office, that they had missed. It was funny—the camera took pictures at ten-second intervals but caught none of the robbery. When we watched the tape, in one frame the display case was intact, and in the next frame the cases were smashed and empty.

"I hear you're on the wagon," Lieutenant Farrell asked when we were alone.

I guess he'd been talking to Vince Puletti.

When I didn't answer he said, "I've been there a time or two myself." He was still looking around as he said it.

"I plan on staying there," I said with feeling.

He smiled indulgently. "So did I." He started to whistle as he walked away.

I didn't care what he said. I was staying on the wagon.

We took the report while the evidence collection unit dusted for prints and gathered their evidence. We used the bathroom to wash up, brushing as much dust off as we could. It was now almost 3:30 and we were hot and tired. We had a 5:00 meal, and I wanted to sleep.

Fiore and I parked on the east side of 8th Avenue. We had an hour and a half to kill, so we went to Fiore's place on 43rd Street for coffee. Rooney pulled up next to us in a scooter.

"Hey, guys." He smirked. "What are you doing up here?"

"What are you doing on a scooter?" I countered.

"Ah, I was an hour and a half late, and the boss put Romano with Sean." He looked mad.

"I saw Romano driving with Connelly. I figured you banged the day," I said.

"The boss gave Romano my seat and gave me his foot post," he explained.

"So what's with the scooter?" Fiore asked.

"I saw the scooter behind the precinct and figured I'd get myself a ride."

"Are you even scooter qualified?" I asked.

He laughed. "I'm not qualified, but I ain't walking."

As we talked, a white male ran around the corner from 42nd Street northbound on 8th Avenue with O'Brien and McGovern in hot pursuit. They had the turret lights going and were right on the guy's heels.

"What's up with this?" I said.

Right then the white male began weaving in and out of parked cars on the east side of 8th Avenue, avoiding apprehension by McGovern and O'Brien. They stopped the car in the street but didn't get out.

"I'll be right back," Rooney said and took off with the scooter.

He went in front of our car and did a U-turn up onto the sidewalk. As he drove toward the fleeing man, the guy started doing a "catch me" shuffle, darting between the cars and running across the street onto the sidewalk where Midtown's largest and most famous triple-X emporium is.

As the perp sped across the street Rooney drove in between two parked cars, scraping the front end of the scooter as it came off the curb. He scraped the back end of the scooter as the back tires came off the curb. Ouch, that was gonna leave a mark. As he crossed 8th Avenue he turned on his lights and sirens and went up on the curb. He bounced the front tire up a couple feet and dragged the back end of the scooter on the street. The back tires hit the curb, scraping the front end onto the sidewalk.

The man was now walking under the overhang of the peep show joint, looking back at Rooney. He looked confused until he heard Rooney hit the gas. He bolted a couple of car lengths and went in between two more parked cars, stopping to see what Rooney was doing.

Rooney's Irish temper made him misjudge the height of the overhang of the triple-X marquee. He gunned it full force, lights and siren going, and smashed the turret light into the marquee, sending the front end of the scooter up in the air. As the front end of the scooter came crashing down to the sidewalk, the turret lights were still flashing, hanging down by their wires off the back of the scooter. The siren sounded like a 45 record playing at 33 speed until it coughed and died.

The only sound aside from the *waaaa* of the dying sirens was the hysterical laughter coming from me and McGovern and O'Brien. Rooney took off after the perp on foot but then changed his mind and ran back to the scooter. McGovern and I followed with the cars to where the scooter was under the marquee.

"What were you chasing him for?" Rooney yelled in between gasps for breath.

"We were just playing with him," O'Brien said, still laughing.

"You were what?" Rooney yelled.

"Hey, we didn't tell you to chase him," McGovern called out. "Where'd you learn how to drive?"

"He didn't," I yelled out. "He never got qualified."

This brought on a new wave of laughter, and even Fiore couldn't hold it in. He had panicked for a minute when he thought Rooney was hurt, but then he busted out laughing with the rest of us.

We followed Rooney back to the precinct and watched him park the scooter where he'd found it and place the turret lights back on top. I wish I could have been there to see the next guy take it out.

We dropped Rooney back off at 42nd and 8th and drove to the Sunrise Deli. Our coffee had gotten cold, and we needed another jolt to stay awake. We were still laughing about Rooney, but for once I wasn't scheming up ways to throw this in his face. I'd noticed that about Fiore—he never brought up anyone's past screwups.

We took our coffee back to 37th Street and sat drinking it in silence. I stepped out of the car to smoke a cigarette, feeling the change in the air. The temperature had dropped pretty suddenly; a cold front was moving in, and we were expecting rain for the next few days. The air now felt cool and thick compared to the heat and humidity of earlier. Fiore closed his window while I smoked, and I saw him give a cynical laugh while he flipped through the paper. I knocked on the window.

"Whatcha reading?" I asked.

"I don't believe this," he said, shaking his head.

"What?" I peered in to see what he was reading.

"Listen to this." He opened the window. "U.S. Is Found Blameless for Waco Deaths." He started quoting the article, stating that a special investigation council cleared Attorney General Janet Reno and the government of any wrongdoing in the deaths of David Koresh and the Branch Davidians when they burned their compound to the ground with everyone in it.

He was incredulous. "It took them seven years to figure this out?"

"Did they say whose fault it was?" I asked. You never knew what the government was gonna come up with.

"Yeah, it took a special council and probably a billion tax dollars to figure out it was the cult leader's fault. Is it me, Tony, or could they have just gone to the videotape?"

Now this is the kind of thing that really aggravates cops. The Waco thing happened right after terrorists drove a truckload of explosives into the parking garage of the World Trade Center in an attempt to blow up the building. We were still dazed by the trade center bombing when this psycho decides he's Christ and it's the end of the world.

"And listen to this," Fiore continued. "It says that they hope the report begins the process of restoring the faith of the people in their government."

"If all it took was seven years to figure that out, then hey, my faith is restored!"

"Unbelievable," Fiore said.

He put the paper on the seat, and I picked it up to read the article. Getting annoyed with it, I browsed through the rest of the paper. I moved on to the sports pages. The Yanks beat the Orioles four to three. I noticed Fiore had pulled out his Bible and was reading one of the Psalms. I alternated between scanning the paper and stepping outside to smoke. The night wound down without any more jobs.

14

*T*wo days after we had dinner I called Michele to ask her out again on Saturday. I wrestled with how soon I should be calling. If I called her the day after we had dinner, it would look like I was desperate; on the other hand, if I waited too long it would seem like I wasn't interested. I called her at 9:30 on Wednesday morning when I got back from the boardwalk. I guzzled a bottle of water and smoked a cigarette to cool down from my jog and dialed as I took the phone out on the deck.

The cooler weather was a nice change, but August was on the way and it would heat up again. It was one of those clear, fresh days that cook up as the day wears on.

I wanted to take Michele somewhere private so we could get to know each other better. It surprised me how much I'd thought about her over the past two days. I really wanted to see her again. I was going over in my mind what to say to her when Stevie picked up the phone.

"Hello?" he said in a cute voice.

"Hey, Steve, it's Tony," I said. I didn't expect him to answer.

"Tony! Where are you? Are you coming over?" He sounded excited.

"Not today, buddy. Is your mom there?"

"Yeah, but when are you coming over? We could play again like at Josh's house."

I could hear Michele in the background saying, "Who is it, Steven?"

His voice faded as he moved the phone away. "It's Tony, but I want to talk to him first."

He came back on the line, telling me about Clifford the dog and his bike with training wheels and the blue helmet that he wears with it. He wanted me to take him to the aquarium and the water park and play ball and wrestle like we did at Fiore's house.

All of a sudden the phone call didn't seem like such a good idea. This woman had a kid, and kids like fathers, and this kid didn't have one. As a rule I stayed away from the ready-made family situations because they were messy. I liked Stevie. If things didn't work out with his mother and me, he'd get hurt, and I didn't want to hurt him. Why hadn't I thought of that sooner? I felt claustrophobic as Michele got on the line.

"Hi, Tony," she said warmly.

"Hey, Michele," I said quietly.

She paused. "Is everything okay? You sound funny."

I hate perceptive women. "Just tired. I worked last night."

"Did anything happen?"

"What do you mean?" I'm sure I sounded annoyed. Was she asking if I drank?

"At work. Did something bad happen there?" The concern in her voice sounded sincere, but I'm distrustful of females as a rule.

"Nothing out of the ordinary," I said.

"Define ordinary." She laughed.

I really did like her, which clouded my judgment. The next thing I knew we had plans for dinner on Saturday.

"If the weather is good we could ride out to see the light-house in Montauk. There's a great seafood place out there." She spoke quietly to Stevie in the background, saying, "I'll be off in a minute and then I'll get it for you."

"Wherever you want to go is fine with me. What time should I come out?" I asked.

"Are you working Friday night?"

"Yeah, Friday night into Saturday morning."

"It's up to you, Tony. Get some sleep and call me later in the day when you get up." She sounded so pleasant and agreeable, but it's been my experience, women are always that way at the beginning. Six months down the road they're complaining they don't have a life because of my friggin' job.

I said good-bye and sat on the deck, feeling like I got sucked into going out with her on Saturday. It was stupid of me to feel like that, since I'm the one who called her, but I hadn't been thinking about the kid when I was dialing. It seemed like a lot all at once. A couple of weeks ago I answered to no one. Now I was answering to God, and I knew instinctively he wouldn't want me to get involved with Stevie if I wasn't planning on staying. But how could I find out if there was anything between Michele and me without involving him?

I went back inside and rummaged through the fridge for something to eat. I ate some cold ziti with broccoli in garlic and oil, washed it down with a Coke, and went upstairs to bed. I lay awake for a while thinking about Michele and Stevie. The last time I looked at the clock it was 11:10.

I forgot to set my alarm but woke up at 7:30. I could hear a radio on downstairs and the whir of the blender. The irritation I felt before I went to sleep stayed with me as I crossed to the bathroom. There were still no Q-tips, and I had to wash with a piece of soap the size of my fingernail. The shampoo bottle was empty, so I added water to get some suds. I had to go shopping. We were out of just about everything, and of course Vinny wouldn't do a thing. Now that he was getting married, he let Christie do everything for him. He ate his meals over there, and half the time he didn't come home to sleep.

I dressed for work in old Gap jeans and a Yankees T-shirt and went downstairs to get something to eat.

Denise was decked out in a blue FDNY T-shirt and faded jeans and was tossing a salad. I saw bags of groceries on the table: the soap, Q-tips, shampoo, and conditioner I could have used about twenty minutes ago. There was a case of soda next to the fridge and big packs of paper towels and toilet paper.

Sal came in from the deck wearing sweatpants and a Haz-Mat T-shirt, and I saw smoke coming out of the barbecue. He came over to shake my hand, a goofy smile plastered on his face.

"I'm grilling some steak. You hungry?"

I shook back. "Sure," I said.

"You and Vinny owe me forty bucks each. I went to the Price Club and stocked up," Denise said as she fussed around the kitchen. I pulled out two twenties and handed them to her.

"You could have put the stuff in the bathroom. I had nothing to take a shower with," I said grumpily.

She raised her eyebrows. "You could have shopped yourself," she shot back pleasantly.

"Fire department having a sale on T-shirts?" I asked.

"They're Sal's. He is a *fireman*," she said as if I was a moron.

I nodded toward the blender. "What are you making?"

She looked away. "Strawberry daiquiris."

My mouth watered, and I fleetingly resented my decision not to drink. I put ice in a glass and poured a Coke instead, leaning against the sink as I drank it. Sal checked the oven, where he was roasting several heads of garlic.

I set the table for three, knowing Vinny wouldn't be home. Sal had grilled portabella mushrooms along with the steaks, and we put them on top of the roasted garlic we spread on the meat. It was delicious. They had a store-bought tortellini salad with fresh mozzarella, artichoke hearts, red peppers, and Greek olives. The green salad had sweet balsamic vinegar and oil dressing, which I dunked with seeded Italian bread.

Denise and Sal talked about a piece of furniture they were restoring. He was teaching her the ropes on how to do that, and she seemed genuinely interested in it. They talked about furniture stripping, sanders, and using lacquer with a sprayer. I didn't know much about it, but I've seen some of Sal's work, and it's beautiful.

Apparently these two were closer than I'd thought, and I noticed their eyes lock and grow mushy throughout the dinner. Good for them. If there were any two people who deserved to be happy, it was these two. It's funny, though. I never pictured Denise with someone like Sal. He was too nice, too goofy to have a knockout like her. He was a plain-looking, everyday Joe. Denise looked like she should be on a magazine cover. She was used to men falling all over themselves with her. Since Denise is my sister, her looks never impressed me, but a lot of my friends had drooled over her in the past. I got the distinct impression that her looks weren't the only thing Sal saw when he looked at her. He's a good guy. I hope she doesn't hurt him.

I left at 10:00. I had to stop for gas and cigarettes and was on the road by 10:15. There wasn't enough traffic anywhere to slow anything down, and I got to the precinct by 10:55. Fiore had my coffee waiting for me in the muster room, and we shook hands as I came in.

Rice and Beans had an accident on the four-to-twelve. Well, Beans was driving, so he'd had the accident. A cabby blew a red light on 8th Avenue and 36th Street, broadsiding the RMP.

Technically it was the cabby's fault, but the department makes us walk a foot post for thirty days for a car accident. Both Rice and Beans were hurt, not seriously, but they were taken to the hospital by ambulance.

The sarge cautioned us on safe driving before we filed out, which annoyed me. It wasn't Beans's fault that the cabby blew the light, and everyone knew it. I was in a bad mood. It still hadn't left me from when I'd talked to Michele that morning. Fiore's upbeat attitude was grating on my last nerve. He was saying something about his little girl.

"She was a preemie, Tony, but she's progressing so fast. She's doing things for her age that preemies usually can't."

I nodded as if I had a clue about what he was saying. "Hey, that's great," I said as I wondered what a preemie was.

"What are you doing this weekend? If you're going out to see Michele and Stevie, maybe we could barbecue or something."

"I'm taking Michele to dinner on Saturday, but we're not taking the kid," I answered shortly.

I saw Fiore's eyes flash when I called Stevie "the kid," but he didn't say anything. I was suddenly in the mood to argue with Fiore about it.

"So how does it work with these church ladies?" I asked.

I could tell he didn't like my tone. He paused and said, "What do you mean?"

"You know, is Michele allowed to go out alone with me, or do you or her son have to chaperone?"

"What you and Michele do is up to the both of you. I'm sure Michele knows her limits. I can't speak for her." He didn't look mad, just maybe a little disappointed.

We stopped for coffee. Since Rice and Beans had crashed the car and didn't leave me the paper, I bought the *News* and the *Post* to keep in the car. On our way back we were driving southbound on Broadway when we watched a cabbie go through a steady red light and hit a white Chevy Celebrity. We pulled over and walked to the scene. Both drivers were alone in the cars and looked uninjured. I asked both of them if they wanted an ambulance, and both declined. The driver of the cab was your typical Scud missile operator and instantly started yelling at the driver of the Celebrity. The driver of the Celebrity was a middle-aged man wearing a green work shirt and pants. He looked dazed enough that I thought he should get checked out, but he wouldn't budge. The cabbie kept saying, "I did nothing wrong, you do what you want." I issued him a summons for disobeying a steady red light and issued the driver of the Celebrity a summons for not having his license.

At around 2:30 I was driving eastbound on 40th Street, patrolling our sector. I had been quiet most of the night, reading the paper in between jobs and stepping out of the car to smoke.

"You okay, Tony?" Fiore asked.

I nodded.

"Did I do something to offend you?" He leaned over so he could see my face as I looked straight ahead.

"No, Joe. I'm not mad at you," I said tiredly. That wasn't entirely true. I was pissed at him. I wanted to blame him because I couldn't have a drink. Tonight I wanted that strawberry daiquiri. I wanted to feel normal, not like an alcoholic. Not only that, but I was feeling the reality of having made a commitment to God. I would have to honor it. No booze, no sex, and no more Tony. I didn't feel like myself anymore, and I was afraid I couldn't measure up to who I was supposed to be. How was I supposed to get into something with Michele when my mouth still watered at the thought of a drink? I didn't want her little boy looking up to me when I was nothing but a drunk who wasn't any good at loving people. His real father had let him down enough.

It was Fiore's fault that everything had changed. If he had left me alone, I wouldn't be feeling like this. I ignored the part of me that said if he'd left me alone I'd be dead.

At 3:00 we were patrolling our sector. As I approached the corner of 39th Street and 7th Avenue where the needle and button statue sits, there was a male white talking on a cell phone and flagging us down. He looked about forty-five years old. He was conservatively dressed in a pale yellow golf shirt and tan pants. He had gold wire-framed glasses and a clean shave, and his face was full of blood. He said something into the phone and hung up as we pulled over.

He told us he'd just gotten robbed. His nose and mouth were swollen and bleeding, and he had a nasty gash on his bottom lip. He kept dabbing at it with his hand as he talked. He told us that he'd been talking to a guy on the corner of 39th and 7th and out of nowhere the guy punched him in the face and took his wallet. He said the guy just ran down 40th Street.

"Get in the car. Let's see if he's still around," I said.

I saw a white male running westbound on the north side of 40th Street about three-quarters of the way down the block. Given the way he was running, I figured he was the guy. He looked behind him as he ran and slowed down to a walk when he saw us approach him.

The guy was wearing black shorts and a white shirt with a beer logo on it. His hair was cropped short, shaved at the sides and greased down flat on his head in the front. He had a small hoop earring through his left eyebrow and a row of stud earrings in both ears. He looked young, maybe nineteen or twenty. He stopped walking and watched us as Fiore got out of the car.

"Where are you heading, buddy?" Fiore asked him.

"Is this the guy?" I said to the bleeding man in the backseat. "Is he the one who hit you?"

He peered out the back window at him.

"Take your time, get a good look at him," I said.

"I—I'm not sure," he stammered. I nodded to Fiore through the back of the car.

"I was just running to catch the train," the guy said.

"Would you mind emptying your pockets and placing your things on the car?" Fiore asked.

He shrugged. "Sure, no problem. What happened?" he asked, trying to look innocent.

"Nothing to worry about. There was a robbery not far from here, and we're just checking the area." Fiore smiled in a fatherly way. "This will only take a minute and you can go catch that train."

The kid was nervous, but I guess being stopped by the cops would make anyone nervous. Personally, I thought he was our guy.

"Take another look. Are you sure this isn't the guy who hit you?" I turned toward the back again. "He's running away from the scene not five minutes later."

"No. I don't know, I'm sorry." He looked away.

"If you were talking to the guy, you must have gotten a look at him," I said impatiently.

"I really don't know." He looked down again, swiping at the blood on his face.

"He's got nothin' on him, Tony," Fiore said from the back of the car.

Unless the victim confirmed he was the perp, we couldn't search him. Frustrated, I called out to Joe, "Then let him go." Joe gave him his stuff back and let him catch his train.

Fiore got back in the car, and I drove up 40th Street. On

the northwest corner of 40th and 7th was a fashion school with a line of shrubbery on the side. A man jumped out from between the bushes and froze as we approached.

"What are the chances of this?" Fiore mumbled and we both burst out laughing. I pulled the car up next to the guy and asked him what he was doing.

"I was looking for something," he said.

He was big, maybe six foot three, and wearing a blue-and-white-checked button-down shirt over white shorts. His feet were huge, at least a twelve or thirteen in big white sneakers with glow-in-the-dark piping. At closer inspection I got the impression of him being slow, maybe mildly retarded.

"Stay there," I ordered. I turned to the guy in the back again. "Is *this* the guy?"

"No," he said matter-of-factly. "It's not him."

I got out of the car and opened the back door and leaned in. "Listen, we just grabbed two guys running from the scene, and you're telling me neither of them fits the description of the guy who hit you?" I was getting angry now.

"No." He shook his head. "It's not him."

"Have him empty his pockets. I'm going to search the bushes," I called to Fiore.

At the entrance to the school there was a courtyard that sat beyond the row of shrubs. Cement benches were placed throughout, with big cement planters holding flowers and greenery. Fiore stood outside the car as I walked up into the courtyard where the man jumped out. I used my flashlight to look under the benches, in the planters, and under the shrubs, but didn't find a wallet. Since there was nothing to connect him to the robbery, we had to let him go.

I was sure that the first guy was the one who hit him—this guy was probably using the bushes as a bathroom. But that was beside the point. Our witness wasn't cooperating. If he wasn't going to point the perp out, why waste our time? I walked back to the RMP and radioed Central for an ambulance to meet us at 40th and 7th. While we waited for the ambulance, I tried to talk to the victim again.

"What happened? What were you talking to this guy about?" I asked.

"I wasn't talking to him, he just walked up and punched me in the face," he said, not looking at us.

"Wait a minute," Fiore cut in. "You told us you were talking to the guy."

"First you can't identify anyone, and now you're changing the story." My voice was rising. I went up to his face. "Why don't you just tell me the truth?"

He hesitated then took a deep breath. "I was at my hotel, and I was hungry, so I took a walk to get something to eat."

"What hotel are you staying at?" Fiore asked.

"The Hyatt on 42nd and Lexington." His head was still down as he spoke.

"So why are you all the way down here on 39th and 7th?" I demanded.

He shrugged.

"Why would you come all the way down here for something to eat when you could get something at the hotel? Even if you didn't want to eat at the hotel, there are plenty of places by Grand Central Station. But now you're down here where it's totally isolated from everything and there aren't even any restaurants open." I was in his face, but he still wouldn't look at me.

"I felt like getting some air," he said to his feet.

I hate being lied to. We spend most of our time sifting through the lies, trying to find out what really happened. I knew what the deal was here, I looked over at Fiore. He knew too. I know he doesn't like being lied to either, but he was letting me handle this one.

Our guy then decided he didn't want to pursue this any further. "I'm okay. I need to get back to my hotel and get some sleep." He moved to step out of the car when Fiore motioned him to sit down.

"No way, buddy. We have to do a report. How much money did you have on you?" Fiore asked.

"About six hundred dollars." He appeared to be thinking. "But I don't want to file any report."

Now I was mad. "You wave us down because someone smashes you in the face and takes six hundred dollars of your money. First you say you were talking to them, then you weren't talking to them. Do you really expect me—"

I cut off when I saw that he'd gotten blood all over the back-seat and door. He opened the door so he could spit blood and mucous out onto the street.

"Hey! Clean that up! That's disgusting!" I pulled open my door and grabbed a bunch of napkins from the storage pocket and threw them to him.

"I'm sorry," he said as he cleaned it up. He looked pitiful. He knew I knew what had happened, and he was ashamed. I ignored him as he groveled, and EMS came on the scene. They worked on his nose and mouth to stop the bleeding. He wouldn't need stitches. His yellow shirt was very blood-stained, and his face, now free of blood, was red and swol-len. His nose looked broken but he declined a trip to the hospital.

Fiore was taking the report as EMS worked on him, which made me more irritated.

"Don't even bother, Joe. If he doesn't want a report, then leave it," I spat out.

"We better do a report," Fiore said. "Even if this guy seems re-luctant, if something happens at least we covered ourselves."

"Do what you want," I said. He knew I disagreed.

As Fiore took the report, we found out the guy had lost his driver's license, three credit cards, and an ATM card, along with the six hundred dollars. He said he'd also lost his credentials.

"What credentials?" I asked suspiciously.

"I'm a state legislator from Connecticut," he said quietly.

"State assembly or the senate?" I saw the surprised look on his face when I asked. I'm sure he figured I couldn't spell *legislator*, let alone know what it meant. He told me which one, and I nodded, unimpressed.

"What are you doing in the city?"

I could see him debate lying to me. "I'm speaking at a function tomorrow, honoring World War II veterans." He told me where it was.

I had gotten some alcohol pads from EMS and gave them to him to wipe off the door and seat. He kept apologizing throughout the whole thing, and now I started to feel sorry for him. I realized why he didn't want to file a report.

"Listen," I said as I leaned in closer, "I'm sorry I got so mad at you, but I know you weren't down here at 3:00 in the morning to get something to eat." He stared back at me. "I think you were looking for some companionship that maybe you didn't want anyone to know about. It sounds to me like you found some companionship that wound up belting you in the mouth and taking your money instead of going through with what you were looking to do. I wouldn't have been so angry if you'd just told me the truth."

He put his head down, holding his face in his hands. When I looked up, Fiore was smiling at me.

"What?" I barked.

"Nothing," he said, still smiling.

Fiore turned his attention to our politician and while talking to him in a soothing voice explained the process of the complaint report. He gave the man his name and shield number and the complaint room phone number, along with the name and address of the precinct.

The politician thanked us both for our help and continued to apologize for not pointing out the perp. He thanked us for getting him medical attention and stood to leave.

"Can we give you a ride back to your hotel?" I asked.

"No, thank you. I appreciate it, but I'll just get a cab."

"How are you gonna get a cab with no money?" I asked. "Get in, we'll drive you." We dropped him off at the Hyatt.

Fiore was still smiling as we pulled away from the hotel.

"Okay, Joe, what's so amusing?"

"You're okay, Tony." He was still smirking. "Why don't you tell me what's on your mind."

"What are you, my shrink?"

"No, I'm your friend, and I know something's on your mind." He wasn't smiling anymore, just amused. "You called Stevie 'the kid' before and made a remark about dating Michele."

I sighed. I might as well fess up—apparently Fiore could read me like a book. "I don't know, Joe. I don't want to hurt the kid. What if it doesn't work out with her? What if I start drinking again?"

"Did you start drinking again?" He looked concerned.

"No, but I wanted to. My sister and my neighbor had dinner at the house with me and made strawberry daiquiris. I wanted to guzzle some from right out of the blender." I played with the steering wheel.

"You're doing better than you think, Tony. You just need to remember to pray it through. Christ in you is bigger than having a drink. The Bible says that we are more than conquerors through him who loved us. As far as Michele and Stevie are concerned, you need to be honest with her. She doesn't want Stevie to be hurt either, and she's not going to use him to rope you in."

"Him who loved us is Jesus, right?" I asked.

"Yeah." He smiled.

"Where does it say that?"

"Romans 8, I think it's 37." He whipped out his pocket Bible and flipped through the pages. "Yup. Verse 37."

I nodded, feeling better. I made a mental note to read Romans 8 when I got home and to call Michele and talk to her.

It was now almost 4:00 when Central called for us to return to the command and we went inside. At this time of night the muster room was usually empty. The lieutenant was talking on the phone. He acknowledged us by peering over the glasses perched on his nose and holding up his index finger in a "hang on a second" gesture. He nodded while he listened, added an occasional uh-huh, and ended the conversation with, "He'll be up there in five to ten minutes."

Lieutenant Coughlan was in his early fifties. He had salt-and-pepper hair that looked dark because he greased it back. He had ice blue eyes and the dry sense of humor that seems to favor the Irish.

"Did you 10-2 us, Lou?" Fiore asked.

"Yeah. I just got off the phone with Midtown Court. They've been waiting for a prisoner that's been locked up since the day tour. Can you do me a favor and run this guy up there? They're expecting him, so it'll just take you five minutes." He looked at me funny and then turned back to Fiore.

"Sure, no problem, Lou," Fiore said.

He gave us the arrest papers. I scanned them to see what the arrest was for. If it were any kind of violent crime, we'd be especially cautious. It turned out to be misdemeanor drugs, crack specifically. We put our guns in the locker behind the desk. I spotted Vinny Begaducci, the assistant station house officer.

"Hey, Vinny Bag-of-donuts," I called.

"Hey, Tony, Joe, what's going on?" Vinny was a nice guy. He

had a little less time on than me and was a real gun buff. He collected them—rifles, shotguns, antiques, semiautomatics. He loved to hunt, so every year he saved all his vacation for November and spent his time off hunting. When he got married two years ago, he scheduled his honeymoon to be back in time for opening day. He was even packing at his wedding reception. His wife complained that his shoulder holster showed up in some of the pictures. He was a full-blooded Italian but had frizzy blond hair and blue eyes. He leaned toward me and signaled me to come closer. Confused, I leaned in.

"Hey, Tony, is everything okay?" he said in hushed tones.

I backed up. "Yeah, why?"

"I heard you went to the farm." He looked troubled. The farm is the rehab where alcoholic cops go. They called it the farm because it's upstate.

"Obviously, I'm not at the farm." I shook my head as Fiore and I walked away.

Fiore chuckled. "You gotta laugh, Tony."

"It's amazing how the rumors spread," I answered.

We headed to the gated door that buzzes people into the cell area. Dave Fishman, or "Fish" as he was called, did the arrest processing. He printed the perps, kept a log on them, and then checked every thirty minutes to make sure they didn't kill themselves or beat the snot out of each other. He's five foot ten, 250 pounds with no muscle tone. He has a doughy look to him, round eyeglasses, brown eyes, and a crew cut. His lips are always wet, and he has a big schnoz and a ready smile. He whined when he talked but he was still a good guy.

"Hey, Fish," Fiore and I greeted him.

"Tony, Joe. You doing the transport?"

"That'd be us," Fiore said.

"Great!" Fish was thrilled. I guessed this was his only prisoner and now he could take an extended meal.

Fish hit the buzzer on the wall and held the door for us to come in behind him. We grabbed the manila envelope with the prisoner's papers and personal effects from the box next to Fish's desk. As we looked into the cell we found the prisoner asleep on one of the benches inside the cell. We smelled his feet before we saw him; his torn, dirty sneakers were on the floor at odd angles.

Fiore went in to wake the prisoner, who was curled up in a fetal position. He shook him on the shoulder. "Time to go, buddy."

Nothing, he was out cold.

On the second shake the guy turned his head and looked at us. He was disoriented, coming down off the crack, so it took him a couple of seconds to realize where he was.

"Dude, put your shoes on," I said as I kicked the shoes toward him.

"I told him to keep his shoes on. He must have taken them off when I left the room," Fish called over.

"What time is it?" the prisoner mumbled.

"Four-fifteen," Fiore said.

"In the morning?" He looked surprised.

I checked through the envelope as Fiore cuffed him. I matched the face to the mug shot just to be sure. It wouldn't be the first time someone mixed up the prisoners. I stuck the envelope in his hands behind his back. He was in his early twenties, wearing brown baggy cutoff shorts and an ancient T-shirt that may have once been white. His dark hair was chaotic, sticking up all over. The tongues of his sneakers were sticking straight up as he shuffled out in front of us like the walking dead.

We picked up our guns before stopping at the desk. The lou noted the time and that we were taking the prisoner to Midtown Court.

We took 9th Avenue up and parked in front of the precinct. After we walked inside, we spoke to the sergeant on the desk and put our guns away behind the desk there in a similar locker to our own.

The sarge asked the prisoner if he was sick or injured and did he want to go to the hospital. The prisoner had his head down, and all three of us waited for him to respond. When he realized we were talking to him, he looked up, surprised that the sergeant was addressing him. The sarge repeated the question, and the prisoner said he didn't need medical attention.

We went back into the cell area to an officer who could have been Fish's twin except that he was Italian and not as friendly. Because he was getting the prisoner, he wouldn't be able to watch his portable TV.

We went back to the precinct at 5:00 for our meal. Fiore went to the lounge to read, and I went up to the third-floor gym to work out. Our gym is one big room, mirrored on three walls with a wall of windows in the back. Anyone who worked out there paid annual dues of twenty bucks. We had two stationary bikes, a treadmill, a bench press, an incline press, free weights, a leg machine, and a curling bench. The gym is usually empty this time of night, and I had the place to myself. I threw on some shorts and a muscle shirt and did some curls, then I worked out my back.

Fiore and I went back out at 6:00, patrolling our sector until 7:30, when the city was just starting to get moving.

I left the precinct by 7:50. The outbound Brooklyn Battery Tunnel was down to one lane for the inbound rush hour, slowing the traffic. I was clear through to the Verrazano but the "low balance" light went on when I used my E-Z pass. I would have to shoot down to the payment center sometime today and throw some money on it.

When I pulled up in front of my house I saw that Denise's car was still there. I had planned on calling Michele as soon as I got home and had been going over in my mind what I would say. But I didn't want to have this conversation in front of Denise. I heard music from upstairs when I came in and went up to my room to put my bag away. She couldn't hear me with the radio blasting away, and I knew I was going to scare her. I yelled "Hey!" and she screamed, just like I knew she would.

"That's not funny, Tony!" she yelled as I laughed.

"What do you want from me? Don't keep the music so loud. What are you doing home?"

She seemed to be thinking of what to say. "Mr. Ellis died last night," she said quickly.

"Mike's father?"

She nodded. "He had a heart attack. Mike called you about 1:00."

"Why didn't you call me?"

"I would have, but Mike said not to. I think the wake is at Davis's." She continued to fold her clothes. She's one of those people who cleans when they're upset, and I could see she'd been at it a while. I could smell the bleach from the bathroom, and the vacuum was in the hallway.

"I have to go see Mike, but I have stuff to do before I go to sleep." My mind started racing with everything I had to do.

"Anything I can do?" she asked.

"I need to throw some money on my E-Z pass."

"I'll do it," she said.

"Are you sure it's not a problem?"

"No, go see Mike."

"I have to make a call first," I said as I went to my room.

I changed into shorts and a tank top and went back down to the kitchen. I took the cordless out onto the deck and dialed Michele. I glanced back at the clock as it started ringing—9:05. I hoped she wasn't sleeping.

"Hello," she said. I was glad she answered; I didn't want to talk to Stevie again so soon.

"Hey, Michele, it's Tony," I said.

She paused a beat. "Hi, Tony, how are you?"

"Good, how 'bout you?" I asked.

"Fine."

We were getting awfully polite here. I could tell she thought something was up. I had spent some time praying while I was stuck in traffic. I'd tapped my fingers on my steering wheel as I prayed so it looked like I was singing along to music instead of talking to myself. I hoped Fiore was right and that telling her the truth was the way to go.

"Listen, about Saturday—"

"Tony, if you don't want to go, it's okay," she said.

"No—it's not that. It's about Stevie." I waited for her to say something, but there was silence on the other end. I thought she'd hung up.

"You still there?" I asked.

"I'm here," she said quietly. "What about him?"

I took a breath. "I feel funny about you having a kid."

"Oh."

Bad move. "I mean, I like him and all, it's just that . . ." I couldn't think of what to say next.

"It's just what?" she prompted.

"I don't want to hurt him," I blurted out. "I don't want him to get attached. He needs a father, and I don't want him thinking I'm it and then be disappointed if things don't work out."

There was silence for a moment. "I appreciate your honesty, Tony. Steven's getting old enough to notice that other kids have fathers and he doesn't. He even talked to Joe about it." She gave a quiet laugh. "He asked Joe why he didn't have a father, and Joe said he should pray for one. When you came here last week, he asked me if you were going to be his father, and I realized we had to be careful. I told him we were friends, and I figured you and I could leave him out of this for a while. If things change, we could always involve him later."

"I don't want you thinking it matters that you have a son. It wouldn't matter to me. I just want to take it slow with him."

"I think that's a good idea," she agreed.

"So, are we still on for Saturday?" I asked, my tone more upbeat.

"Sure," she said.

We talked a little longer, making plans for Saturday. I told her about Mike's dad and that I might have the funeral Saturday morning. Since I didn't have work Saturday night, I could crash on Sunday to catch up on my sleep. She wanted to change our date to another day, but I had already started to think ahead to the wake and the funeral. Mike's family were big drinkers, and if I had to work both nights of the wake, I could turn down a drink without drawing too much attention to myself. My plans with Michele on Saturday would get me out of drinking after the funeral.

Mike Ellis and his family lived two blocks north of my house. Mike and his sister, Debbie, had gone to St. Michael's with us, and his father coached us in Little League with my dad. Our parents were pretty close until mine got divorced, and even now my father stops up at Dave's for a drink if he sees Mr. Ellis's car outside.

I was stunned to hear he died. I wondered how Mike was handling it. I felt funny about going to the house, but Mike and I had been friends too long for me not to show up. I had a hamper full of dirty clothes, and I threw them in the washing machine before I walked up to Mike's.

The sun was warm as I walked the two blocks. Since I wouldn't make it to the boardwalk this morning, this would have to serve as my exercise for the day. As I turned the corner I could see two cars in Mike's driveway and a black Jeep double-parked next to Debbie Ellis's new red VW Beetle. The front door was open, and the screen let me hear the sound of someone crying in the living room. The block was quiet for the most part. A couple of kids were playing roller hockey two doors up, and I could hear the *thwack* of the stick hitting the street as they took their shots.

Mike's mother, Joan, was sitting on Mr. Ellis's lazy boy chair, and Debbie was kneeling down in front of her, talking in low tones. I tapped on the door.

"Come in, Tony." Debbie hugged me as she opened the

door. "I guess you heard about Dad." She started crying as she hugged me.

Debbie Ellis was two years younger than Mike and me. She was cute, short with brown hair and big brown eyes. She's a sweet girl who loves her older brother and never gives him any of the problems Denise gives me.

"What happened, Deb?" I rubbed her back. "You okay?" She nodded and walked back over toward her mother.

"Hi, Tony," Mrs. Ellis said through her tears. "John had a heart attack last night. I called an ambulance, but it was too late." She started to cry again.

"I'm sorry, Mrs. Ellis," I said for lack of anything better. "Where's Mike?"

"He's in the kitchen." She sniffed.

Mike walked into the living room to see who'd come in and shook my hand. He had a beer in his hand and looked like he'd been at it a while. I could remember being half in the bag by 9:00 in the morning, but suddenly the thought of it made me sick. I wondered if I had some kind of alcoholic schizophrenia where one minute a drink made my mouth water and the next it made me nauseous.

"I'm sorry about your dad, Mike," I said.

"Unbelievable." He shook his head. "My old man is dead. I never thought it would happen. Fifty-eight years old, retired two months ago, and now he's dead." He shook his head and took a hefty swig. "Want a drink?"

"No thanks, I need to get some sleep," I said.

He looked at me funny and shrugged. Mike had that all-American look that women seemed to love. But in the early morning light and without the tint of alcohol in me, I could see the wear and tear from the booze. Lines crinkled his forehead, around his mouth, and the corners of his eyes. His nose had a broken blood vessel and his face a pasty pallor. As we walked toward the kitchen I could hear the people in there talking about Mr. Ellis.

Richie Patterson, Mike's roommate from down the shore, was there, along with Laura, Mike's girlfriend, and Debbie's boyfriend, who I'd never met before. I shook hands all around and kissed Laura hello. Everyone was drinking—I guess the occasion called for it. It felt strange to be around Mike, and I was uncomfortable with all the socializing in the face of sudden death. Mike isn't Italian, and I guess they have a different way of handling it. If it were my father, you'd hear the screams a mile away.

I made small talk and listened to the burial arrangements. They would have the wake tonight and tomorrow afternoon and evening at Davis's Funeral Home on Bay Street. The mass would be Saturday morning at St. Michael's and the burial after that. The post-funeral gathering was at Dave's Tavern. Mike said his dad would have wanted it there.

Although it hadn't been that long since I'd hung out with Mike, I was out of the loop. Mike and Richie had apparently gotten closer, and I felt like an outsider as I heard them talk about all the things they'd been doing down the shore. They weren't doing anything different from what we did every summer at the shore. You'd think the thrill would be gone by now.

I stayed for half an hour and made all the right noises before going home. The kids were still playing hockey outside, although it looked like a couple more had joined in. I thought about Mike as I walked home. We were different now, and he knew it. He wasn't rude to me, just kind of ignored me. I wondered what he would think if I told him about church and Fiore. He'd probably laugh and tell me to have a drink and get over it.

I threw my clothes in the dryer and ate a bowl of cereal

before going to bed. It was 10:30, so I set my clock for 5:00, giving myself time to eat and shower before the wake. I put my air conditioner on low, letting the hum lull me to sleep.

I woke up at 4:40, twenty minutes before the alarm, and jumped in the shower. Our bathroom was now stocked with shampoo, soap, Q-tips, and tissues, starting my night off right. Denise was downstairs with Vinny, Christie, and Sal, all dressed in their mourning clothes. Vinny and Sal wore suits, Denise wore a black dress, and Christie had on a blue suit. I was wearing my new gray suit but would wait to put it on until after I ate dinner.

"Did you guys eat?" I asked.

"We ordered pizza and got you a hero." Denise pointed to a white paper bag on the counter.

I ate my chicken cutlet sandwich, now cold with the mozzarella solidified. I didn't bother to heat it; they looked like they were in a rush. The family gets very somber at the subject of death, and I knew they wanted to be there on time. We left the house by 6:20. I took my truck, Denise drove with Sal, and Vinny had Christie's Saturn.

Davis's Funeral Home is located about a block from the projects. I popped off one of my hubcaps and tossed it in the back of my truck. The neighborhood was pretty bad, and I doubted I'd find the hubcaps on if I left the whole set. The funeral parlor was an old Victorian house, tastefully decorated in floral patterned rugs in beige, green, and rose. Music was piped in overhead, and everyone moved quietly, speaking in hushed tones as if they could wake the dead if they got too loud.

My father and Marie were there, consoling Mrs. Ellis by the door to the viewing room. Mrs. Ellis seemed to have aged since this morning. She wore black pants and a gray button-down shirt. She looked dazed as she greeted those paying respects and seemed to be looking around for Mr. Ellis to help her with it. Occasionally her eyes would rest on the coffin where he lay, and she would stare until someone snapped her out of it.

A lot of people from the neighborhood were there. People I hadn't seen since the eighth grade must have read the obituary and come to offer condolences. I said hello to Mike's cousins, aunts, uncles, and grandparents that I'd known from over the years. I saw firemen Mike worked with, and Dave from Dave's Tavern. Grandma Jean, Mr. Ellis's mother, was sitting in front. She looked like someone slipped her a valium, her eyes vacant and emotionless. I bent over to give her a kiss, but she didn't seem to recognize me.

As the room filled up, people gathered in groups and the noise level rose until everyone realized they were at a wake and shouldn't be socializing. The viewing was over at 9:00, and everyone planned to go across the street to the Loft, an old-time Staten Island bar that had been there since the sixties.

I signed my name in the visitor's book and knelt in front of the coffin and said a prayer for Mr. Ellis. I didn't know what to pray, so I prayed that God was merciful with Mike's dad and added that I needed some help with all the drinking that was sure to be going on for the rest of the night.

I went downstairs to have a cigarette in the smoking room. Mike's Uncle Tommy was sitting there staring straight ahead.

"Hey, Uncle Tommy." I walked over and shook his hand.

"Hi, Tony."

He looked stunned, that look I'd seen so many times over the years when tragedy strikes unexpectedly. I tried to remember something about him, to strike up a conversation, but nothing came to mind. I remembered seeing him at Mike's for the holidays, drinking and laughing with the family. He'd never had any kids, so I couldn't ask about them.

"How's the job?" he asked, trying to be polite.

"The job's the job," I said.

He nodded. "I better go back up and see how Joan's doing."

We shook hands again as we stood.

"Take care, Tony."

"You too."

He shuffled slowly up the stairs.

At 8:30 I heard a murmur in the crowd, and I looked up to see who had caused the commotion. It was Kim, my old girlfriend. This would be interesting. She spotted me from the doorway as she hugged Mike and Laura. From there she stopped at my father and Marie. I could hear Marie say, "You look great!" as she hugged her.

My father and Marie were in their element. My father was making his rounds with Marie, showing off his trophy wife to his middle-aged friends. He made all the right noises to Mike's mom while Marie paraded her cleavage around the room. I couldn't believe she showed up at a wake looking like that. She had on a black cocktail dress, something more suited for a night on the town. As I watched Kim and Marie gush over each other, I realized how thankful I was that Kim was out of my life. If only getting rid of Marie were that easy.

"Hi, Tony," Kim said as she walked up and hugged me. "You look good."

"You too. How are you?" I said casually.

"Great." She smiled.

She did look good. Her hair was straight and very blonde. Her extension nails were painted in what Denise calls a French manicure, white tops covered in light pink. She wore a sleeveless black silk dress with a gold link chain around her very tan neck and diamond studs in her ears. The results should have looked elegant, but instead she looked bogus, trying to be something she wasn't. I was thinking how much better I liked Michele and how glad I was to have met her. My mind must have drifted because Kim said something, and I had to ask her to repeat it.

"I said do you want to go get a drink?" She tilted her head to the side.

"I think everyone's going over after the wake."

"You too?" She smiled.

"For a little while, before I go to work." I got a little nervous when she sat down. We sat in silence for a couple of minutes.

"So—are you seeing anyone?" she asked.

"As a matter of fact, I am," I said brightly.

Her eyes narrowed. "Anyone I know?" Her smile was forced.

"No, she's from Long Island."

"A cop?" A little more threatening.

"Nope."

"Is it serious?"

I almost asked how her boss was. Considering the fact that *she* left *me* I didn't think she had any right to ask me anything. "Serious enough that I don't want to screw it up," I said honestly.

Denise and Sal came over to where we were sitting, and Denise, tactful as ever, said, "So Kim, how's your boss?" If I cared I would have laughed, but I just wanted to finish the night and go to work where it was safe. Kim stared at Denise, who stared back. It was the equivalent of a cat fight at a wake.

"Have some respect for the dead, Denise," Kim said before she walked away.

Denise rolled her eyes. Then she looked upset. "Do you believe Dad had the nerve to tell me my dress was inappropriate for a wake?" She looked like she was going to cry.

I was stunned. "Are you kidding me? Did you take a look at what Marie was wearing?"

"Which part, Tony? The wonder-bra dress or the sandals with stockings? Her outfit is so tacky."

Denise's dress was a little short, but nothing as revealing as Marie's.

I heard my father laugh at something someone said and resisted the urge to start something with him. It wasn't the time or the place, and I'd learned a long time ago that fighting with him was useless. I'd also learned that Marie takes great pleasure in getting Denise and me to explode.

Denise checked her watch again, willing the time to move so she could leave. I checked mine, 8:50, ten minutes until we could go to the bar. I had already decided to order Sprite or 7-Up so it would look like vodka if you didn't get close enough to see the bubbles. I'd bet that Marie and my dad would stop for a drink and so would everyone else in the room.

"Denise, I'm gonna say good night and get an early start across the street," I said.

She raised her eyebrows. "Are we drinking?"

"No, but you don't have to broadcast it," I snapped.

"Wait, we'll come with you," she said.

We made our way back up to the coffin, where we hugged Debbie and Mrs. Ellis. I didn't see Mike, so I couldn't say good night to him. Denise and Sal were still talking when I exited through the front and crossed to the bar, leaving my truck in the parking lot. The air was thick and hot. It was cloudy, and a mist had settled on the cars and pavement.

The Loft was a one-room establishment. There were a good number of people at the bar, with a few of the tables occupied. A lone bartender moved up and down, tossing ice, washing glasses, refilling glasses, and using the cash register. He was a veteran, using both hands, dumping as he refilled, putting money in his tip cup as he rang up an order. I spotted Mike at the far end of the bar and ordered a 7-Up before he spotted me. Armed with my drink I made my way toward him. He was downing a shot of something amber, and as I got closer I could see how drunk he was.

"How are you holding up, Mike?" I asked.

He nodded. "I'm okay."

"Anything I can do?" I took a sip out of my drink, trying to look comfortable.

"No, there's nothing anyone can do. He was a good man," he said with feeling.

"Yes, he was," I agreed. We clinked glasses and toasted. I sipped, he guzzled.

By 9:15 the funeral crowd had made its way over, and the place was filled with well-dressed mourners. The mood was more upbeat as drinks flowed and tongues loosened. My father and Marie stopped in but didn't stay for a drink. Vinny and Christie were there, but Denise and Sal had left. Kim was ignoring me, talking to a fireman and laughing up a storm. I said good night to Mike and spoke to Vinny and Christie before leaving.

I stopped home to change. I was feeling like a liar and a coward for not telling everyone I'd found God and quit drinking. I laughed out loud at the thought of their reaction. I could picture their baffled faces followed by waves of hysterical laughter. I should probably ask Fiore how to handle it. I couldn't go through the rest of my life ordering clear soda so it looked like vodka.

I searched through the fridge for something to eat. There was a piece of pizza with meatballs and ricotta that I popped in the microwave while I went upstairs to change. I put on shorts and my "Midnight Tours" T-Shirt that had Bugs Bunny, Daffy Duck, the Road Runner, Elmer Fudd, and the Coyote dressed in NYPD uniforms and standing outside our precinct. I grabbed my bag and a clean set of clothes in case I collared up.

For once I watched the 10:00 news while I ate, checking for accidents, severe weather, or anything else that would hinder my ride in. It had started to rain while I was inside, and a steady drizzle rubbed across my windshield, blurring my view. The rain makes people afraid of hydroplaning, and traffic slowed my commute. It took me close to an hour to get to the precinct, but I made it for the fall in at 11:15.

Maureen Courtney, a new sergeant from the north precinct, was calling attention to the roll call. Sergeant Hanrahan leaned up against the desk behind her, shuffling through the notifications as she addressed us. I had met her a few times over the past several weeks. She was in her late thirties, with an easygoing, pleasant nature. She's about five foot five, skinny with blue eyes. She was pretty in a worn kind of way, with her curly red hair spilling from the clip that held it back from her face. She had some time on. You could tell by how comfortable she was around the other cops, unaffected and tolerant.

She gave out the sectors and the color of the day (red). She ended the roll call by telling us a little bit about herself, where she came from, and how much time she had on. She began instructing us on the use of bug spray to combat the West Nile mosquito virus when a disturbance interrupted her address. Tonight was our night to be sprayed for the virus, and we were warned to keep the car windows closed. I wondered what the foot posts would do. We were reminded to pick up our bug spray as we filed out.

Fiore had signed for his radio and was waiting outside. I picked up my radio and stopped to talk to Vince, who asked me about my trip to the drunk farm.

"Where do you get this from, Vince? I've been here every night. Who's saying I went to the farm?" I was getting tired of this crap.

He held his hands up. "Tony, you know I can't say who told

me. I told them you were here every night, but people have noticed you're on the wagon." He waited for an answer.

"Whether or not I'm on the wagon is nobody's business, Vince. Pass it along." I left without saying good night.

Fiore was outside talking to Romano. I think Fiore felt bad for the kid; he was always going out of his way to be nice to him when most people ignored him or goofed on his hair. Romano was young, maybe twenty-two, twenty-three years old. His dark hair was cut short and spiky with the tips bleached blond. He was a good-looking kid, olive skin, dark eyes. He clearly worked out and was pretty built.

"Hey, Mike Piazza," I said.

"Why does everyone call me that?" He was clueless.

"It's the hair, birdbrain," I said. I don't know why I always get sadistic with rookies. I guess because everyone tortured me when I came on.

He shook his head and started to walk away.

"Hey! Where are you going?" I called after him. He waved me away and kept walking up the street. I shrugged and started walking toward the car. I stopped when I realized Fiore wasn't with me.

"What?" I asked.

He seemed to be thinking. "Let's get Romano. Something's bothering him, and he seems to want to talk about it."

"What's bothering him?" I asked.

"I don't know. He started to talk to me before you insulted him."

"The hair thing? The kid's too sensitive."

"The hair thing," Fiore said absently.

We cleaned out the car; there were no newspapers again. We put our hats in the back, books on the dash, and radios in the side armrest before moving out. I caught up with Romano near the corner of 8th Avenue.

"Romano!" I called out.

He kept walking.

"Hey!" I yelled, my voice stern.

"What?" he said, still walking.

Something *was* up with him. He looked upset. "What's his first name?" I asked Joe quietly.

"Nick," he said.

"Hey, Nick! Come on, let me give you a ride." The first name must have got him, because he stopped walking and came over toward the car. He got in the back, moving our hats over and adding his to the pile.

"Where are you going?" I asked. The clean smell of his cologne filled the car.

"They got me on a fixer at a synagogue on 6th Avenue," he said.

A fixer is a foot post assigned to guard a specific location. In this instance the synagogue had been having some problems with vandalism and needed someone to watch the place. Fixers are boring, because you often stand alone for the whole tour. You get relief for a one-hour meal, and then it's back to looking at your watch. Rookies always get stuck on fixers. They also get stuck watching dead bodies until the coroner gets there, or sitting on front breaks where a burglary leaves a building vulnerable to looting.

"What's the matter, Nick?" I looked at him in the rearview mirror.

He shrugged.

"Is it the job?"

His eyes met mine in the mirror, and he shrugged again.

"It's a lot of things," he said.

"So talk to us, maybe we can help," Fiore said, turning toward him.

At first Romano looked doubtful, but then he started to

spill his guts. "I don't even feel like a cop. I feel like a security guard. I don't get to do anything, I don't know anything, and I don't know if the job's for me."

"Listen, we all did this for our first two, three years," I said.

I remember feeling the same way. The old-timers when I went on weren't half as nice as me and Fiore. They would have driven right past me and let me walk to my fixer. I remembered one of my first days at the command—an old-timer pushed me out of the way, saying, "Move it, rookie, I've got more time in the trial room than you've got on the job." At the time I'd never heard of the trial room, never mind been there. Over the past ten years I'd learned a lot about it. It's the place you go when you get suspended or fight a command discipline and go before a department trial judge.

"Why did you become a cop?" Fiore asked.

"My father was a cop," he said.

"Where did he work?" I asked.

"In Brooklyn."

"Is he retired?" I asked.

"No, he was killed. Line of duty," he said quietly.

We were stunned. It was quiet in the car until Fiore broke the silence.

"How?" he asked.

"Shot in the face in a domestic dispute."

"Why would you become a cop if your father was killed in the line of duty?" I asked.

"I don't know. I'm on the list for the fire department too."

"You may get called for FD and decide to take it," I said.

"I'd definitely take it," Romano said with feeling.

"How old were you when your father was killed?" Fiore surprised me by asking.

"Ten, and my brother was eight."

"I'm sorry to hear that," Fiore said. We both got quiet, thinking about Romano's father. I didn't remember the incident; it would have happened before I was on. Fiore would have been a rookie at the time, but he showed no recognition of it.

"Is it me, or does everyone hate us?" Romano asked, changing the subject.

"Not everyone, but most people. What else is on your mind?" I asked.

"My girlfriend and I broke up, and she won't let me see my daughter."

"You have a kid?" This surprised me, but a lot of the younger guys were doing that, having kids without being married.

He nodded. "A little girl, she's two."

"How old are you?"

"Twenty-three."

"Why didn't you get married?" I asked.

"I wanted to get married, but she didn't want to. She's still in college and she's not sure she wants to marry me. I thought if we lived together it'd be better, but she wants to stay at home so her mother can help her with the baby. We broke up at the beginning of the summer, and she's been going out a lot, seeing other guys."

"I don't get this," I said. "She has a baby with you and lets her mother take care of it so she can go out with other guys? You have a right to see your daughter." He'd even offered to marry her, the old-fashioned Italian boy that he was.

"I know. I hired a lawyer, and I'm taking her to court for visitation rights. Cost me five grand up front, and the lawyer gets like three hundred bucks an hour."

"Have you tried talking to her?" Fiore the peacemaker asked.

"I can't get her on the phone. She leaves the machine on. I

go to the house, and her mother says she's not home. But I got loud with her mother today, and she let me see my daughter for a little while."

"Be careful with that, buddy. If you lose your temper over there, it'll work against you," Fiore said.

"But I don't know what else to do," Romano said dejectedly.

We parked outside the fixer. As long as we didn't have a job we could stay and talk to Romano. He talked about his family. He grew up in Staten Island, which surprised me. He lived on the south shore. He went to college in Ohio for a year on a football scholarship. He got hurt playing ball and came back to New York and did another year of school at St. John's. He took the test for the department and came on two years ago. He was pretty high on the list for the fire department but got called to the police department first.

He met his girlfriend in a club. She was three years younger than him and got pregnant in her first year of college. Now she went to school, went out on the weekends, and even went to Mexico during spring break with her friends. I thought of Michele and Stevie. Michele was a single mother too. Granted, she'd been older when she had Stevie, but she was the one responsible for her son. Romano's girlfriend sounded spoiled and selfish, and I told him so.

"I know that now," he said. "But at the time she was so excited about the baby, so excited about us, that we were gonna be a family."

"I'll pray for you Nick," Fiore said.

Romano smiled. "I forgot, you're the Jesus guy."

"I'm not Jesus. But he's the only one who can help you with this one."

"It's true, Nick," I added.

Romano looked shocked. "You too?"

"I'm talking from experience here," I said.

"What experience?"

"That's none of your business."

He looked skeptical. "You guys are gonna pray for me?" He sounded skeptical.

"Fiore's gonna pray for you; he's better at it than I am. But listen to what he's telling you and don't be thick like I was."

"You weren't thick, Tony," Fiore said.

"You went to the farm, right?" Romano threw in.

"What's with the farm?" I yelled. "I haven't even taken a day off! How could I go to the farm? I bet Rooney's passing this around because I missed the game."

Fiore smirked. "Baaahhhh."

"What's 'baaahhhh'?" I barked.

"A sheep. Isn't that what they have at the farm?"

"How would I know? I've never been there! I'm going to get some coffee," I said, getting out of the car. "What do you want?" I asked them.

"Regular coffee," Fiore said.

"Me too," Romano added.

There was a twenty-four-hour deli across from the synagogue. I got three coffees and three blueberry muffins and brought them back to the car. It was now midnight, and we still hadn't gotten a job. Thursdays were usually pretty busy in the summer but not as busy as the weekend. A minute later I realized why we had no jobs when the mosquito sprayers made their way up 6th Avenue. Everyone was inside, afraid to breathe in the pesticide.

A highway patrol car led the spray truck, announcing on the car's public address system to get indoors and close the windows while the truck was spraying. The truck had a flashing yellow light on top, and a heavy mist gushed out in a steady stream. We closed the windows and kept the air conditioner off so none of the fumes would get in the car.

"Good thing you guys are here, or I'd be off post not breathing this in," Romano said.

"All right, we gotta go, you can get out now," I joked.

"Thanks a lot, Tony," he said.

It took about ten minutes for the smoke to dissipate, but it would probably take about a thousand years to get rid of the effects of the chemicals.

"I was talking to a friend of mine who's an exterminator," Fiore said.

"I heard this fog won't kill anything," I said.

"It'll kill some of them, but that's not the way to control it. To control it you have to treat the larvae in the standing water. They have these chemical donuts that you place in the standing water, preferably in the spring before they hatch, and follow up throughout the season," Fiore said.

"How could you treat all the standing water in the city? You'd have to treat every puddle, lake, pond, garbage pail full of water. You could never do it," I said. "All the buildings with flat roofs that get water, how can you control that?"

"I guess you treat the areas that breed the most," he said.

We went with this mindless conversation about mosquitoes and the West Nile virus for a while. Since none of us were exterminators, we were riding on hearsay. The West Nile epidemic wasn't as widespread as the press would have liked us to believe. They thrive on putting fear and panic in people so they stay glued to their TV, waiting for the news to tell them what they have to worry about.

We got a job from Central, an alarm on 39th Street, so we booted Romano out of the car while he cried about toxic fumes from the mosquito spray.

"Go across the street to the deli and watch from there," I told him.

"Thanks for the coffee and muffin, and for the conversation. I appreciate it." He grabbed his hat, memo book, and radio.

"No problem, buddy, just be careful," I said.

"Everything's gonna work out, Nick," Fiore added.

He waved us off, and we drove back toward 39th Street to answer the alarm.

16

I talked to Fiore about Mr. Ellis dying and the wake.

"I felt like a coward for not telling them I quit drinking," I said.

"You're gonna have to tell them, Tony. Otherwise they'll never leave you alone."

"What should I say?"

"Say you quit drinking," he said.

"They'll want to know why. Then I'd have to tell them about church and God." I could just picture it.

"You don't *have* to tell them anything. Sometimes when people get saved, they're so excited they shove it down everybody's throat, and that's not good either. If you don't want to tell them because you're afraid they'll make fun of you, that's a different story," he said.

"But that's exactly why I don't want to tell them," I pointed out.

"You just talked about God to Romano," he countered.

"Yeah, but Romano's a rookie. Nobody listens to him anyway."

"That's your pride talking," he said. "And pride is a dangerous thing."

"I thought pride was a good thing."

"Not according to the Bible. There's a lot written about pride, and if you look in the book of Proverbs, you'll see pride isn't a good thing," he said. "Taking pride in your work and being proud of your family is a good thing, sure. But I'm talking about being concerned about what people think of you and about denying you know Jesus. Jesus doesn't want us to deny him at any time. The Bible talks about it, I think it's in Luke 12." He took out his Bible and flipped through the pages. He was Johnny-on-the-spot with that Bible. "Here it is, Luke 12:9: 'But he that denieth me before men shall be denied before the angels of God.'"

"It's different for you, Joe. Everyone knows how you are with God. They know me as a drinker and a manly man," I joked, flexing my arm. "If I start talking about Jesus, they'll think I'm a wuss and expect me to turn the other cheek and crap."

"Jesus wasn't a wuss. He's the toughest guy that ever lived, and he's got the scars to prove it."

"But it'll change the way they see me."

"Everyone we work with respects you. They see you as a good cop who knows the job. Granted, you've partied a lot and have a reputation for that, but I think you'd be surprised at how much they'll admire your decision for God."

"I don't know about that. I think they'll torture me over it."

"Maybe for a while, but they'll get past it."

By now it was almost 12:30. We saw a news truck pulling away from the corner of 37th Street and 9th Avenue on the northeast side. A male black, possibly six foot one or six foot two wearing denim shorts, a black T-shirt, and sneakers, approached the corner. He grabbed one of the bundles of newspapers that had just been tossed from the truck and hoisted it over his shoulder. He started walking away. I drove to where I could pull the car in front of him.

"Hey, where are you going with those papers?" I called to him.

"They're my papers. They drop them off, I pick them up." He moved his head from side to side as he said it. On closer inspection I could see he was in his mid to late forties with short, black hair threaded with gray.

"Really? And where are you taking the papers?" I asked.

"Uh, I'm picking them up for my boss."

"What's the address on that?" I asked as Fiore and I stepped out of the car.

He gave us the address 330 West 37th Street. If that's where he was going, he was on the wrong side of the street. I got out and took the bundle. There was a yellow sheet of paper on top of the newspapers, and they were wrapped up with plastic tabs. I looked at the top sheet, and sure enough, 520 9th Avenue was scrawled in black magic marker.

"What's your boss's name?" I asked, putting the bundle on the ground.

"Joe," he said.

"Joe who?"

"I don't know his last name." He smiled. I love comedians.

"Why are you telling me these papers are for your boss and you're walking away with the papers for 9th Avenue?" I asked.

"Oh. They must've gotten the address wrong," he said flippantly.

"Nah. I think you got it wrong." I took out my cuffs.

While I turned him around to toss him and cuff him, he tried to talk his way out of it. "This is a big mistake," he babbled as Fiore put him in the backseat.

I opened the driver's side door to hit the button to open

the trunk, and I picked up the bundle of newspapers to put it in the trunk.

"Uh-oh," I said.

"What?" Fiore came around to the back of the car.

"Take a look at this," I said, pointing to the first page insert.

"Go to page two," Fiore said.

I pulled the top paper out of the bundle and turned to page two. Fiore and I stared at the picture for a second and then simultaneously busted out laughing. There in black and white taking up half of page two was our politician from last night. He was smiling with his face busted up and his arm around the mayor. The caption read: "HIZZONOR TO THE RESCUE!" The smaller headline said "Mayor Aids State Legislator."

Fiore started to read the article that said a Connecticut state legislator visiting the city to honor World War II Veterans was robbed last night of over six-hundred dollars plus credit cards and his credentials. Since he couldn't identify himself at the ceremony where he was supposed to speak, security wouldn't let him in. He was able to catch the attention of the mayor, who was invited to the celebration. I guess the mayor didn't like his cronies getting robbed on his turf.

The story didn't match what happened. The politician said he was robbed and "brutally assaulted" while on his way to a restaurant near his hotel. He said he still loves New York and that the NYPD officers arrived quickly and helped him. He called the officers "extremely professional."

"Maybe he doesn't mean us," I cut in. "Do you think he was robbed again after we dropped him off?" I started to laugh. "At which point was I extremely professional, when I made him clean up his own blood or—"

Central came over the line. "South David."

"South David," Fiore answered, looking at me.

"South David, 10–2 forthwith." Which basically means, "Get your butt back to the station now."

I guess they just got the early edition.

"It's a good thing we did those reports," Fiore said.

"You're not kidding."

Fiore radioed back that we had an arrest.

As we drove back Fiore and I got our story together. He was calm and I was mad. I'd seen this happen before, where a cop was totally innocent and got in trouble because some big shot opened his mouth to the brass.

"I can't believe we're gonna get yelled at for what this guy did. We know he wasn't looking for a restaurant," I seethed.

"Let me handle this, Tony," Fiore said calmly.

"No. I'm coming with you."

"No. You handle the prisoner, and I'll straighten this out. Trust me," he said.

"Yeah, famous last words," I mumbled.

I took 9th Avenue to 36th, entering through the back of the precinct. Fiore was out of the car and inside before I could open my door. I took the prisoner out and held him by the cuffs as I checked the backseat. I left the papers in the trunk for the time being and walked him inside.

Behind the desk Lieutenant Coughlin was smirking, and Vinny Bag-of-donuts looked scared.

"The mayor's office called," he said.

"What's their problem?" I said.

"I don't know. They talked to the squad, and the squad called down here and wanted to talk to you guys." The squad is the detective squad, which is located on the second floor of the precinct.

Vinny looked so upset that I started to laugh. "Did they want to thank us for cleaning this guy up for his charity luncheon?" I asked.

The lou looked over and said, "Maybe you guys are getting your shields." I could hear scattered laughter around the desk. He meant our detective shields. Fat chance.

"They didn't sound too happy," Vinny said.

"Then I guess I'm not getting my shield."

"Who's this?" the lou asked, nodding toward my prisoner.

"A paper boy with amnesia," I said.

I brought him to the back and gave him a second toss. I had him take his shoelaces off and empty his pockets, which had nothing in them. I put him in the cell and started to fill out the prisoner log when he got talkative.

"I've been arrested twenty-nine times for this," he called to me.

I ignored him but wrote down what he said in my memo book. I make it a practice to write down any spontaneous utterance no matter how trivial it may seem.

"I'm the news bandit," he called again. "I've been doing this for ten years!" He puffed at me, that sound that is supposed to make you feel unimportant. "The judge is just going to let *me* go and tell *you* to go arrest someone else." I kept writing. I knew the judge was going to appreciate that when I read it to him. Judges love it when people undermine their authority.

I left the arrest process room to go run his name in the computer behind the desk. While I was back there waiting for a hit on his priors, Fiore came in and closed the door. He was calm and cool.

"Well? What happened?" I asked.

"The mayor's office called the squad upstairs to get information on what happened last night and why no arrest was made." He held up his hand when I started to interrupt. "Just let me finish, Tony. I told them we had two possibles but that the complainant refused to identify one as a possible and was adamant the other wasn't him. They also wanted to know why we didn't notify them that this had happened. They asked if we searched the possibles, and I told them it would be illegal to search them unless the complainant pointed them out as possibles. They implied that we were looking to get out of making a collar, and I told them that my partner was looking to make a collar last night. I also told them this guy was punched in the face by someone he was talking to, that he knew exactly who hit him but wouldn't identify him. I also said that it was my impression that his location suggested that he was looking for something other than a restaurant, probably companionship, and I would be happy to speak to the mayor's office directly and relay all this to them."

I smiled. "Pretty good, bro. What else did they say?"

"They said that they would handle it from here and that we just have to give them a copy of the complaint report and the aided card."

By the time Fiore finished the story, the report came back on the news bandit. It gave his name, address, date of birth, height and weight, and the color of his eyes and hair. It didn't give a list of prior arrests, it just said "misdemeanor recidivist." He had no outstanding warrants, but being a recidivist, he had to go through the system.

I processed the arrest and waited for Vinny Bag-of-donuts to come back with an arrest number. I didn't have a complainant yet, because the deli that he stole the papers from wasn't open. I filled out the complaint form but left the complainant's name blank. I'd have to go over there later and get the information from the storeowner before I finished the complaint report.

I took two photographs of the paper thief, printed him, and put him back in the cell. I also took pictures of the newspapers and vouchered them. Fiore stayed with me while I waited the hour it took for the prints to come back verified. I had to be sure Albany got them before I could transport the prisoner.

Had this been a felony, I would have had to wait until morning when the ADAs come in, and I would have made some overtime. Since it was a misdemeanor we would take him over to Midtown Court once he was processed.

We went out to get food so we could eat early and sleep through our meal. We walked across to the all-night deli on the corner of 9th Avenue and 35th Street to pick up sandwiches. We both had turkey on a roll and two Cokes and two bags of potato chips and took them back to the arrest room.

The perp was already asleep, snoring annoyingly as we ate. Fiore went back to our earlier conversation about Jesus being a tough guy.

"When I said Jesus was a tough guy, did you understand what I meant?" he asked.

I shrugged. "I think so."

"I said he had the scars to prove it. He has scars in his hands and his feet from the nails on the cross, and the one in his side from the sword. Those scars aren't like some soldier coming back from a war with battle scars. He knew before he ever came to earth that he would die that way. He sacrificed himself for us. Everyone. Good, bad, or the most evil, vile person that would ever walk the earth, he died for them."

"Why?" I asked.

"Because he loved us. Even if we didn't love him, he still loved us."

I didn't understand it. "How could he love us if we didn't love him?"

"Because that's who he is. Love. I don't think you're getting this, Tony. There was more to it than dying. The Bible says in Isaiah 53—"

I thought he was gonna whip out his little Bible again, but I guess he decided to go on memory.

"He bore *our* grief and carried *our* sorrow. He was wounded for *our* transgressions and bruised for *our* iniquities. The chastisement of *our* peace was upon him, the guilt and iniquity of all of *us* was upon him. He was oppressed and afflicted but didn't open his mouth. He was like a lamb led to slaughter."

"We used to say something like that in church," I said, remembering a prayer I never understood.

"He took our sins and paid for them. He was innocent."

I was getting a glimpse of something here. I'd heard the story of Calvary, but it never meant anything to me. As a cop, I'd seen things—innocent people hurt or killed at the hands of someone evil. I often wondered at the futility of it. Some kid with a promising future cut down in his youth by some scum over twenty bucks. But Fiore was saying it was the scum that Jesus died for, along with the innocent. Something inside me disapproved of him dying for the scum. But a couple of hours ago, I was ashamed to tell anyone I'd given myself to him. I wasn't innocent either.

I was distracted, thinking about all my shortcomings. My temper, mostly, and my pride, worrying about what the guys would think of me. Fiore was a better man than I was, a good example for God.

"It makes me feel . . ." I searched for the word, "guilty for being ashamed of him."

"He doesn't want that, Tony. He loves you. You took the first step and gave your heart to God. He'll show you what to do with the rest."

"That was deep, man," said a voice from across the room.

Fiore and I turned to see the paper bandit, now awake and sitting on the bench and watching us intensely.

"Shut up. Who asked you?" I yelled over to the cell.

"No, really. I never heard it explained like that," he said.

I looked back at Fiore, who was shaking his head. "He wants to know, Tony. Why don't you explain it to him?"

Realization hit me. "I'm sorry, Joe. He died for him too, right?"

Fiore smiled. "That's right."

"Why don't you tell him? I could never explain it like that," I said.

This night turned out to be one of the strangest nights on the job. Fiore talked to the paper bandit and wound up praying the prayer of salvation through the bars in the cell.

I used the phone on the file cabinet by the printing machine and called Albany to verify that they'd received the prints on our perp. Once I got confirmation and a number, we were set to transport him up to court.

On the way back from dropping off the paper bandit at Midtown Court, we drove toward the Sunrise Deli to get a cup of coffee. A black female of indeterminate age was standing by the curb just before 7th Avenue looking very distraught. She was emaciated, wearing a ragged blue T-shirt and ripped dirty shorts. She was barefoot and filthy, and she eyed Fiore with suspicion. That happened sometimes—an EDP would take to one of us and be agitated by the other. Usually it was Fiore they connected with, but this time he scared her.

Her eyes darted all around as she told me that she had been kidnapped. She looked scared enough for me to take her seriously, and I asked her to tell me what happened.

"They took me in the van and dumped me here," she said, her body moving in quick, jerky motions.

I saw no visible marks or bruises, and she wasn't bleeding. Her face was worn, probably from years of drugs and abuse. I looked down on the ground and saw some of the cornrow braids from her hair lying there. I tried to calm her down again, thinking that something might have gone on here.

"Who was it? Did you know them?" I asked.

She shook her head no.

"What kind of van was it?" I tried again.

"A blue van," she said, looking around. "Blue, right there! Did you see it?" She looked up with confused eyes. She pointed at a building across the street, looked over at Fiore, and backed up again.

I nodded to Fiore, and he walked off to the side.

"They took me and wouldn't let me go." She rambled on, her eyes constantly moving, looking for her assailants. Then she reached up and pulled her hair out, dropping the braids onto the street.

There was no van or kidnappers. She had overdosed on something and was seeing some imaginary bad guys.

I tried to talk to her in a calming voice. For some reason she responded to me, and I got her to sit down on the curb. I didn't want to cuff her as long as she wasn't violent. She was dirty, and she smelled of body odor and urine. There was filth caked to the bottom of her feet.

"Joe, get me a bus," I called over to the RMP. "Tell them we have a voluntary EDP that needs to go to the hospital."

"Don't let them get me." She focused on me for the first time. I saw frightened, crazy eyes. She reached out her hand to me; it was yellowed and grubby with broken, filthy nails.

"I won't let them get you," I said.

Compassion replaced repulsion as I took her hand. I could always wash mine later. I stood in front of her on the curb, speaking soothing words as I heard the sirens in the distance.

For God so loved the world . . .

Epilogue

New York had a subway series in October. The city went wild as the pennant race heated up. The Mets upset San Francisco in a three game to one division series, the high point being Benny Agbayani's game three winning solo homer in the bottom of the thirteenth. The Yanks cracked open the cases of champagne after barely escaping Oakland with a seven to five win in game five. The Mets went on to beat the Cardinals in five games, and the Yankees beat the Mariners in six. The World Series games were close, and though the Mets were only able to win game three, they broke the Yankees fourteen-game series-winning streak. This was the Yankees' third consecutive World Series and their fourth in five years. They're calling them the Team of the Century.

Fiore caught the Yankee Stadium detail, game two, in the Bronx with Roger Clemens as the starting pitcher, the game when Clemens threw the bat at Mike Piazza. Personally I thought it was an accident, but the Mets were pretty mad about it. The Yanks won that game six to five, and Fiore got to stay inside the stadium, near the Yankee dugout. He even got autographs. He bought me a T-shirt that said "Subway Showdown" with a picture of Mike Piazza on one side and Derek Jeter on the other. I gave it to Grandma, who fell asleep during game five and woke up just as Piazza flew out to Bernie Williams to end the series.

Fiore and I led the precinct in felony arrests for July, August, and September. Rumor has it that the CO is considering putting us in the anticrime unit.

Mike Rooney had been kinda standoffish with me since I stopped going to the bar with him. When I started changing into a suit on Sunday morning so I could go to church with Fiore, he really started harassing me. One morning he lobbed enough verbal grenades to get me really mad, and I put him up against his locker.

"What's your problem, Mike?" I yelled.

"Is church man losing his temper?" he asked. "Jesus might not like it."

"Jesus is the only reason you're not eating my fist!" I yelled. I was sick of Rooney—ever since I got saved he had been baiting me.

"You gonna hit me, Tony?" He looked hurt.

I let go of his shirt. "Why don't you tell me why you keep busting my chops?" I asked, calming some.

"Why don't *you* tell me why you're too good to come and have a drink with me," he spat.

So that was it. "I'm sorry, Mike," I said. "I'm sorry I haven't hung out with you. I just don't want to go to the bar anymore." I paused to think of how to say it without giving too much away. "It's just that the drinking was getting out of hand."

"You think I didn't know that? Who do you think told the whole precinct you were going to the farm? Why couldn't you talk to me about it?" he asked, sounding insulted.

"I guess because I would have had to go to the bar to talk to you about it," I said.

"You don't have to go to the bar to talk to me. We could go someplace else, I don't know, get coffee or something."

"Okay." I nodded. "We'll have coffee."

He put his hand out for me to shake, and I pulled him in for a hug.

"Get off me," he said, his face turning red.

I chuckled as he walked away.

They closed on my house on September 18. I had talked to Denise about staying with me and told her it was time for all of us to move on. She looked scared as she nodded, and I felt the old big brother tug. I didn't give in, though. I'm trying not to ride on emotion these days.

Denise found an apartment not far from our old house, a small studio in one of the new houses they built up by the service road. It has a little deck off the kitchen area. Sal and I helped her move in. Denise and Sal have been seeing each other for a while now, and it looks like things are working out pretty good. He's started to see his kids again, and Denise seems to like them. His ex-wife is as psychotic as ever, but Denise has had experience with crazy women.

Vinny moved in with my father and Marie. He's staying with them until his wedding. Marie hovers over him like a mother hen; I guess her maternal instincts are kicking in. I still can't stomach the sight of her, and I keep holding off making peace.

My mother called me about a week before I moved out to ask what I would do once the house was sold. She wasn't sarcastic for once when I told her I would be moving into an apartment. She asked about Denise, and I told her she'd have to call her to see what she was going to do.

"Will you miss it?" she asked.

"I probably will," I said. "But it's time for all of us to move on. Dontcha think?"

"I guess it is," she said quietly. "You take care of yourself, Tony. Come up and visit with your new girlfriend and her son."

I guess Vinny had told her about Michele. "I'll do that," I said, and I meant it. This was the first real conversation we'd had in a long time. It wasn't much, but it was a start.

I found an apartment on Greeley Avenue. It's small, a one-bedroom with a short walk to the beach. I had looked for apartments on Long Island, but they were too expensive. I'm trying to save money, and my rent is only seven hundred a month. The cheapest I could find in Long Island was eight-fifty, without utilities. The seven hundred I pay in rent here includes electric, heat, and hot water. I just pay my phone bill.

The week before they closed on the house I didn't go to Long Island at all. I stayed home to pack up my stuff. Michele and Stevie surprised me by coming out to help me. My father had stopped by to pick up some boxes with Vinny, and I could tell right away that he wasn't happy. He nodded to Michele and ignored Stevie. He surprised me a few days later by coming to talk to me about it.

"Tony, before you get all boxed in here, think about what you're doing," he said, his face stern.

"What are you talking about?"

"I'm talking about that church you go to, this woman you're seeing. You changed your whole life. You don't see your friends, you don't have a drink, you meet a woman who already has a kid. How do you know she's not just looking for someone to take care of her?" He looked me in the eye. "You walk away from your church—"

"Dad, I never went to church," I pointed out.

"You went to church—you went to school at St. Michael's, your whole life you went there." His voice rose.

The irony of it was incredible. "You know something, Dad,

you haven't spoken to me in twelve years." I held up my hand when he tried to interrupt. "No, hear me out. I know we've spoken about trivial things when the family got together, but we never really talked. When you left, you stopped caring about what happened to me, or Vinny and Denise, for that matter. You watched me drink and party and sleep around, and you found that amusing. Did you know that right before I stopped drinking I almost killed myself?" I let that sink in.

He stood speechless.

"That's right," I continued. "I was going to come home and eat my gun. In all your years on the job, how many cops did you know who ate their guns?" He didn't answer. "My partner, Joe Fiore, knew something was wrong. I didn't even know the guy for a month, and he knew more about me than my own family. He stayed with me for three days, talking to me, telling me about God and how much God loves me. Do you know how much I needed to hear how much God loves me? Enough to make me not blow my head off, that's how much I needed to know." I couldn't believe I told him that, but I guess a part of me wanted to.

"But Tony, those people are obsessed. They aren't right in the head. You think you're like them because you got a little depressed, but this is crazy." He pointed at me. "Don't get sucked in by them."

He just didn't get it. My temper flared, and I lashed out. "Don't you ever try to tell me what to do again. I stopped caring about what you think a long time ago." My voice was deadly. I knew as I said it that I was wrong but it had to be said.

He put his head down, and when he looked up again I thought he was going to cry. I didn't feel sorry for him—he threw his family away, and we all had to pay for it. I'd been praying for him, but right then I could have hit him.

"Michele and Stevie are a fact of my life. If you don't like it, I don't want to hear about it. If you don't treat them right, you won't see me." I walked outside and got in my truck, my hands shaking.

I didn't see him again until we all went to my grandmother's for Denise's birthday in October. I brought Michele and Stevie with me. To give her credit, Marie bought Stevie a plastic ball and bat, two bags of M&M's, and a Yankee hat. My father shook Stevie's hand and was hesitant but polite to Michele. When he hugged me, he held on for an extra second or two. I pulled him and squeezed hard. Denise hugged Michele and wrestled with Stevie, tickling him until she worked him up into a frenzy. Grandma made him cookies and let him help her make macaroni, showing him how to shape cavatelli using the tips of his fingers.

I met Michele's parents when she had us all for dinner after church one Sunday. I like her father—he's a quiet man but keeps his end of the conversation going when we talk about baseball and my job. He's tall and lanky, over six feet with thinning light brown hair threaded with gray. He has a serious look about him; I guess that's where Michele gets it from. The thing that impresses me most about him is his way with Stevie—patient and encouraging, letting Stevie know that a four-and-a-half-year-old is worth listening to. Michele's mother fusses over me.

I started to do some work on Michele's house. I'd always had some project going when I lived with Vinny, and I missed working with my hands. Her house is solid but hadn't been updated in a long time.

Michele and I have gotten pretty serious. By Labor Day weekend we decided that we wanted to bring Stevie into the picture. I know it hasn't been that long, but in my gut I know she's the one for me. I was gonna have to be serious with her—she wouldn't just put out. I don't know which was worse sometimes, not drinking or keeping my hands to myself. I felt like I was twelve years old again, trying to make out behind the parish center of St. Michael's.

She's not immune either. Last week I was painting the new back door I'd put on her house. The old one was falling apart, so I bought one at Home Depot and spent an Indian summer Saturday afternoon painting it white. I had taken my shirt off and was sweltering in the heat.

"Hey, babe," I called out. "How about some ice water before I melt out here?"

She brought me a big glass, set it down next to me, and picked up my shirt to throw it at me. "Why don't you put some clothes on," she snapped.

I wiggled my eyebrows. "Why, is the sight of my bare chest making you rethink those morals of yours?"

"Not at all." She laughed then said seriously, "Put your shirt on."

I chuckled, admiring her legs as she walked away. I put the shirt on. I want to stand by those principles almost as much as she does. I've been thinking about getting married—not now, but not so far from now. Right now I'm working on my walk with God and building something solid before I take the plunge. Between what I've been saving by not drinking and the money I got from the house being sold I have twenty-eight thousand in the bank. A nice ring will cost me about five grand. I figure that leaves me enough to add a second story to Michele's house. I want to extend the living room and add a dining room and a family room. I think I'll put two nice-sized bedrooms upstairs, a bathroom with a jacuzzi, maybe a nursery.

I have never been so close to anyone else in my life, not even Denise. I'm amazed at how good Michele and I are together. I really like her. Aside from love, I like being with her. She's funny in a dry, quiet kind of way, the perfect lady to counter my rough edges. I probably spend at least two hours a day on the phone with her, talking, praying, and laughing. And Stevie makes me feel like a father—we fish together, play ball, and talk. On my days off, I stay at Fiore's house and get to read Stevie a story and say prayers with him when he goes to bed.

Michele and I have started talking about marriage in the hypothetical. My only question was if she would let me adopt Stevie. She answered in that quiet thoughtful way of hers and said yes.

I think a lot about what Fiore told me, how God always has something better for us. I thank the Lord, like I always do when I think about Joe Fiore, about how he reached out to me when I was so lost and broken. My brother in Christ, my partner, my friend.

Acknowledgments

*T*he authors would like to acknowledge the following people:

Mike Valentino of Cambridge Literary Associates for taking a chance on a couple of unknowns from Staten Island. You're an okay guy for a Red Sox fan.

Lonnie Hull DuPont, transplanted New Yorker, editor extraordinaire, and risk taker. You're the best, Lonnie. Bada bing.

Reverend Thomas Mann, whose preaching on Gideon touched our hearts. Sorry you couldn't be here to see how we butchered your sermon. Today you are in God's glory, but you are deeply missed.

Frankie and Georgie for being patient with us, even when we said, "Just let us finish this," for the thousandth time. You make our lives complete.

F. P. Lione is actually two people—a married couple by the name of Frank and Pam Lione. They are both Italian-American and the offspring of NYPD detectives. Frank Lione is a veteran of the NYPD, and Pam recently left her job as a medical sonographer in vascular ultrasound to stay home with their two sons. They divide their time between New York City and Broadheadsville, Pennsylvania, in the Poconos.